Jenna's Coin

Book One of The Island Fever Series

BY

Stuart Leland Rider

Forward:

While this is a work of fiction, all the locations and environs used in this book are today, and were, real in 1956. The characters are loosely taken from an amalgam of people that populated my life on the island between 1946 and 1960.

In April 2011, I revisited most of the locations uses in preparation for finishing this book.

There are historical figures scattered throughout the book. For the most part, they are portrayed in their normal role or used as cameos in fun situations. I hope that I have not stepped on anyone's historical dignity. These people are an integral part of the fabric of the island's true historical character.

If any of you, my old friends or enemies still living, recognize yourself in the characters portrayed herein, and you wish to protest or sue, please contact me first. I would be delighted to hear from you again. I loved my time on the island and remember fondly all the people who populated my life at the time. I miss you one and all.

Stuart L. Rider

Scottsdale, AZ – 2011

Table of Contents

Chapter 1 - Wednesday
The Colony Club, St. James, Barbados, BWI

This morning started like most mornings in Barbados, the sun came up quickly, shining brightly on the fluffy white billowy clouds scudding along over and past the island, and adding a sparkle to the gentle chop of the Caribbean sea. The usual trade winds were lazily moving the palms and the rest of the landscaping around. Birds, lizards, and even land crabs were going about their business; ignoring the stirring people who were emerging to start their day. The Colony Club was perched on the edge of the sea in St. James Parrish; part of a small neighborhood known as Porters Plantation. It nestled between the coast road and the beach, adjacent to the Coral Reef Club. It's starkly white limestone buildings were topped with red clay tile roofs and trimmed with lattice around the edges. The landscape was lush, with bright blue pools scattered throughout the property between the buildings. Down on the beach, just at the northern tip of the property, partially screened from the main beach area was a small wooden shack, perched uncertainly on a crumbling foundation of coral rocks. The multilayered paint was peeling, revealing successive layers of ancient and different colored paint. The front door hung open drunkenly by one hinge, and the screen gaped open where it was torn from the frame. It was here that Norman lived; he was, as usual, at home.

Norman regained consciousness very slowly. A loud rhythmic pounding pulse was moving his body back and forth on the hard surface he was lying on. He felt hot sun on his face. Gradually a sickening, yet familiar, stench registered in his fogbound brain. The sensation was like that of a putrid wet wash cloth being sucked up his nose. The pain in his head was intense, pulsating when he breathed. He could see nothing, perhaps he was blind. His mouth was bone dry from a night of mouth breathing, and his sense of taste was either gone, or mercifully numb. His tongue felt like a piece of cardboard scraping against jagged wooden gums.

Cautiously, he forced open one eye. Relieved that he could still see, he was instantly alarmed by something large moving vigorously about, two inches from his eye. It was an ominous, predatory looking creature, waving its antennae near his only currently functioning eyeball. A large cockroach was enthusiastically feasting on his vomit. Alarmed by the sight, he jerked his head up, pulling out substantial clumps of hair from his head and beard as his head rose from the floor. His hair had been stuck to the surface he was laying on, held in place by a malodorous, solidified, pool of vomit. He had apparently, again, passed out on the floor of his hut, puking all over himself and the floor in the process. The rhythmic pounding in his head turned out to be his headache, which was threatening him with blindness, from the intense pain. He sat up deliberately; purposely remaining on the floor while carefully planning his next move. Experience had shown him that precipitous action invariably ended in disaster. He slowly and painstakingly made his move. Holding his breath to keep the pain in his head at bay, he struggled to his knees and looked around. His head started to throb so alarmingly, that he kneeled over and rested his forehead on the floor, waiting patiently for the pain to recede to a more manageable level. As usual in this situation, he was alone. Cautiously, he looked up again to access his situation. Fighting the pain whenever his eyeballs moved, he carefully glanced around the room. He could see the sun shining through the doorway of his one room shack; the door stood open, hanging from only one hinge, the screen hung down in two pieces. Apparently, he had trouble getting it open again last night, and had resorted to the tried and true method of kicking it in. The resulting damage was familiar, and not surprising. The door had been repaired so many times, that it was hardly worth closing. He had nothing of value that would prompt a thief to break into the shack anyway. He paid it scant attention. Struggling to get a grip on his current condition, he pulled himself up by the counter, and took inventory. He was wearing his best shirt, a fashionably faded cotton hula shirt of dubious origin, and even more anonymous and unidentifiable color, and a vomit stained, wrinkled pair of khaki shorts. Only the sandal on his left foot seemed to have survived the prior evening. The other was nowhere in sight. Both garments, coated in chunks of solidified vomit, gave off an unbearable stench. Even for Norman, in his less than functioning condition, it was more than he could bear.

Not daring to look in the cracked mirror hanging over the counter, he staggered to the door, peered out, looking up and down the sandy beach. Finding it relatively deserted, he lurched down to the water and fell face first into a small wave. He floated there; face down, for a few minutes, trying to get his brain in gear, letting the salt water unstick his eyelids so he could see properly.

Finally, needing to breath, he sat up in the shallow water and started to scrub his face, hair, and beard with hands full of sand. It was his customary morning toilet, whether or not he needed to get rid of the clinging filth. After ten minutes, somewhat satisfied with the results of his labors, he removed his shirt and shorts, and scrubbed them with sand. Drawn by their eternal quest for food, a cloud of silver bait fish had gathered around him to feast on the floating chum. Their thin silver bodies sparkled in the sunlight. Norman became irritated, as they pecked harmlessly at his body in their feeding frenzy. When his clothes appeared to be relatively free of the caked on gunk, he pulled on the shorts, and tossed the shirt onto the dry sand above the wave line. Wading into deeper water, he started swimming out past the club's moored raft, toward the inside of the reef. After a few minutes, he passed the raft and picked up the pace; he covered the last hundred yards in fairly good order, halting between several of the moored boats. Treading water, he turned around and looked back at the raft and beach beyond it. Not overly given to introspection, today he felt that he ought to take stock of himself, at least in a superficial way. He knew he was marking time. Since he deserted the Australian Army, he had not been able to sustain any form of permanence. His tenure here at the Colony Club as a water ski instructor, depended on the good graces of a local entrepreneur who was clearly less than enchanted with Norman's usual performance. His home, such that it was, slated for demolition sometime soon when the club's manager got around to it had been his only permanent home in the past few years. As usual, he was teetering on the abyss; he had no real future prospects. Strangely undaunted, he shook off his hangover and actually looked around at the magnificence of his surroundings. He acknowledged that despite his dismal situation, he loved it here. Once again reconciled to his fate he turned back to the beach and looked up and down.

He observed only one person on the beach; a pale woman, clad in a smallish two piece swim suit was walking leisurely along the beach toward the Colony Club, from the direction of the adjacent Coral Reef. She appeared to be oblivious to Norman and his casual observation. He did not recognize her. Based on the pale skin and colorful suit, he thought that she was, most likely, a newly arrived tourist, out for an early morning stroll on the beach. She looked happy and beautiful. From what he observed, she was athletic, medium busted, with long blond hair. She was very attractive. He hoped that she was staying at one of the two hotels, because, faithful to his daily routine, he was certain to run into her later in the day at the water sports shack or the beach bar. If he didn't run into her before, he'd check her out that evening when she showed up at the bar. Sooner or later, everyone showed up at the beach bar.

As Norman tread water, it finally started to register in his addled brain that today was Wednesday, and he had to work. His boss Lyle Farmer was expecting him to have the ski boat and equipment ready for their first reservation at ten o'clock. For all he knew, it might be mid-afternoon. Furtively, he glanced at the sun. He was relieved to see that it was still early morning, probably about eight o'clock, or thereabouts. As he swam back to shore, he started sorting out his day, first a hair of the dog, then some coffee, then fetch the boat from anchor, and haul the skis and lines from the back of the water sports kiosk onto the beach.

As he swam, Norman struggled to remember if he had gassed up the boat yesterday after work. He couldn't remember, so he'd have to check first thing. If the boat needed gas, he'd have to hustle to be ready on time. He was becoming wary of his boss, who, although he was an easy going bloke, had become increasingly irritated with Norman's constant tardiness and slipshod approach to the business. Lyle kept telling him that, even though his business was, at present, the only waterskiing venture on the gold coast, they still had to give good service to keep out any potential competition. More than once, he had fired Norman, only to relent and let him come back to work a few days later.

With his hair slicked back, he emerged from the Sea and walked over to pick up his newly laundered shirt. He stood up, shaking the sand from the soggy shirt, intending to return to his shack. The woman walking on the beach chose that moment to glance his way. She paused, about to turn into the Colony Club beach terrace. She looked at him, and he looked at her. With her hand shading her eyes from the early morning sun, she looked him over. What she saw was an unshaven, good looking, bleached blond, tall man, with the beginnings of a paunch. He was well muscled and burned dark brown from the sun. She could see a white line just above his sagging shorts, where the sun had not tanned him. She smiled at him, turned and walked past the mancheneel tree, into the dining pavilion. Ever vigilant where good looking women were concerned, Norman caught the smile. With his heart lifted once again, he set off to start his day. Life, once again, had some potential. He would worry about the future later; something always came up.

For Norman, this particular day, like all others in Barbados in November 1956 had definite possibilities. The bookings were good, the fees large, and the tips generous. The tourist ladies always seemed anxious to rub up against the local color. Norman was one of the last of a passing breed, a true beachcomber. Unknown to most of the people on the island, he was a deserter from the Australian army. He had gone AWOL, out to sea, signing on to serve a series of rusty coastal steamers, changing berths frequently as he tried to put some serious distance between himself and the deserted army. Satisfied that he had gone far enough and tired by the endless drudgery of ship life, he had jumped ship one night off Bridgetown. He took his kit bag and swam ashore. After a few false starts and some near brushes with the local law, he now had a rent free shack on the beach, with no running water, no toilet, no real kitchen, and a board floor. The Caribbean Sea was fifty yards from his front door. His shack was a strange color. Successively ancient layers of paint peeled away in the sun to reveal a variety of faded colors, and rotting boards beneath. The roof was tin, and his bed, a true, battered and sagging king size with one gray sheet with multiple stains, and two moth eaten pillows, was the only intact piece of furniture in his domain. His wardrobe consisted of a decent blue Speedo, two pair of faded blue swim trunks, three pair of ragged khaki shorts, two T shirts, and two hula shirts. They were laundered to perfection, every morning, in the sea, and hung on one of the hooks on his wall to dry.

His working uniform was solely the blue Speedo. To prepare for the day, he took a generous swig of Eclipse rum, from the gallon jug he kept handy under the bed. He could not afford Mount Gay, unless a tourist was buying. He brushed his teeth, and pulled on a pair of swim trunks. His preparations for the day complete, he walked back down to the water, and pushed a six foot wooden dinghy into the waves. He rowed leisurely out, to an obviously homemade twenty footer, moored about half way to the reef. He tied the dinghy to the mooring, and clambered aboard. The first thing he did was check the gas tanks. He was relieved to see that all three tanks were full and ready to go. He lowered the motor into the water and with two pulls on the old, but lovingly cared, for sixty horse motor, the boat's Evenrude purred to life. Leaning over the bow, Norman untied the boat from the mooring, and headed to shore. Expertly killing the engine, he lifted the prop out of the water, beached the boat, and climbed out. One quick drag on the bow line, and the boat was secure above the gentle waves. Since he didn't have to get gas, he knew he had time for breakfast. Walking up the sandy lane, along the north side the Colony Club, he skirted behind the building to the kitchen. He was welcomed and handed his coffee and a toasted bun with butter. As usual, when he was not late for work, he sat on the kitchen stoop and exchanged gossip with the kitchen staff. It was a great way to start the day. He was accepted as one of them, even though he was white. Due to his circumstances, he had truly become an islander, a Bajan thru and thru. He had been there long enough to ignore color. Even though the population was ninety five percent black, there seemed to no racial overtones anywhere. Occasionally a tourist stirred the pot, but they were so thoroughly rebuffed and ignored, they tended to go away confused. It was, in fact, the locals against the tourists, no matter what their color. Other than tourists, sugar, and rum, there was no other real work on the island. The bustling service industry kept it all going smoothly. Norman was an integral cog in that well oiled machine, keeping the tourists happy.

Few people knew that Norman was an illegal immigrant. He could not legally take a real job. Since jumping ship, he had moved from one cash-in-hand job to another, before landing this job with Lyle Farmer's new water ski enterprise. His basic qualification for the job was that he could fix any motor. At six two, bleached blond, and darkly tanned, he was also a magnet for the tourist ladies, who signed up to ski each week. Even though his boss at thirty five was younger, more fit, and equally tanned, Lyle was hard pressed to compete with Norman, for the favors of the tourist ladies. Fortunately, there was enough to go around and then some. Lyle also had an off and on again, local girlfriend named Eileen. She split her time between helping Lyle, and the charter captain Quincy McKenna. As far as Norman was concerned, the spin-off social life was one of the best perks of the job. Lyle paid in cash, and could always be counted on, for a loan between paydays. It was a perfect existence, at least so far. If he kept his nose clean, and worked steadily for six hours a day, six days a week, he was literally living in paradise. Eclipse Rum was five BWI dollars per gallon, at the factory, if you brought your own jug. The fish and the breadfruit were free for the taking. He could cook over a driftwood fire on the beach. More often than not, when he was not the guest of one of the tourists at the hotel restaurant, he cooked for two on the beach. He then, retired early to his shack, with his company and his bottle of rum. He lived a life that was only a fantasy for thousands of pale skinned refugees, from cold country winters.

He was in fact, thoroughly hung over, and blissfully unaware, that his life was about to change forever. It would not be pretty.

Chapter 2 – Wednesday
The Colony Club Beach

That morning on the Island was once again typical of the latitude, but more varied than the day before. Far off clouds, fluffy white, were interspersed with dark grey, rain filled cumulus. Patches of heavy air spread under the darker clouds where they were drawing water from the sea. Everywhere else, the bright sunlight sparkled off the water which varied from beige to light blue to deep green over the reefs that stood off the beach about one hundred yards. The beach itself was off-white, coarse sand sloping sharply to the wave line, broken only by the creek running into the sea between the Colony Club and The Coral Reef. Lazy waves, typical of the leeward side of the island swished steadily onto the sand with a gentle hiss. That's why this side of the island was referred to as the Gold Coast; it was calm, serene ocean for people who were afraid of the more active water elsewhere around the island.

On the beach, a good looking woman in a brief, two piece swimsuit, with a gauzy sarong tied loosely around her hips was meandering past the outdoor dining of the Coral Reef, searching for shells and generally enjoying the novel sensation of the trade winds sliding gently over her bare body. The combination of the view, the breeze, and the feel of the crisp sand under her feet put her in a mood that spoke well for the rest of her day.

Jenna White was truly a refugee. Her normal daily existence consisted of fourteen hour work days, confined to a large, but cluttered office or conference room. Her desk was always piled high with weighty legal briefs. Her secretary spent her entire, ten hour day, churning out more reams of documents that had to be corrected, retyped, and processed. The only relief from her daily routine was the frequent phone calls, bringing a new load of problems to be solved. The real excitement in her day was usually a stale sandwich, partially eaten, and then forgotten at some point during the long day. She was burned out. The mind numbing weight of all that paper, and the oftentimes esoteric meaning contained within, weighed her down. After four years, she had started to wonder why she was doing it in the first place. When had the excitement of the vital legal contest, degenerated into the ceaseless quest for a partnership in the firm? Did she really want to be a partner? If, and when, she attained that goal, would she be happy, or merely busier than ever? She was fresh out of answers, discouraged, frustrated, and bored out of her mind. Her personal life was becoming increasingly boring. It seemed that she did not have time to date, far less get involved. Her social life had atrophied in law school, and had not appreciably improved since she hired on with the law firm. While she considered herself a modern woman, she had neither the time not inclination to cruise the bars, and the two experiences she had with one night stands convinced her that this was not a behavior suited to her. While she was a physical person, she was not drawn to mindless encounters, and contented herself on a routine basis with a vigorous workout at the gym and a more intimate workout in the evenings with a clever appliance. So far it had distracted her from her present situation. Apparently, however, it was no longer enough. She had caught herself, in the last few days, looking up from her pile of papers and staring wistfully out the window at the dismal city skyline. She was starting to panic; she was definitely missing something, and her desperation was mounting daily. Her secretary had started to look at her in a quizzical manner as she hauled the piles of paper in and out of her office each day.

Seventy two hours ago, at eight thirty two on a Monday morning, she had abruptly stood up from her desk, grabbed her purse, and walked out her office door. In passing, she told her secretary that she was going out for a while. Startled, but not particularly alarmed at this unprecedented occurrence, her secretary merely shrugged, and returned to her typing.

Jenna had walked out of the building, turned right along the sidewalk toward the subway station. She was searching for the storefront travel agency that she vaguely remembered passing, every morning for over ten years. Almost passing it by, she stopped, looked in the window, marched over, and opened the door. A well dressed, pleasantly plump, pretty, middle aged, woman looked up at the sound of the opening door. Fixing Jenna with a dazzling smile, she said, "Welcome, may I be of service?"

Momentarily speechless and unprepared for even this banal remark, Jenna finally stammered, "I need to get away, I need to get away right now; somewhere warm and sunny. I want to be gone at least two weeks, and I don't care where I go, as long as it's warm, sunny, and peaceful." The woman looked her over. What she saw was a good looking, well dressed, but wrinkled, harried looking woman, with blond hair escaping from a carelessly wound bun. To the woman behind the desk, Jenna looked as strung out as she sounded.

Eager to be of help, the travel agent thought briefly and replied, "I have just the place, and the busy season has not yet started. It should be very peaceful at this time of year. A month from now I wouldn't recommend it. Right now, though, it's perfect for you. When do you want to leave?"

"Tomorrow," said Jenna, handing over her Diner's Club card. "If you make the arrangements, I have some shopping to do, and I'll stop back later today, and pick up the tickets."

"Do you have a passport?" asked the woman.

"Yes. I'm not sure why I do, but I do. My secretary always makes sure that it is current. I haven't used it in years," replied Jenna.

"Great, you won't need a visa," the woman said. "You're all set. Enjoy your shopping, and I'll see you later. Everything will be ready for you by three o'clock this afternoon."

Jenna exited the office, humming softly to herself. She felt better already. The decision made, she was off. She turned right again, and headed for Bergdorf's.

The next morning, she took her phone off the hook while she packed. She knew it was the office calling every twenty minutes. She had no intention of changing her mind. Jenna made sure that she included all her slinky stuff, especially the new swim suits. She had purchased three of them yesterday. She had rejected the scandalously brief new bikinis in favor of the more traditional two piece suits. She did, however choose the briefest of those available. Satisfied that she would not be conveying the wrong message, she had paired up the suits with several sarong type scarves. Busy, she packed and repacked, sorting, rejecting, and selecting, what she wanted to take. She was scrupulous about not taking anything that reminded her of her daily life in New York City. By noon, she was on her way in a cab to the East Side Airline Terminal, to connect to a shuttle to Idyllwild airport.

Jenna did not care that she knew virtually nothing about her destination. Barbados, before this Tuesday, was just a name she had heard occasionally when her friends and acquaintances talked about vacation plans. She had a vague notion that it was somewhere very south , near the equator, in the British West Indies, a few hours south of New York. It was supposed to be warm and beautiful, and she was ready for that. Her BWIA flight left promptly at one thirty, and landed right on time. She had arrived yesterday, exhausted, from the surge of emotions, guilt, at deserting her post, elation at her escape, and hope that something wonderful was going to happen to her. She felt way overdue for wonderful. When she arrived at the Colony Club, she checked in, taking the complimentary rum punch with her to her room. She started to unpack and sat down on the bed to sip her drink. Enjoying the exotic taste, she quickly finished the drink, and fell asleep before she had finished unpacking. Still in her travel clothes, she had awakened this morning, to a sunny day, and gentle breezes. Ignoring the rest of the unpacking, she quickly changed into one of her new suits, grabbed a scarf, and left the room headed for the beach. That was two hours ago. As she returned from her walk, she was excited, rested, and looking forward to her first day. She was thoroughly in love with her new found location. The sun, the sand, the breeze, and the ocean combined to put her in a mood to relax and let her hair down. It was a strange feeling, unfamiliar, exciting and disquieting at the same time. Her newfound openness to what was going to happen next, frightened and exhilarated her at the same time. For the first time in years, she was wide awake and fully aware of her surroundings. It was intoxicating, and she loved the unaccustomed feelings coursing through her. Perhaps, she thought to herself, I might even meet a man. Even if it only amounted to a vacation fling, at least it would not be a one night stand. Her new surroundings were making her feel that she could be someone different here, someone more open and receptive. Her first impression was that she was already in exotic and uncharted territory, and she was conscious of a growing feeling of eroticism and optimism in her private self. She was eager for each day and what it might bring.

Before turning in to the breakfast patio at the Colony Club, Jenna looked north along the beach. She saw a man walk out of the sea, and pause to pick up something off the beach. By shading her eyes, she was able to see he was a real hunk, slightly older, but a genuine hunk none the less. She realized that it had been years since she had seen a man not wearing a business suit. He looked so good; she smiled involuntarily with pleasure, and saw that he caught the smile. Slightly embarrassed, she turned to go into breakfast. Floating on her mood, she walked into the pavilion, wondering who he was, and if she might see him again. Only here for only two weeks, she wanted to make every day count.

Glancing over to the beach bar, she spied the elderly black bartender who had served her the welcome rum punch the night before. On an impulse, she diverted to the bar to thank him for the delicious welcoming drink. She walked up and said, "Hi, I'm Jenna, and you served me a great drink last night. What's your name?"

"Manny," he replied. "Yes mistress, I remember you too. You left before your second drink. The policy of the house is two rum punches per guest upon arrival. You can have your second one anytime; just come over and get it when you are ready."

"Thanks," she said. "I'll see you after lunch." She turned and went into the dining patio.

The breakfast patio was a colonial style, open air pavilion, looking out toward the beach bar and thatched roof covered tables, overlooking the beach. Jenna unconsciously chose a table looking out over the beach, toward the sea. She studied the menu, and selected nothing familiar. She wanted to taste the island as well as experience it. She ordered chilled sliced mango, a bowl of cold sowersop, and a pot of tea. After she ordered, she resumed her perusal of the beach and the sea beyond. She noticed the man she had seen earlier coming out of the sea. He was dressed this time only in a blue Speedo. He came out of a small shack, and sauntered down to a dingy, grey/white, dinghy resting on its side on the sand. He pushed it into the surf, jumped in, and rowed out to another boat, anchored off the beach about fifty yards.

This one was a stripped down looking speed boat of indeterminate make, dirty white, with a red slash along the side, and a big outboard strapped to the transom. He reached down under a seat, adjusted something, lowered the outboard into the sea, and fired it up; he switched the mooring line to the dinghy, and drove the larger boat back to the beach. As he neared the sand, he slowed the boat, raised and shut off the engine and allowed the boat to slide up onto the packed sand at the edge of the beach. After pulling it further up onto the sand, he strolled up to the water sports kiosk, and disappeared inside. Intrigued, Jenna called a waiter over and asked if he knew who the man was, and what he was doing.

"Yes Mistress" the man replied. "That's Norman, and he's getting ready to start the water skiing for today."

"Can anyone go?" she asked. "Yes Mistress, just sign up at the front desk or the water sports kiosk."

Happily, she thanked the man, and tucked into her breakfast. Smiling to herself, she thought that meeting the man would be as easy as signing up for water skiing lessons. It sounded like fun, and, who knows what might develop. He might turn out to be single, and possibly as interesting as he was good looking. While eating, she happened to look out to see and spotted another man climb out of a cabin of a rather large boat moored about two hundred yards out from the beach. He was too far away to distinguish his features, but she noticed that he was wearing only a pair of khaki shorts; he was heavily tanned and powerfully built. While she watched, picking idly at her papaya, he casually vaulted to the roof of the salon, grasped one of the ropes hanging down from the boat's mast and almost casually climbed hand over hand to the top of the mast. Astonished, she considered what strength would be required for a feat of that nature. He fiddled with some ropes at the top of the mast, then stood erect on the crosstree a few feet lower than the top of the mast. She gasped in shock as he casually let go the mast and started to fall toward the deck of the boat. He abruptly executed a perfect jackknife and parted the water almost without a ripple. Unaware that she had been holding her breath, she exhaled with relief. She realized that she had been afraid he would sash himself insensible on the deck of the boat. Embarrassed to be observed staring openly, she returned her attention to her breakfast. Later, as she signed the bill for her breakfast, she casually asked the waiter who owned the large boat at anchor offshore.

"Captain McKenna, Mistress, he is a charter captain, and cruises around the island and takes people scuba diving." Well, she thought, two interesting specimens within a half hour. Her vacation was definitely shaping up, and it was only the beginning of the day. Apparently both men were accessible because of their businesses. She resolved to meet them both.

This was the first vacation that Jenna had taken in many years. Her job as lead attorney, in the fraud division for a prestigious law firm, kept her so busy that her social was a distant memory. All her cases had become a meaningless blur in her mind. She nodded to herself. She needed this, and she did not care that her office had no idea where she had disappeared to. She deliberately did not tell anyone, because she knew that would track her down, and drag her back. She half hoped that they would fire her for her irresponsible conduct. She doubted, however, that they would. Where would they find another willing slave?

Now that she was so far from home, she could be whomever, and whatever, she wanted to be. She could reinvent herself. This was the first time, since her college years, that she had felt truly free. No one knew where, or who she was. What a golden opportunity to try out some things she had only read and dreamed about. With her current feeling of well being, just the thought, of the seemingly limitless possibilities, gave her a thrill.

At one pm Jenna found herself at the water sport kiosk, eagerly anticipating the skiing lesson. She had been thinking all morning, about what might happen when she tried to ski. She had decided in advance that she would lean back and enjoy the ride. Looking forward to meeting Norman was fun in itself. She watched him as he greeted the people in the group. His manner with the ladies suggested that he was not a married man. He definitely did not act like he was married, so she felt that it would be ok to flirt with him a little and see what happened. It was obvious that he had noticed her. There were five other people on the beach for ski lessons, two couples and a good looking, dark haired, man who appeared to be on his own. He too was not wearing a wedding ring, and he also had noticed her and was subtly moving in her direction. She turned to listen to the group as Norman got them organized. There were, including her, six people in the group.

Janice and Trent Carver were from Manchester England, on their honeymoon. They had never skied before, and having been married only for a week, couldn't keep their hands off each other. This was certainly the perfect place for such delights. It turned out, that Janice worked in a bank, and Trent sold real estate. They had dreamed of this time in the islands since they first decided to honeymoon in Barbados. It would be an amazing change from Manchester, and the dismal gray weather. They also hoped to meet people who were from some exotic locations, other than Manchester. They were off to a good start. Janice was looking forward to a little adventure, and eager to experience it with her new husband.

The other couple, clearly middle aged, named Chloe and Tedd Whiting were from Wales. They were waiting patiently for the ski session to begin. On their island holiday, they were looking to rekindle their dwindling passion. Chloe, an author with a successful series of children's books to her credit, was looking for some more salacious content for books of a different bent. Modestly successful, she enjoyed book signings, travel, the publisher's parties, and, mostly getting away from Tedd. After he inherited his father's tire business, Tedd had morphed into a complete bore. Chloe had hoped that this island vacation, a definite departure from their daily lives, would jolt them both into a better place. At middle age, she felt that their fun time was running out.

The fifth person, waiting while Norman was explaining what they were going to be doing, was a fellow American, Ellis Caulfield, an apparently wealthy, self styled, adventure enthusiast, eager to renew his skiing skills. He would try anything that was even mildly risky. This attitude definitely appealed to Jenna. He had that bad boy look, with tousled black hair, and an athlete's build. It seemed to her, that Ellis had not yet found himself, but was looking, and looking hard. He was definitely interested in getting to know Jenna. Somehow, both Norman and Ellis were aware of the other's interest and were already vying for her attention.

Finally, Norman led his group over to the boat, shaking Jenna out of her reverie. He was ready to begin the ski session. He loaded the six guests into the boat, and shoved off the beach, motoring out to a spot about one hundred yards offshore, directly opposite the Colony Club raft. The sun bathers on the raft sat up and watched, as each person in the group slipped on a pair of skis, and tightened the bindings to fit. The onlookers, accustomed to the daily ski routine, were anticipating some entertainment, watching a bunch of neophytes tackle a new sport. The man from the yacht was also clearly interested, as he perched himself on the roof of the boat's salon and sipped idly on a cup of tea. He appeared eager to view the show. Once the skis were properly adjusted, they were taken off, and stowed so that the first skier could enter the water.

Norman, wanting to evaluate the level of competence or incompetence that each student exhibited, selected Ellis as the first skier. After Ellis was safely in the water with his skis on, tips pointing in the air, he handed Ellis the tow rope, and slowly pulled the rope taut, to start Ellis on his journey. Norman anticipated that, because of prior experience, Ellis would know how to position his skis, so that when the ski boat began moving forward, he would simply stand up out of the water on his skis, and ski properly. Ellis' exalted opinion of himself sadly resulted in failure, as he was pulled forward, over the skis, onto his face. Coughing and choking, he clung to the side of the boat after it circled back to pick him up. He quickly regained his composure, as Norman patiently explained to him again, that he should keep his knees bent, his arms straight, and let the boat pull him out of the water. Ellis elected to try again, and this time, successfully launching himself on top of the water. He skied confidently around the bay, pleased that he had redeemed himself. He skied well, crossing the wake several times and gaining confidence as he zoomed around the bay before dropping off the tow rope right where he started.

The next adventurer to rise out of the ocean was Janice Carver. Athletically inclined, she miraculously grabbed the tow rope, spaced her legs apart, and managed a wobbly rise out of the water. She quickly gained confidence in her new found ability, and did a complete circle around the bay, dropping off the line, directly opposite the raft, to a fun round of applause. Her husband Trent followed the same path, and likewise, did a commanding job for a first timer. Chloe and Tedd, experienced skiers, took their turns, and also managed a credible effort.

Now it was Jenna's turn. She was itching to try the skis, thinking that it looked so easy, except for Ellis's fall. Jenna had been known, to her many friends in college, as something of a klutz. Although graceful on a dance floor, she had a history of tripping and falling in unlikely places. After strapping on the skis, she carefully lowered herself over the side of the boat. Norman gave her the standard pitch, and eased the line taut, waiting for her signal to start. She grabbed the tow rope hard, and let Norman know she was ready with a quick nod of her head. Her first try to get up was a total failure. She over compensated for the pull and fell forward over her skis. As the boat lost power, the tow rope somehow wrapped itself around her neck. Jenna fought the fear and panic that wrenched her, desperately trying to free herself, and get some air. When she felt Norman's hands around her waist, lifting her, she collapsed against him with relief. That was enough skiing for her first day. She would try again tomorrow.

She was embarrassed that she alone had not managed to get up on the skis, but everyone assured her that it was ok, and that she would be fine when she tried it again later. Both Norman and Ellis went out of their way to be solicitous. After the boat was back at the beach, the group decided to meet next door for drinks before dinner. They all wanted to see the Coral reef Club, and they had plenty of time to enjoy the sunset from the bar before they had to return to the Colony Club for dinner. Mollified by the obvious male attention, Jenna shrugged off her failure and set off for her room.

Chapter 3 – Wednesday
Aboard the Billfish

Later in the afternoon, as the ketch pulled away from the anchorage at the Paradise Beach Club, owner and captain Quincy McKenna eyed the sails, the pennant on the mainmast, and the riff along the water to seaward. He adjusted the wheel slightly to starboard, and nodded with satisfaction when the sails billowed out full with a satisfying snap. As The Billfish headed out to deeper water, the color of the sea turned from turquoise to dark green. He debated setting the staysails, just to show off a little for the dozen or so tourists littering the deck; he decided that it was too much work. It was a perfect day, a few far away squalls passing to the west, and a steady trade wind pushing the boat along. Loosely hauled, the yacht would make about six knots back to the anchorage at Colony Club. His guests were all obviously pleased by their excursion. They had snorkeled, picnicked, and drunk a load of rum punches. Judging from their sunburnt faces, they looked to be a happy bunch. Eileen the stewardess was kept busy filling glasses and replenishing ice. They were all mildly drunk, and loving it; another successful cruise.

Black haired, with a dusting of gray, and six feet tall, Quincy appeared at first glance to be a little squat due to the heavy muscles of his upper torso. He was a little top-heavy, but his strength was well earned. He had sailed the Billfish from Liverpool to Barbados, single handed, through two hurricanes, and assorted tropical squalls. His slightly irregular features were also earned, when he was blown up with his SAS squad, on a clandestine raid, on some nameless beach in North Korea.

How he got back to the rubber boat, he still did not know. When he regained his senses, they were rendezvousing with the submarine. The only other man in the boat looked as bad off as he did. The rest of his men were dead, or missing. He was grateful to be alive.

He had lost most of his friends that ill fated night, and, when he was discharged from the hospital later that year, he decided to cash in his commission. The incident had left him with a sense of predestined fate, and some rather spectacular scars, slowly fading in the tropical sun. After two years on Barbados, his skin was approaching the color of finely tanned leather. What scars that remained visible, were thin white lines on his heavily tanned, muscular torso. His daily uniform as captain of the Billfish consisted of one garment only, a pair of old, khaki military shorts. He had about a dozen pair, and that was uniform enough for him.

A year after his discharge from the Special Boat Service, his father had died, leaving him the family pub in Liverpool. With most of his friends gone, and no romantic ties of any kind tying him to his home town, he decided to dramatically change his life, and head for warmer climes.

While pondering his next move, Quincy encountered a man named Sam in the pub one night, who was asking around where he could sell his boat. Inexplicably, Quincy was immediately interested. He was an indifferent sailor at best. He, like all his mates, had learned to sail as pre teens and teenagers, in sailing dories, on the Thames, and up the coast in summers past. The two men discussed the boat at length, and made arrangements for Quincy to look it over the following day. Sam bragged that it was a handsome boat, a fifty four foot, pilot house ketch, with a copper clad, wooden hull. The twin masts and rigging were in excellent condition. The hull and deck were in need of some sanding and varnish. The two men spent the next day going over the entire boat, from bilge to bowsprit. Sam was obviously, a very experienced seaman. He had, apparently spent the last ten years cruising the Mediterranean, the Channel Islands, and the British Isles. It seemed to Quincy that the boat had been very well maintained. A full on marine survey should verify his opinion. He was definitely interested, and had spent the day mulling over the prospects of simply taking off in this boat for parts unknown. The idea was appealing, but also a bit daunting. Even so, he reasoned, he could start slowly and get his sea legs back before he set out over the open ocean. As the day wore on, Quincy became more and more excited. The engine room was spotless, with the small Lister diesel and genset in perfect working order. The boat was about fifteen years old, with minimal instrumentation. It was obviously lovingly cared, for despite the benign neglect of the superficial spit and polish.

When the inspection was finished, Quincy invited Sam back to the pub for a fry up, and some serious conversation. It turned out, that Sam wanted fifty thousand pounds for the boat. Quincy was quite dismayed. His mustering out bonus was only ten thousand quid, and that, against the price of the boat, was a just a drop in the bucket. As the evening wore on, and the pints of bitter piled up, the two men seemed to take each other's measure, liking what they saw. It turned out that they shared a common, but somewhat vague, service background. As soldiers often do, they started swapping war stories. It came out, somewhere toward the end of the conversation, that Quincy was the current owner of the pub. He explained how he had come by it, and his desire to head to a warmer climate. Sam was immediately entranced; he said he envied Quincy the business, and the stability it offered. After knocking around for a dozen years, he had decided that he wanted to settle down. He hoped that, one day, he could achieve the same type of situation for himself.

In a flash of inebriated brilliance, Quincy blurted out, "Let's trade, my pub for your boat."

Sam was silent for a moment. Then, looking Quincy in the eye, he held up his hand, spit on the palm, stuck it out to Quincy, and said simply, "Done."

Quincy spit on his palm, reached for Sam's hand, and shook it vigorously.

In a flash, two lives had changed forever. Quincy reckoned that, despite Sam's evident satisfaction, he had got the better of the deal. Ruefully, he acknowledged, Sam probably figured that he had, also.

Thinking back on that day, Quincy realized what an insane idea it was for him to have set sail, all by himself, for the tropics. He knew how to sail, and he loved the boat, but he had come to realize that he had made a very fortunate choice. A ketch rigged boat is a forgiving boat for a single sailor. One man can handily raise the jib, set the tiller, and then trim out the rest of the sails. In a hard blow, a ketch rigged boat could be sailed on a storm jib handily. If things got serious, he could rig a sea anchor, batten down, and ride it out. It was, however, a lot of work. The leave taking was longer than Quincy had expected. There were numerous details to consider. First, he had to report back to his regiment that he was going to leave Great Britain, perhaps for good. He had retained a reserve commission when he mustered out and needed to make sure that he could do as he wished and still retain that commission. He was more attached to the service than he had realized. As it turned out, he was only required to touch base with the service when he changed countries. As long as they could find him, he was free to wander. That taken care of, he had to square away the boats papers, have it officially renamed the Billfish, inspected, and certified so that he could enter foreign ports with a clean bill of health; and then there were the provisions. Relying on his military background he stocked the boat as if he was off for an extended campaign in the bush. He knew he could fish, so he loaded up on freeze dried foods, vitamins, medical supplies and gin. After a few short trips up and down the coast with Sam supervising, he was pronounced proficient and bid Sam a hearty farewell. Upon hoisting anchor, he realized that the only people he had said goodbye to were his regimental commander and Sam. I guess I am ready for a new life he mused as he motored away from the wharf for the last time.

Fortunately for Quincy, the first two weeks proved to be time enough for him to resurrect his sailing skills, and learn his new boat from top to bottom. His only real problem was sleep. He had to set the boat on autopilot, with light sails, whenever he had to rest. Since the boat had no radar, he stayed well out of the regular shipping lanes. He dozed for no more than two to four hours at a time. It was safer sailing, but risky, if he needed to hail some other boat for help. It might be a long and fruitless wait for a rescue.

After two weeks of sailing, the love affair between Quincy and the boat he named the Billfish, was full on. He could feel the boat and its performance through the vibrations of the wheel, and the taut hum of the wind in the sails. The Billfish had become the love of his life. He felt that they were one, united against the elements. He loved the feel of the hull leaning to windward, the leeward rail awash as the boat sliced through the water with an evil hiss. As the shorebirds fell away, flying back to land, he was alone with his new love, on empty cobalt colored ocean. He was headed for paradise, and he loved the journey.

The weather turned serious, and, two months later, when he dropped anchor in Bridgetown to clear customs, both he and the boat showed signs of severe trauma. Two hurricanes, and assorted squalls, had challenged him and the Billfish to the limit. Despite a few close calls, the Billfish never let him down. He lost count how many times he had to go hand over hand to the top of the rigging, to free up some snarl or cut down some ripped canvas. He learned to appreciate the two-masted ketch design, and the snug pilot house, which kept him alive. Quincy felt that, without the rigorous SAS training, and his already superbly conditioned body, he might well have perished on the crossing. Instead, he had survived, and the Billfish was intact, albeit a bit battered and worn.

He arrived in Barbados, with six thousand pounds sterling in his sea chest, determined to embrace his new life.

After clearing customs the next day, he had meandered up the coast, inspecting prospects for a permanent mooring for his boat. He needed time to refit after the crossing, and there were some changes he wanted to make in the rigging, to render the boat easier for him to handle alone. In Bridgetown, the customs officer had recommended the Paradise Beach Club, and the Colony Club as good, sheltered locations with permanent moorings available for a price. He decided on Paradise Beach, as it was only about three miles from Bridgetown. He would need access to a good ship's chandlery for his refit. The owner of the Paradise Beach Club was congenial, and agreed to let him use one of their permanent moorings gratis. He felt that a good looking yacht, parked just off the hotel beach, couldn't hurt the club's ambiance. It gave the place a little flair for the tourists. Quincy's frequent forays to the hotel bar did wonders for the morale of the lady tourists, especially the single ones, and the dinghy was frequently seen heading back to the beach, late in the morning, with a succession of lovely ladies onboard, in various states of deshabille.

Quincy was in heaven. He worked steadily on his boat, sailing frequently around the island, acquainting himself with its reefs and anchorages. He quickly decided that the Gold Coast was the place to moor the boat on a permanent basis. The leeward side of the island was calmer, even in bad weather. If the weather was really bad, he could put to sea and ride it out until the storm blew through. In the tropics, the weather was never bad for long. The Billfish was soon in better shape than it had been when he bought it. The spit and polish was back. As his refit progressed, he soon realized that his money was running out, and there was no work available for a non citizen on the island. One day, as he was talking to Quarrel, the bartender at the Paradise Beach Club, about the situation. He mused that he might have to move on to the Keys for work, when Quarrel said, that he had overheard the guests, on many occasions, wish that they could have a ride on the Billfish. Most of the hotel's guests were from the England, the Continent, or the US mainland, New York, or other major eastern cities, and were landlubbers to a man. It was then that Quincy came up with the idea of chartering his boat. A quick call to the authorities reassured him that, while he could not hold a job on the island, he was free to operate a business, and pay taxes on the profits.

Two years later, here he was, sailing along with a full complement of guests aboard, usually about ten or twelve, with Eileen, his pretty stewardess, serving drinks. He also had a handy man, when he needed one, to help with the heavy lifting. All he had to do was sail, maintain the boat, and smile at the guests. By now he had it down to a routine. He knew all the silly questions and answers that pleased the guests. As long as he kept his shirt off, the ladies were content during the day. The tips were generous, and the fringe benefits without peer. He had, last year, moved his permanent mooring to the Colony Club. Their front desk seemed to generate most of his bookings, from their guests and the Coral Reef's next door. He had re-established a respectable balance in his checking account, and, was well along the way to becoming one of the most eligible bachelors on the Gold Coast. He was not yet ready to settle down, but he felt that he was establishing himself within the island's society. His reserve commission as a Major in the service gave him automatic access to the Governor and the other senior officials in the colonial administration. The island was working its way to total independence from Britain, but it was so firmly British in nature that there was no doubt that Barbados would remain within the Commonwealth. He had met several of the local politicians who were gradually assuming more control over the island's affairs, and was very happy that he was well received. It appeared that he had indeed found a new home. The unofficial name for the island was Little Britain; it was even shaped like the mother country. He seemed to be in demand socially, and was enjoying himself hugely. Recently he had met Bobbie Chastain, a neighbor of the Colony Club, and an amazingly enticing woman. Not quite sure exactly what to make of her, he was enjoying getting to know her and her children. She was very good looking in a busty athletic way, dark-haired, and tall for a woman. She water skied, spear fished, and sailed like a man. She was reputedly filthy rich. All in all, she was a very intriguing woman. Quincy was looking forward to their dinner date later that evening and hoping that it would develop into a long evening. The only thing about her that was disconcerting was her wealth. He had come from more humble origins, and although he was, by decree, an officer and a gentleman, he was more at home in shorts and at the wheel of the Billfish, than all dolled up at a cocktail party. The island custom of dressing up for social occasions had forced him to buy a dinner jacket. He was not quite comfortable with it, but he was secretly pleased with the way he filled it out; the response from the ladies more than justified the minor discomfort. Fortunately, he mused, he could go most places in shorts and a shirt and sandals. When he was required to suit up, he was resigned to it. Lately, however, the Governor was letting him know that he should attend functions at Government House in his uniform. He felt that as a reserve officer, he should show the colors.

On one such occasion he had attended, he had run into an old member of his regiment, a Sergeant Smythe-Caulley. The two men despised each other. Unfortunately, it was a small island, and they crossed paths often enough to keep their enmity alive. It seemed that neither man elaborated on their relationship; people who encountered them both were slightly mystified at their mutual disdain. They remained tight lipped.

As the Billfish rounded the point south of the Colony Club, Quincy steered the boat toward the beach. He called to Eileen to man the wheel while he pulled down the sails. When they were all down, tied off and stowed property, he went aft again and started the auxiliary engine. Eileen went to the bow with the boat hook, and they approached the mooring. This was always a tricky maneuver as the inebriated male guests always wanted to demonstrate their manhood and help Eileen. Often one of the guests or Eileen was knocked overboard in the process. He had to be very careful not to run them over. Usually, the guests were all excited and having fun, so no harm was done. Male dignity was somehow always preserved. When Eileen went for a swim, however, she had to struggle to maintain her composure. Today everything went smoothly, and Eileen expertly snared the mooring line and ran it through the Billfish's bow cleat. Quincy cut the power, and the billfish swung into the wind on her mooring. Three trips to the beach in the dinghy, and all the tourists were safely off his hands. He and Eileen expertly cleaned up after the party, and then Quincy ran her ashore and returned to the boat to make ready for his dinner date.

While he was going to dimmer with Bobby Chastain, he idly wondered if he might run across that good looking blond he had watched trying to water ski that morning. There was something about her infectious enjoyment of the day that drew his attention. She was a beautiful woman who seemed unconscious of her effect on the male half of the population. He had noticed that the two single men in the boat were trying to outdo each other for her attention. Can't blame them, he thought, they had good taste. Humming to himself, he went below to shower and change. You never knew, the day was still young. It was just the shank of the evening; he had time for a sundowner before he had to pick up his date at Porters.

Chapter 4 - Thursday Evening
The Coral reef Club

Back in her room at the Colony Club after her failed attempt at water skiing, Jenna was tired and discouraged. Her muscles ached from the unaccustomed activity; a hot soak was in order. If she wanted to enjoy herself tonight, she would have to regroup rest up, and start all over. Her ski group seemed to have gelled into a nice companionable bunch of people. Their geographical diversity was interesting to Jenna. To date, she had lived an urban but sheltered life, and her contact with foreigners had been very limited to mostly Canadians. Vaguely, she realized that she and Ellis were the only Americans in the group, and the Brits seemed quite exotic to her. For some reason, Norman did not seem British; she surmised that he might be an Aussie or another variety of colonial. She was enjoying the easy camaraderie, and the attentions of the two attractive single males during the ski session had been very flattering. Briefly, she recapped her experience to date; she had met Norman, and embarrassed herself trying to ski. She had met Ellis and not had a chance to get to know him at all, and she had spied a very attractive looking boat captain, admittedly from afar. She had noticed that the skipper had sat with a cup of something and watched the ski session. It might be her imagination, but it seemed that he was looking mostly at her. After her first day, she was tired, sunburnt, covered with sand, and just a little depressed. A full on reappraisal was in order. First, she called room service, and ordered some shrimp and two rum punches, then she stripped off her suit and rinsed off the sand in the shower. Her plan to reinvent herself a little, in a place where no one knew her, was so far, not meeting with much success.

Her room faced the ocean; she could look over a terrazzo patio, with thatched beach shelters, lining the separation between hotel and beach. Huge casurena pines, and the occasional mancheneel tree, lined the patio, and provided generous shade to the guests stretched out on loungers at the water's edge. Her sliding doors overlooked the scene, and the room, furnished simply in rattan and wood furniture, had a breezy island flavor. It was a total change from her overstuffed, carpeted existence in New York. The cool tile floor, relieved by a woven Dominican rug, was cooled by open shutters and a large central fan. A generous, stark white, mosquito net was hung over her bed, gathered over the headboard for the day. Later that evening, the maid would turn down the bed, and drape the net to keep the mosquitoes at bay.

While waiting for room service, Jenna lazily drew a very hot bath, tossed in some bath beads, and put on her robe to answer the door. Surprised that the bathroom was equipped with a Jacuzzi tub, she was looking forward to relaxing in its embrace. She arranged the drinks and the shrimp on the table next to the rose marble tub, turned the Jacuzzi on low, and slowly sank into the hot water. The bubbles soothed her skin, tender from the hours in the unaccustomed sun. A sip of rum punch, several nibbles of shrimp, and a face masque, completed her relaxation package. Letting her mind drift over the day, she speculated about the prospects for the evening. The group from the ski session had agreed to meet at the Coral Reef bar for drinks before dinner back at the Colony Club. Lying back in the water with her eyes closed, she became slowly aware of the water gently lapping over her nipples. Her large areolas, turned bright pink in the hot water, and her nipples, quite large to begin with, gradually became painfully rock hard and prominent. Without even having to stimulate herself, she was becoming aroused, relaxed, and definitely ready for an exciting evening. The building sensations in her body set her mind to thinking.

Her dedication to work had left her deprived of any real private life. What was she going to do with her future? What kind of a woman was she really? Before leaving New York so abruptly, she had not spent any time recently examining her private life. She needed to decide who she wanted to be. She was definitely consciously of a growling loneliness. It was not just a feeling of being alone, but a growing ache for some real intimacy in her life. She recalled fondly how her parents were with each other. They seldom passed each other at home without a soft touch or a pat on the butt. They seemed genuinely connected and content with their relationship. She envied that and had always assumed that she would, one day have a similar relationship with some special man. Her life, however, had taken a different turn; she suddenly realized that she had been diverted by her ambitions. Ruefully, she realized that her precipitous exit from New York was most likely due to an unconscious panic attack. Time was slipping by. Women today were more open than the generation she had grown up with. She could see it during the working day, and realized that she had been frozen in a generation gap, focused solely on her work. The sexual revolution was just starting, bras were being burned; women were becoming more overt about their sex lives. How did she fit into all this? Was she an old fashioned girl, or was she destined to be a more modern woman? Conscious of her body and the very sensual feelings currently stimulation her, she realized that she was an intensely sexual woman; sadly, she was to date unfulfilled. Her previous, brief sexual encounters had been quick, inadvertent, and very unsatisfying. She conceded that the lack of emotional engagement had ruined the two experiences for her. In fact, during the last few years she had relied on satisfying herself, instead of taking time from her career to seek real emotional engagement with a man. She had been sidetracked by her career, and was feeling very sorry for herself. While she was not yet interested in marriage, she was overripe for a good relationship and, definitely ready for some great sex. I'm definitely not the slutty type, she decided, but I won't pass by a promising encounter. I'll just keep my wits about me, and take it as it comes, she decided. Building on her growing mood, she let the fingers of one hand drift downward between her legs, while the other hand gently pinched her nipples into a further state of excitement. She stimulated herself languidly into a stress relieving mini orgasm.   As the tension left her body, she decided that this might turn out to be a great vacation after all. So far she had met two good looking men who seemed interested in her, and spied another that intrigued her somehow. Chuckling to herself, she acknowledged that she hoped their intentions were going to turn out to be less than honorable. She had no illusions that there might be a future for her with either man.

Lost in her musings, she finally became aware that the bubbles had cooled off the water sufficiently to make it less enjoyable. Deciding not to refill and continue, she rose languidly from the tub, grabbed a fluffy white bath towel, and slowly rubbed herself down. She rubbed especially hard between her legs, to relieve the gentle ache. When dry, she wrapped the towel around her hair, and stepped into the bedroom.

The afternoon sun streaked between the shutters, spilling fragmented light all over the room. Her bed was awash with dappled afternoon light, making a short nap seem like a perfect end to her little pick me up ritual. She stretched out on the bed naked, and, letting the gentle breeze from the slowly turning ceiling fan caress her bare skin, slowly drifted off to sleep.

When she awoke, Jenna looked out the window and saw that the sun was almost down, creating another spectacular sunset. She needed to hurry so that she would not miss the group gathering at the bar. Surveying her wardrobe, she picked the sexy little violet silk number she had bought just days before leaving on her vacation. Spaghetti straps, with a flared full skirt, the silk dress probably weighed three ounces. It lay over her body like a second skin. She moved around in front of the mirror, and was startled to see how erotic an impression she made. The glow on her face from the sun required no makeup; she could not improve the look. Her breasts and her nipples showed dramatically through the top, and she reluctantly reached for a bra to tone down the effect. The braless look had just started to surface in the States, but, so far, it was just espoused by college students and very young, hip professional women, and the occasional wanton needing male attention. Well, she conceded to herself, she wanted and needed some male attention. Defiantly, she threw the bra to the bottom of her closet. She decided to let it all hang out for the duration of her trip. No one on Barbados knew her, so what did it matter what they thought? It might turn out that she was baiting a very attractive hook for her fantasy vacation. She slipped into a very lacy pair of sheer white panties, checking to see that they did not show when she swished her rear. To complete the effect, Jenna added a pair of strappy heals, and sauntered out the door.

Jenna walked quickly through the winding walkway between the bungalows, lined with Hibiscus bushes and Coconut Palms. She headed for the walk that led next door to the Coral Reef. The hotels encouraged their guests to mingle and there was an established path from the Coral Reef to the Colony Club. The breeze was gently blowing through the open bar. Bright cushions topped the rattan and bamboo stools and chairs. The lights were dim, and the music was playing softly. In the distance, the sun was setting over the swishing waves, silhouetting the Billfish, just offshore, bobbing gently at anchor. Jenna took a deep breath of the sea air and sashayed into the bar and spotted her group. She greeted the Carvers, the Whitings, Norman, and Ellis. Taking the proffered drink handed to her by the bartender; she sank gracefully into one of the comfortable bamboo chairs, and crossed her long legs.

"You look delicious," said Ellis. "We were wondering if you had changed your mind, and I, for one, am very glad you came along. Norman is definitely not my type."

Bridling slightly that his intended compliment had been preempted, Norman quickly agreed and pulled up a chair next to Jenna, leaving Ellis standing alone nearby at the bar.

"What are your plans for this evening?" asked Norman.

"I've not given it any thought," she said. "I'm a little tired from the skiing and the sun. I'll probably just have dinner at the hotel tonight, take a short walk on the beach, and call it a day."

"Some of us were discussing going to Paradise Beach Club for the Calypso night and some dancing," said Ellis. "Would you like to join us? Norma Stout is singing tonight. She is one of the island's best calypso singers."

"No thanks, not tonight. They told me at the concierge desk that the show moves daily from hotel to hotel up the gold coast. It will be available all week, and here at the Colony Club on Friday night," replied Jenna.

At that moment, Jenna glanced up in time to see a very striking couple walk into the dining room, from the direction of the lobby. At first glance, the man seemed short, but when she looked carefully, it was because his massive shoulders made him seem shorter. He was actually quite tall, over six feet she guessed, dark haired, and a bit weather beaten. He was dressed in pressed khaki shorts and a loose, white, short sleeved shirt. His dark tropical tan topped off a very handsome package. Startled, she suddenly recognized the man from the yacht. He was incredibly attractive up close. Equally striking, was his companion. She also was also tall, about five feet seven, Jenna judged, athletic, quite busty, and dark haired. She was wearing one of those oversized scarves that wrap around and tie behind the neck. She could possibly be totally naked underneath. Jenna wished that the man would glance her way, but he was being a proper, attentive escort, focusing his attention exclusively on his companion; the couple passed by and entered the dining room. As if prompted by her telepathic command, he urged his escort ahead of him and he glanced her way. His gaze fell directly on her and his intent scrutiny made her heart start to hammer. She had completely forgotten the two men in her party competing intently for her attention. The moment passed, and with a wicked grin, the tall man turned once more to his date and followed her into the dining room. Flustered, Jenna reluctantly returned her attention to her group.

It was obvious that all the men had noticed the woman; conversation had come to a halt at the bar. Jenna was grateful that the men's attention had been distracted as well, and they had failed to notice her brief encounter with the mysterious captain. From the way the couple was greeted by the Maître D, it was evident that they were well known at the Coral Reef. They were shown to a table overlooking the beach and the candles were lit. The maître D summoned a waiter, and a brief consultation ensued. Satisfied that the couple was in good hands, the Maître D smiled and returned to his post at the restaurant entrance. The waiter bustled off to bring refreshments.

Turning to Norman, Jenna asked, "Who is that, or rather, who are they?" She did not want to be too obvious about her curiosity about the man. She was, however, also very curious about the woman.

"That's Quincy McKenna and Bobbie Chastain," said Norman.

"That doesn't tell me much," said Jenna. "There must be more to the story than that. Are they a couple?"

"They spend some time together, but they are not married. The man, Quincy McKenna, is the captain of the Billfish that you see anchored offshore. He charters out to tourists for cruises and scuba diving expeditions, when the mood strikes him. He's British, ex military and a hell of a sailor. That seems to be all anyone knows about him."

"What about her?"

"Bobbie Chastain is a real mystery woman. She moved here about a year ago and rented Porter's Great House across the street. She must be filthy rich. She loves water sports and lives with her two children, who are about eight and twelve. She skis a lot with Lyle, and scuba dives off Quincy's boat at least once a month. No one seems to know much about her. She's European, according to the rumors, but she speaks English like a Brit, and she is fluent in French and German. She entertains a lot and seems to like to meet people visiting the island. You might get an invitation to one of her well known cocktail parties"

"Why well known?" asked Jenna.

"Apart from the generous drinks and delicious finger food, the guest list is often pretty exotic. It's usually a mix of some well known local dignitaries, a selection of nefarious characters, a handful of the more colorful planter families, some local blacks, chosen for their talents rather than their breeding, and usually, a nice mix of tourists and visiting celebrities. Her home is unbelievable; two pools, one indoors, the only one on the island, two Rolls Royces that come with the house, a private temple, a tennis court, and a generous staff." Norman replied.

"Do you go there often?" asked Jenna.

"Not anymore," said Norman, "I wore out my welcome there a long time ago" he replied wistfully. "I did something foolish that I deeply regret, but it's water over the dam, and I don't like to talk about it."

Interesting; mused Jenna, to herself. She was now thoroughly intrigued and determined to meet the captain.

Her eyes lingered on the couple for a while, noticing that Bobbie seemed to be pulling out all the stops, trying to be as attractive as possible for the man. Being a woman, albeit rusty in the seduction department, Jenna noticed the subtle feminine moves Bobby was pouring on. Most men were oblivious to the actions, but enchanted with their effect upon the male libido. She leaned forward eagerly, her shiny black hair cascading over her shoulders, frequently touching his hand. She was obviously listening intently to what Quincy was saying. The man, however, seemed engaged, but slightly detached, obviously holding himself a little in reserve. Clearly, he was enjoying the attentions of a very beautiful woman, but not abandoning himself to the moment either. Jenna found herself powerfully drawn to the man, and jealous of Bobbie; she wanted to be the one vying for

Quincy's attention. Reluctantly, she turned back to the group, noticing that Ellis, by comparison, now seemed just a little slick, and Norman mostly ingratiating. Both men had been instantly diminished in her eyes after she had seen Quincy McKenna.

Well, she thought, the week's not over yet. Who knows what can happen tomorrow? Perhaps I will go for a sail.

"I think it's time for dinner," Jenna announced. "Is anyone else going back to the Colony Club, or are you all eating here?"

The Carvers, the Whitings and Ellis rose at her suggestion and joined her as she headed out to dinner.

"See you later," said Norman, as he turned back to the bar for another drink. He could not afford to eat at the club, and usually made it a practice to drink his dinner unless he was being pursued by some interested female tourist and she was buying. He shrugged, tonight was not one of those nights. At least he could afford a few drinks.

After dinner, Jenna begged off of an invitation from Ellis for a nightcap, and, taking off her shoes, she wandered down to the water's edge. By this time, the sunset had long gone; a quarter-moon had taken over. The silvery moonlight kissed the wave tops that continued to lap at the sandy shore. The stars seemed so bright compared to the city. Here on the island, there was little man-made light to block the view of the sky, and the moonlight seemed to lay a silver path over the water aimed directly at her. As she wandered to the right, she passed the shack that she had seen Norman emerge from, on her first day. It lay in darkness, but the moon threw enough light for her to see someone sitting by the door, drawing on a cigarette. As she passed by, he stood up, flicked the cigarette away into the dark, and walked toward her. Jenna was momentarily nervous, but then relaxed when she recognized Norman. He was wearing only his khaki shorts and a smile. His entire manner was relaxed and quite appealing.

"Join you?" he asked.

"Sure," Jenna replied. "I'm just getting my feet wet before bed."

"How about a swim instead?" He asked.

"Isn't it dangerous at night with all the fish?"

"Not at all" said Norman, "I swim every night before bed."

"OK," she replied. "I'll just get my suit."

Norman looked at her. They were far enough along the beach that they were completely out of the pool of light cast by the hotel dining patio. Suddenly, he grinned at her and said, "Why bother?"

He pulled down his shorts, revealing a rather well endowed and partially tumescent manhood, and started toward the water. Stopping at the edge, with the waves lapping his ankles, he turned toward Jenna, displaying his growing erection, and held out his hand with a quizzical look on his face. "Coming?" he asked.

Her thoughts flashed back to her ruminations in the Jacuzzi, and she decided more or less on the strength of those thoughts. This was a moment that Jenna had contemplating since she had come to the island. Should she? Was Norman the one to be with? Can anyone see us? Thoughts raced through her head until, with a sigh, she dropped her shoes, unzipped her dress, stepped out of it, and, wearing only her very brief, sheer lacy white panties, ran down the sand and dove into the water. She swam out from the beach for a few strokes, stopped and turned toward Norman. Her feet rested on the sandy bottom. Only her head and shoulders showed above the water. Norman, still standing at the water's edge, looked intently at her and then slowly waded out to her. It was obvious to Jenna that the brief glimpse of her all but naked body had quite roused his interest. He came right to her, reached for her shoulders, and slowly pulled her to him. She went willingly, and immediately encountered his erection, poking her in the belly. Her breasts, firm and urgent, were squashed against his chest, as he bent down and covered her slightly parted lips with his. The kiss was a long one. She could taste the rum and cigarettes on his breath. In the middle of the kiss, he reached down and ripped her flimsy panties off her body, tossing the remnant up on the beach. Her rising passion overcame her distaste for the taste of cigarettes. She responded by taking his tongue in her mouth and sucked gently, but insistently on it. She was wet from desire. The ache in her belly made her sex swell and open. She parted her legs, angling herself so that Norman could slide between her legs. She felt him drag through her pubic hair towards her eagerly waiting vagina. Then, inexplicably, he started to wilt. He pressed harder, bearing down on her mouth with increased ardor.

She reached down to fondle him, and realized that he had completely lost his erection. Gently, but firmly, she disengaged herself.

Norman looked stricken. Gone was his confident manner, and in its place was a sad look of resignation. The booze had done him in again, and like most nights, he would drink himself to sleep alone. Abandoning Norman to his fate, Jenna quickly waded ashore, slipped on her dress, not bothering to zip it up and, with the dress clinging to her wet body like a second skin; she retrieved her shoes, and, walked quickly up the beach to the path by her room. Quickly glancing back at Norman, to make sure he had not followed her, she saw him standing waist deep in the sea, staring out at the horizon. Unlocking her door, she slammed it shut and sagged against it. She was devastated, her cheeks aflame with lust, embarrassment, and disappointment.

A total disaster, she thought. The only consolation was that apparently no one had witnessed the scene. She was not sure why Norman couldn't follow through, but she was sure it was not her response to his overtures. She had been ready and more than willing. In retrospect, she had not even been a bit coy about it. Perhaps that's what had thrown him for a loop; her lack of reticence might have done him in. She would never know, because she would never let Norman near her again. She rinsed off the salt water in the shower, shampooed her hair, and curled up in the bed.

Comforted by the wall of mosquito netting hiding her from the rest of the world, she finally drifted off to a restless sleep.

Chapter 5 - Friday Morning
Sandy Lane beach

Driving to work that morning, Lyle Farmer chuckled to himself at his encounter with the man filling his car at the Holetown Shell station.

"Morning Sah, fill it up?" asked the attendant.

"Yes please, with regular," said Lyle.

While the man filled the tank, Lyle was stretching his legs beside the car and just enjoying the morning. The attendant looked at the license plate and said,

"I saw your car, X2151, at The St. Lawrence Hotel last night."

Lyle chuckled. The island was so small, even if you were not personally acquainted; sooner or later most people knew who you were, and the license plate number on the car you drove.

"Yes, I was there, enjoying some of their famous pepper pot. Have you had it?"

"No mon, I never be dere, but someday I try it."

"When you do, you'll like it," Lyle said with conviction.

He paid the man and drove off through Holetown toward the Colony Club.

Lyle was a local, a white Bajan; his father's family had been here for generations. His father had married an

American tourist who was visiting and became seduced by the laid back lifestyle of the island. When the family was eased out of the sugar business, they started a guest house in St. Lawrence gap and became innkeepers. Lyle decided growing up in the new family business that it was not for him. He wanted a little more glamour. For seven years he worked in the airline business, first for BWIA then BOAC, always hoping for a posting in England or some other country. His lack of higher education was the sticking point, and he finally became reconciled to the reality that he was not going to be more than a glorified clerk for the airline. From what he could see, the only real benefit was the free travel option. One summer, he ran across some youngsters, children of expats who were trying to make some money for college. They had started a poor man's version of a waterskiing business. He skied with them a few times and became intrigued with the concept of a water sports business. After a few months, he decided to throw in with them. They were amenable to his suggestion, but pointed out that there was not enough work for one more man. If he was serious, the fledgling business needed to expand dramatically. Lyle scrounged up enough money to equip two boats, and the business was soon quite busy on the gold coast. The understanding was that when the others went off to college, Lyle would take over the business and treat the others as junior partners. It was a loose arrangement, and it suited all of them quite well. Eventually, the college kids phased out of the business, and Lyle was left with a more or less thriving enterprise. He had three employees running the boats and Warrell who was a floater. Norman was the mechanic and instructor, and so far, each year, the business had grown.

During this time, he had met and taken up with Eileen Hunt, a twenty two year old local girl who was looking for some fun part time work. They soon became an item, and he was constantly torn between desire and the reality of a potential marriage. He loved her, he thought, and he was mad with desire for her, but she would not sleep with him unless they married. Local girls were still old fashioned. Luckily, the occasional tourist lady was able to tame his appetites, but tension was building in their relationship. He was going to have to make a decision soon. He was also getting frustrated that Eileen was spending more and more time with Quincy McKenna on the Billfish, acting as stewardess for his day cruises. Although Quincy seemed indifferent to Eileen's charms due to the age difference between them, it nagged at Lyle all the time. Quincy was a formidable male in Lyle's estimation. All these considerations were whirling through his mind as he drove on to the Colony Club.

Eileen has the day off, he thought. Quincy is taking a few days to tend to the housekeeping aboard the Billfish, so perhaps I could cook up something to do with her today. As he drove down the lane to park outside the hotel, he noticed Norman, Eileen, and Ellis on the beach. He parked and walked down to the water; greeting everyone, he was immediately included in the discussion.

Norman said, "Ellis was just asking if I could take him and his friends down the coast to the Sandy Lane beach, for skiing and a picnic today. I was telling him I'm booked up for most of the day."

Lyle pondered this, and then realizing that, while Norman was using the big twenty footer, the fourteen footer was available. Although he kept it in reserve as a spare ski boat in case of breakdown, it was fully capable of carrying the group to Sandy Lane.

"I have an idea," Lyle said. "I can take you down in the small boat if you don't mind sitting on the beach while the others ski. The boat's motor is too small to carry everyone, and pull skiers at the same time. We could take a picnic and make a day of it. I want to spend some time with Eileen anyway."

"Great," said Ellis. "How many can I fit in the boat?"

"Well said Ellis, there will be me, Eileen and Warrell to run the boat, so we could accommodate you and two more."

Ellis went off happily to round up Jenna, ecstatic that he might have her all to himself for the day without Norman breathing down his neck. Eileen scurried off to the kitchen to make arrangements for the picnic. Lyle and Norman set off in his car to fetch the small boat for the expedition. By the time they retrieved it from the car park, gassed it, and launched it, the group was assembled, and waiting on the beach. Lyle had them choose their favorite skis, and then loaded them into the boat. Ellis had persuaded Jenna to join him, and once she had agreed, he did not ask anyone else. As they were heading for the beach, however, they ran into Quincy, who said that he had talked to Eileen and wanted to tag along. He needed a day off from working on the boat; Lyle owed him some ski time anyway. Quincy, who had found out that Jenna was going, made it a point to drop his plans for the day to tag along. He wanted to get to know this good looking blond lady. It seemed that by her ready acceptance of him joining the group, she was interested to get to know him as well. Ellis was definitely not pleased with another single male tagging along, especially one that looked like Quincy. Since there was clearly room for one more, he could hardly object. He had no idea that Jenna was already intrigued with Quincy. They walked back to the beach chatting happily.

They loaded the boat: Ellis took the opportunity to boost Jenna into the bow seat with a manly heave. He then pushed the boat off the beach, and hopped in with what he thought was athletic grace. His day was off to a good start, and his head was full of visions, strolling the Sandy Lane Cove with Jenna while the others skied. Lyle was busy organizing the gear and discussing with Warrell and Quincy about the skiing, and the relative skiing talents of their two American guests. Warrell had been briefed that morning by Norman who told him to be careful with Jenna, as she did not make it up the last time she tried.

Lyle said, "Not to worry, I'll take her up. I never fail."

The boat cruised toward Bridgetown, down the coast past Coral Reef. Once past several large homes, they soon were motoring along sandy, coconut palm infested, deserted coastline, fringed by shallow reef, about 200 yards offshore. Soon they spotted the Sandy Land beach and its distinctive cove angling away from the beach. Warrell pulled the boat up on the beach, and the party unloaded their gear and the picnic supplies. The discussion concluded, it was decided that Jenna would start, with Lyle assisting on the teaching bar, while everyone else watched from the beach. Lyle had developed a system for teaching beginners, and it seldom failed. He explained to Jenna that they would both be on the rope as the boat started up. He would don skis and hold the tow rope with Jenna. She would be on his lap, with her skis pointing parallel to his. Her hands would be next to his on the bar, and the boat would pull them up together. Once she was stable on the skis, the plan was that Lyle would simply drop off, allowing Jenna to ski by herself. Quincy, in a surprise move, told Lyle, "Why don't you spend some time with Eileen, and I'll take Jenna up; after all, I know your system as well as you do." Delighted, Lyle readily agreed, and Quincy smiled at Jenna. Slightly apprehensive, remembering her disaster with Norman, Jenna agreed to give it a try. She smiled back at Quincy, excited to have an opportunity to be close to the captain.

Quincy and Jenna waded into the shallow water, about waist deep, and donned their skis, Warrell handed Quincy the long tow bar, and Quincy positioned Jenna firmly in his lap with her skis parallel with his, but between his. She nodded to Warrell and the boat started with a gentle surge. She had no choice but to stand up properly, as Quincy's body supported hers fully. Soon they were both skiing with Quincy's skis outboard of hers. She gained confidence as he expertly talked her through the start and tow. Soon she was standing correctly, with her knees bent, her arms straight, and a slight lean backwards. As she picked up confidence, Quincy was greatly relieved to back off and put some distance between their bodies. He was having an involuntary reaction to Jenna's bottom pushed into his crotch. He was mortified that she would notice, and he was relieved to drop off as soon as Warrell circled back past the beach where the others were waiting; Quincy wished her luck as he dropped off. She was suddenly alone, on skis, zooming along behind the boat, feeling wonderful, and totally unafraid. She had picked up on Quincy's male reaction and was pleased that she had had that effect on him. She laughed and waived to the beach crowd. Warrell carefully pulled her around in a circle twice and then signaled her to drop off, as the boat came back past the beach. Her dismount was undignified. She plopped on her butt when she let go of the rope; she was ecstatic. She had finally skied, and apparently, the captain had definitely noticed her.

Quincy was next, and he put them all to shame as he donned the slalom ski. Standing in the shallow water on one foot, his other was in the boot of the ski, with the ski resting on top of the water; he nodded to Warrell, and simply stepped up on top of the water. He was instantly skiing. Once the boat was running full out, he expertly cut the wake, and almost passed the boat as it sped around in a big circle. What followed was a virtuoso performance, with Quincy cutting from side to side, jumping the wake, and leaning so far over, that his elbows brushed the water. On the last lap, he cut across the wake, and rode the top of a wave as it washed up on the beach. As the wave petered out on the sand, Quincy delicately stepped out of the ski, and ran lightly onto the sand. He stopped by the group. Jenna clapped excitedly, and Lyle said, "Showoff!"

Lyle skied next, and while he was every bit as proficient as Quincy, he was careful to be a little less flamboyant. He did not want to show up his guests. He saved his good stuff for the Sunday water shows. Each week, Lyle and Warrell journeyed up and down the gold coast, to the five big resorts, putting on a quick exhibition at each resort. They then went ashore to sign up the hotel guests for skiing during the coming week. It was a great system. They had the wholehearted cooperation from the resorts, as the water sports service added to their guests' enjoyment of the island. His three boats were almost always booked up for the full week.

Despite Lyle's forbearance, Ellis was furious. His plans to be the big bad skier impressing Jenna with his flair were permanently dashed for the day. He deferred to the others and went last before the rotation started over. Finally Warrell said that he needed a break, and everyone was hungry. The group attacked the picnic basket with a will. They found not only food, but also a large jug of rum punch. They fell to enthusiastically. Somehow Quincy had maneuvered himself next to Jenna on the sand, and they munched contentedly while getting acquainted. They both seemed delighted with the situation. Lyle, fuming furiously, could hardly get a word into the conversation. Quiet soon descended on the beach, as they stuffed themselves with flying fish sandwiches, sliced mango, and a bowl of chilled sowersop for desert. Replete with their bounty, they were content to stretch out on the sand for a little relaxation.

Soon, however, Lyle and Eileen wandered away from the group and strolled around the bend, up the shoreline of the creek inlet. Jenna idly speculated on the possibilities of their doing a little romancing while out of sight. Soon, she stretched out and was falling asleep. The sun, the breeze and a full stomach had rendered her content. She nodded off with a smile on her face. Quincy and Warrell struck up an earnest discussion of scuba diving. Quincy had recently rigged a refill compressor setup on the Billfish, and was now able to take dive groups anywhere, without having to put ashore for refills. Taking advantage of the busy conversation between the other two men, Ellis was delighted to finally have Jenna to himself. He nudged her awake, and soon he was busy filling her in on his long list of daring do exploits around the world. While Jenna was not particularly impressed with Ellis, she was conscious of envying him the freedom his apparent wealth provided him. He was able to indulge his every fancy whenever it struck him. He loved to snow ski, fly his Cessna 172, travel extensively, and was contemplating trying hot air ballooning, sometime soon. This trip, he was looking forward to doing some wreck diving with Quincy, later on in the week. He was trying, with little success, to persuade Jenna to join him. Finally, realizing that they would be aboard the Billfish, she agreed to go with them, but she would snorkel only. That was the extent of her bravery under water. In reality, she agreed so that she could get to see Quincy in his own environment. She was by now clearly impressed with the man. She noticed that he was glancing more and more in her direction as well.

Warrell finally roused himself, and said that they had enough gas for one final round of skiing before heading back to the Colony Club. As Jenna watched Ellis take his turn, she was idly digging in the wet sand with her toes, when she felt something hard poking her little toe. Thinking it was a rock or a shell; she reached for it and dug it out of the sand. Puzzled by what she had found, she stood up and walked into the water. She scrubbed the object with some sand, and was surprised to find that she had in her hand, an old coin. It had a man's laurel clad head on one side, and what looked like a sailing ship, on the other. It was very crude and oddly asymmetrical. She had no idea what it was but she was delighted with her find. She put it into her beach bag and prepared herself for another try at skiing. Her next attempt was successful from start to finish; she even managed a semi-dignified drop off at the end of her circuit. She blushed at the enthusiastic round of applause from the others, but she was especially pleased when Quincy helped her retrieve the skis and prepare to load everything into the boat for their return to the Colony Club. She hardly noticed the very irritated expression on Ellis' face as they prepared to leave the beach.

On the return trip, she chatted with all her fellow skiers, but she found herself increasingly drawn to Quincy. She did, however, make a special point of thanking Ellis for bringing her along. She was thrilled that she was now a skier. Ellis was somewhat mollified.

Chapter 6 - Friday Afternoon
The Beach Bar

When Warrell guided the boat around the reef, and headed for the Colony Club beach, Jenna said, "I'm buying at the beach bar. I'm so thrilled that I was finally able to ski that I want to celebrate."

Everyone agreed. The plan was to drop off their gear in the rooms, rinse off the salt and sand, and reconvene at the bar in about forty five minutes. Warrell grounded the boat and helped everyone to the sand. Lyle asked him to see that the boat was serviced and ready to go in the morning if needed. If it was not needed, after drinks, he would get the car and trailer; they could load it up, and put it back in the car park. The guests headed for their rooms, Quincy hopped in his dingy and headed for the Billfish, Lyle and Eileen headed straight for the bar after rinsing off in the outside shower, and grabbed some towels from the beach shack.

The group reconvened. An eager Jenna joined Lyle and Eileen at the bar, followed soon by Ellis. Quincy was the last to arrive, rowing briskly back to shore from his yacht. Jenna watched him approach, musing to herself about the possibility of getting to know him better. She was thoroughly impressed by what she had seen of him so far, and was hoping that she might have sparked his interest this morning. He was a substantial looking man, well spoken, if a little on the quiet side. Clearly he was a man in complete control of his environment, and at peace with the world. He seemed to be a thoroughly attractive package. Somehow, she sensed that if they did click, it would not be a casual affair. He struck her as a more serious type of man, not incapable of a casual encounter, but more interested in a substantial relationship. She doubted, however, that he was consciously in the market for a wife. In short, he was intriguing. There is nothing more attractive to a woman than an enigmatic male; especially one that looked as good as Quincy.

"Here's to a great day skiing," said Jenna. "Thank you Ellis and Lyle for putting it all together. It was more fun than the session yesterday, and watching two pros ski today was a real thrill."

Quincy blushed through his tan, and Lyle laughed and said, "Glad you enjoyed it. It's on the house. It's the least we could do after almost drowning you yesterday. I needed a day off, and to pay my debt to Quincy. Having Eileen along, was frosting on the cake. You will be skiing like a pro yourself before you go back to New York."

"Speaking of frosting," said Quincy, "don't drink too much this afternoon, I want you to go with me this evening to a formal cocktail party. My friend Bobbie Chastain, who lives right across the street at Porters, has asked me to bring along some people for her weekly gathering. You will love it. Her parties are well known, and you never know who will be there. Her guest list usually includes some very entertaining people."

Lyle and Eileen had to beg off, but Jenna and Ellis readily accepted. At that moment, Norman came walking up the beach to the bar. He was uncertain of his reception; he had not seen Jenna since that disastrous encounter on the beach, and he was very nervous. He had to tough it out, or Lyle would wonder why he was ignoring their clients.

Sensing the man's unease, Jenna said, "We're celebrating my first ski experience, Norman, how about a drink on me?"

Relieved, and with a somewhat chagrined expression on his face, he readily agreed. The memory of his failed seduction of Jenna was still fresh in his mind. Jenna seemed none the worse for the experience, and was clearly eager to clear the air between them. He shrugged, and took the drink offered by the bartender.

"Thanks and cheers," he mumbled, and took a healthy swig. Another opportunity down the drain he admitted to himself. I'll have to pull myself together, or sooner or later this will get to Lyle, and then I'm going to be out of here with no place to go. That shack and this job is everything I have in the world, he realized.

"All finished for the day," he said to Lyle. "We have a full boat booked for tomorrow, and we might even have to use the fourteen, so if it's alright with you, I'll have Warrell take it out to the mooring when he gets back from the gas station."

"Fine," said Lyle. "As long as your day is full, he and I can look at the bookings this evening and decide how to handle it. There was a message from Paradise Beach that they have some guests interested in a day's skiing, and I think there's a couple at Miramar that also wants to ski. We can put together a day to fit them all in. We'll give everyone a ring when we know what's what. "

Suddenly, Jenna remembered the coin in her beach bag; excusing herself for a moment, she hurried back to the room to retrieve it. She was anxious to show off her find. When she got there, the maid was busily turning down the bed. Jenna hustled in and out, nodding only briefly to the maid. Clutching the beach bag, she eagerly hurried back to the bar. Slightly out of breath, she said, as she arrived, "By the way, does any one of you know what this is?" She produced the coin she had found on Sandy Lane Beach and set it on the bar.

Everyone took a look. Norman and Lyle exchanged a hasty glance as Quincy picked it up to examine it more closely.

"It looks like an old Spanish Doubloon. Where did you get it?"asked Quincy.

"I found it on the beach this afternoon. It was buried in the sand at the waterline," replied Jenna. "Do you know why it might have been there?"

Neither Norman nor Lyle said anything, but they exchanged a pointed look.

Finally Quincy volunteered, "There's an old legend, rumor, or old wives tale, if you will, about pirates around these islands in the old days. People have always said that they buried their treasures on this island. The cove at Sandy Lane had been a favorite candidate for a possible location, because it's the only place on the island you can run a boat up a creek inlet and remain totally unseen from a boat at sea, or at anchor."

After a quick glance at Lyle, Eileen finally spoke.

"From time to time, one of these coins pops up. All the beaches around the island have been dug up by the locals. Everyone is tired of the idea. Some people have even suggested that somebody delights in planting them occasionally just to stir up some excitement among the tourists. No one really believes in pirate treasure anymore. This is, however, the first coin ever found at Sandy Lane, and it appears to be the genuine article."

Lyle offered, "If any buried treasure were actually found, technically, it would be the property of the Crown. There might be a generous finder's fee to the lucky finder, but the treasure would belong to the government. That alone has discouraged most people from wasting their time digging."

"Intriguing thought," said Quincy. "It might be fun to poke around a little and see if we could get lucky."

"How would we go about it?" asked Ellis.

"We could get some shovels and dig around where I found the coin," offered Jenna.

Norman's mind was racing. He knew that there was more to the idea than Quincy did, and he was pretty sure that Ellis and Eileen were downplaying the idea as well. While they were not actively discouraging a treasure hunt, they were not encouraging one either. Quincy and Ellis were enthusiastically endorsing the idea. Ellis was looking for the excitement, and Quincy was looking forward to the challenge.

Thanking Jenna for the drink, Norman excused himself from the bar he slipped away to give his old pal, Sergeant Smythe-Caulley, a ring. Norman knew that this pirate treasure thing was a favorite topic of speculation with Smythe-Caulley. In his position as an officer in the island police force, he was in a position to know more about the ins and outs of the background, surrounding the previous finds, than anyone else. Norman had always suspected that there was more to the Sergeant than met the eye. After all, he knew Norman was an illegal, and turned a blind eye, in exchange for Norman keeping his ears open and doing him the odd dubious favor. He also tipped the predatory policemen to any especially available tourist women he came across. It seemed a good relationship to Norman, but he was well aware that he could be summarily deported, if the time came when Smythe-Caulley got tired of the arrangement. This call might earn him some additional consideration from the man. "Well done, Norman," he said. "We'll see if this is real or not. If you have an opportunity, try to nick the coin. I'll have a look in the Admiralty records to see where it might have come from. I have access to all The Admiralty shipping records back to the 1500s. You never know, it might work out to be something nice for both of us."

The Sergeant quizzed Norman intently for details of the people involved. He was encouraged by the two Americans, he could get rid of them easily as he had in the past, when troubled by some nosy tourists, but Lyle and Eileen would be another kettle of fish entirely. He would have to think about how to get around their involvement. The conversation with the Sergeant ended with Smythe-Caulley saying that he would look into the matter very soon and get back to him. Meanwhile, Norman was tasked with keeping an eye on the group, and, if possible, getting possession of the coin.

After Norman left, Quincy expanded on the possibility of a more organized search. It was finally decided that Quincy would mull it over and see what he could offer, as a plan of attack. He was the only one with the resources and equipment to mount a search on land and in the sea. Ellis and Jenna agreed to rendezvous in the hotel lobby, with Quincy, at seven o'clock for the walk over to Bobbie's home. Jenna and Ellis headed for their rooms, and Quincy strolled down the beach and pushed off in his dingy.

This American girl has turned out to be very interesting, he thought. I really like her. Besides being a real looker with a very appealing body, she had spunk and was interested in many things. I'll just have to pay more attention to her tonight and see what develops. It will be interesting to see how Bobbie reacts to her; I know she will like Ellis. He's her type, rich, smooth, and brash. Humming contentedly, he reached the Billfish, tied off the dingy to the stern rail, and clambered aboard. He took a quick look around; a habit he acquired at some cost, over the last two years. Lessons learned at sea and at anchor, dictated that he make sure all was not disturbed, and that the Billfish was secure at her mooring, no matter what the weather. He opened the hatch to the pilot house and went inside. The familiar aromas of salt, cooking, and machine oil told him he was home. He suddenly realized that the Billfish had, in fact, become home, the first home he had known since he left home as a lad, and joined the service.

Humming to himself, he fixed himself a gin and bitters and went up to the cockpit with a pad and pencil in hand. As long as he had a little time to kill before the party, he thought he'd start a list of items that would help with the search. He realized right away that there were multiple locations that would have to be checked; the beach, the inlet, the adjacent woods, the sea in front of the beach, and the reef protecting the entire anchorage.

He listed the obvious like shovels and rope, and then elaborated with scuba gear, snorkel gear, metal detector, if such a thing existed on the island, lift bags, pry bars and chisels. The miscellaneous list was endless, rope and weights for markers as well as flotation buoys. The list grew and the sun started to set. Finally he looked around and realized that he could finish this over tea in the morning.

Chapter 7 – Friday Evening
Bobby's Party

Quincy glanced west to the horizon where the sun was sliding down below a bank of mixed clouds. Soft fluffy Cumulus were topped by a thin sheet of Cirrus, all turning varying shades of pink, blue and orange. It was a typical tropical sunset, with not one rain cloud in sight. He was mulling over the coming evening at Bobbie's place. He had been somewhat involved with Bobby, in a half hearted way, but he now realized, that he was very attracted to this woman from New York. Was it just an attraction or was it something with more potential? Did he want more than a fling? Pushing forty, he had the world by the tail. He was healthy, solvent, debt free, and in total command of his environment. What could be better than that; Perhaps, someone to share it with? Interesting, he thought.

Still mulling it over, he went below to the master cabin and started browsing in his closet for something to wear. He had tipped both Ellis and Jenna that tropical parties tended to be on the formal side and to dress up rather than down. He was becoming somewhat discouraged by his sartorial choices, when he realized that his dinner jacket was at the cleaners. When he ran across his set of tropical whites, he paused and considered the choice. He had not worn a uniform since his discharge. As a member of the active reserve, he retained his rank of Major, and was entitled to wear his uniform anytime. In fact, at the last Government house reception, the Governor himself had suggested he start wearing it for these formal receptions. He had reluctantly agreed, so if he wore it tonight, it would be a dry run. The last two years aboard the Billfish had added considerable bulk to his chest, arms and shoulders. Luckily, he had just retrieved the jacket from the tailor; the reworked garment fitted him like a comfortable second skin. Regulations stated that if he chose to appear in uniform, it must include all his pips and chevrons. Wearing my uniform will definitely turn a few heads, he thought. It might even make a pretty good impression on both Jenna and Bobbie. Smiling to himself, he rummaged in his miscellaneous drawer for his box of service ribbons. Setting aside the two Victoria Cross Medals, whistling to himself, he started to pin them on the heavily starched, short sleeved, service jacket that was the top half of his uniform.

Surveying the results of his preparations in the limited mirror, on the back of the door to the head, he had to admit to himself that the white uniform, ablaze with his service ribbons, together with his deep tropical tan showed him off at his manly best. This is as good as it gets, he smiled to himself. He took his dress hat off the shelf, removed the dust cover, squared it on his head, and climbed the stairs to the pilot house. With a quick glance around, he stepped out on deck, turned and locked the door. He hauled in the dingy and carefully stepped in. Rowing in, he deliberately planned how to beach the dingy and get out without wetting down his dress whites.

Having successfully pulled off the beaching of the dingy without even soaking his white shoes, he strolled up the beach, across the Colony Club terrace, through the dining room, to the lounge off the main reception area. As he strolled through the bar area and the terrace, he was conscious of the stares from the people seated in the area, especially the admiring glances from the women. He was pleased that his choice of his dress uniform had the desired effect. As he entered the lobby space, he glanced across the fish pond and saw Ellis in conversation with Jenna. He came to an abrupt halt. The light through the arched entry shined through the slinky white dress she wore, revealing her whole body. In one hand, she held a tiny clutch purse that seemed to compliment her dress and high heels. Her hair was loose, long and blond, tumbling around her shoulders. It moved gently with the breeze. The sight of her took his breath away. He paused momentarily, assessing, and thoroughly admiring, the sight of a truly beautiful woman, in a very exotic setting. At that precise moment, Jenna turned and spotted Quincy staring at her. She stopped speaking abruptly. She was completely captivated by the sight of him, outlined against the brilliant tropical sunset in his full dress Major's uniform. Ellis, startled by her abrupt end to the conversation, turned, spotted Quincy, and scowled. He was clearly outclassed in the sartorial splendor department. His elegant white dinner jacket was rendered mundane in an instant. Ignoring Ellis, Quincy walked around the Koi pond, and approached Jenna with a big smile on his face.

Offering her his arm, he said, "May I say, you look smashing tonight. Shall we go?" Jenna, still speechless, just nodded, took his arm, and allowed him to lead her across the drive, to the lane heading toward Porters. Ellis followed along in their wake, totally discouraged. It was plain to him that, after two days of trying his best, he had failed utterly to attract Jenna's interest. Chatting amiably, the pair, trailed by Ellis, walked across the street, and into the driveway of Porters Great House. All three of them were blissfully unaware that they were being carefully observed by Norman, hiding behind one of the large Casurena trees lining the lane.

Just passing through the massive limestone gates, the trio entered an enchanted world of unparalleled tropical luxury. Both Jenna and Ellis were struck dumb by the manicured lawns, stately palms, and marble statuary, scattered around the extensive grounds. Rows of hibiscus and bird of paradise vied for attention, with the peacocks that strolled loose through the grounds. Their sporadic, shrill, unearthly cries, and their arrogantly displayed finery, added a surreal touch to the scene. In the distance, on a small hill, stood a Grecian style temple, its white limestone columns and domed roof washed in pink by the setting sun.

"It's like something out of a fairy tale," said Jenna as the stark white limestone home came into view. "It takes my breath away."

To the left was a collection of cars, all expensive, with uniformed chauffeurs standing around talking and smoking. Quincy started to have a feeling that this was not going to be just an ordinary evening at Bobbie's place.

As they walked through the door, Quincy exclaimed, "Bloody hell, if I knew that this was going to be this type of party, I would have begged off."

Her heart was pounding; this was turning out to be infinitely more exciting than she had anticipated. Ellis was simply speechless.

"What do you mean?" asked Jenna. She busily glanced around, obviously impressed by the glittering crowd.

"She's gone top drawer on us this evening," replied Quincy. "All the political wallas are here, as well as most the Island's infamous characters."

"What do you mean?" asked Jenna. "Who are these people?"

Taking advantage of the fact that their entrance had not yet been noticed, Quincy leaned over, and placed his dress hat on the marble topped entry table. He noticed, in passing, that there was an identical hat already there, equipped with a Sergeant's chevrons. Smothering a frown, he started pointing out to Jenna and Ellis some of the people milling around the glittering room in front of them.

"The tall chap with the white suit in the corner is Brigadier Sir Robert Arundel, the Colonial Governor of the island, and that black chap he's talking to is Sir Grantley Adams, the soon to be Premier of the island. The good looking black woman that also in that group, is Norma Stout, the popular Calypso singer."

He pointed to two men in the corner who were gesturing excitedly, obviously engaged in a lively discussion.

"There's a pair of royalty from the cricket world, Sir Clyde Walcott and Sir Frank Worrell. The chap listening to them is Lionel Bourne. That lot of overfed and poorly dressed people, in the center of the room is comprised of sugar planters and their wives. Their families have been here since the island was first populated. The scrawny little fellow off by himself, in the corner, hiding behind the potted palm, wearing a uniform like mine, is Sergeant Smythe-Caulley, a right bastard if ever there was one. The rest of this crowd are equally interesting. I expect you'll meet them soon enough. If I ever doubted Bobbie's wealth and notoriety here on the Island, I won't anymore. Everyone who is anyone on Barbados is here tonight. You will eventually get to meet them all, the famous, the infamous, paupers, rascals, and the nobility. This is quite a bash."

At that moment, Bobbie walked up to them. She was barefoot, wearing a strapless, Grecian, multi colored gown supported only by her magnificent breasts. Her hair was done up in a long braid flowing over one shoulder with a large, diamond sprayed, hairpin pushed casually into the top of the braid.

"Quincy, you look marvelous," she said, as she leaned over and gave him a proprietary kiss on the lips. "Introduce me to your friends."

"Bobbie Chastain, may I present to you Miss Jenna White from New York and Mister Ellis Caulfield of parts unknown," Quincy replied.

"Welcome to Porters," said Bobbie, as she surveyed the pair. She stepped forward, taking Ellis by the arm. Drawing him close, obviously taken by the dashing urbane looking man, she said,

"Mister Caulfield, may I introduce you around? Quincy here can do the honors for Miss White. He knows most of my guests."

With that, Bobbie led the smiling and obviously smitten Ellis into the room, and steered him expertly through the crowd, disappearing from sight, swallowed by the noisy, milling throng. He was inordinately pleased to be singled out by this stunning woman. It took the entire sting out of having been upstaged earlier by Quincy. He followed her, eager with anticipation, his interest in Jenna totally forgotten, at least for the moment.

"Damn and blast!" exclaimed Quincy.

Recovering from the overwhelming performance by their hostess, Jenna inquired of Quincy, "What's wrong now?"

"Had I known the brass was going to be here, I would never have worn this bloody uniform. Now I have to pay my respects to the Governor and the other officials. I'm afraid you're in for it my dear. Put a good face on it and let's get it over with; then we can enjoy ourselves." Squaring their backs, the splendid looking pair made their way over to the Governor who had spotted their approach.

"Good evening, Norma, Sir Robert, Sir Grantley, it's good to see you all again," offered Quincy, with his hand outstretched to the Governor.

Taking Quincy's hand, and eyeing Jenna from head to toe approvingly, Sir Robert replied, "Nice to see you again, Major McKenna, as well, and who might this delightful creature be who is attached to your arm this evening?"

Turning to shake hands with Sir Grantley, and nodding at Norma with a smile, Quincy said, "Norma, gentlemen, allow me to present my companion for the evening, Miss Jenna White, a distinguished attorney from New York."

Norma Stout smiled and nodded her head, "Lovely to meet you Miss White," she said.

Both men bowed slightly and offered their hands to be shaken.

Jenna smiled broadly and said to the assembled trio, "The pleasure is all mine. I'm very happy to meet you all."

The Governor, with a warm smile on his face clasped both Jenna's hands in his and purred, "Whatever are you doing with such a distinguished rogue as our Major McKenna?"

Jenna laughed and said, "If I'm not mistaken, Sir Robert, there's likely more than one rogue in the room tonight. What makes Quincy so uniquely distinguished?"

"If you look at all the ribbons on his chest, you can see that the good Major here has been all round the world in Her Majesty's service. He's quite a distinguished chap I'm afraid. We're actually quite proud of him. When Major McKenna arrived on the island, I was notified immediately by immigration; I am routinely notified whenever any British service personnel surface here. I was given a lengthy rundown on his background. He's twice decorated for action in the field, and, I notice that both decorations are conspicuously absent from his jacket tonight." Turning to Quincy, but not yet relinquishing Jenna's hand, he continued, "care to elaborate on the oversight Major? You know that it's against military regulations to appear in mufti without your gongs."

"I'm sorry, Sir," said Quincy. "I donned the uniform as a lark, and was unaware that I would be in an official situation. I thought this was going to be just a quiet cocktail party with some of Bobbie's cronies. Truth to be told, Sir, the medals embarrass me a little. I did nothing the rest of my men didn't also do. I have always felt that the citations were earned more by the unit than by me specifically."

"Quite modest as well, our Major McKenna," said the governor. "Since this is not an official function, I'll turn a blind eye this time. It is good to see you showing the uniform, however. We usually only get that rather distasteful chap, Smythe-Caulley, to represent the Crown at these affairs. You should do it more often, McKenna. Mind you, wear your medals next time."

"Absolutely Sir," Quincy saluted. "Duly noted. It won't happen again Sir."

Chuckling at the repartee, Sir Grantley turned to Jenna and said,

"My dear, it is kind of you to put up with us colonial types rambling on. I hope you will enjoy your stay on Barbados, and come back often."

"Yes, I will," replied Jenna. "The island is absolutely lovely, and this evening has turned out to be a marvelously exciting surprise" She turned towards Quincy, "in more ways than one."

Excusing themselves, the pair made their way to the long, marble topped bar, at the back of the room, where they ordered a pair of frosty gin and tonics. Quincy was kept busy introducing Jenna to the curious males, who seemed to gravitate to her, as the party swirled around them. Politely, and sometimes not so politely, Quincy was elbowed aside by the throng of eager males, homing in on Jenna. The selection of eligible ladies on the island was limited, and she was fresh meat, and stunning to boot. Contented to stand close by and watch, as she expertly fended off their advances, while simultaneously charming the men, he realized happily, that his lovely companion had become the center of attention. She was beyond lovely, and he realized that he had become seriously smitten with her. He would have to press his suit, since he knew she was returning to New York within a week's time.

Something at the corner of his eye caught his attention. He observed Sergeant Smythe-Caulley staring intently at Jenna in a manner that belied any acceptable standard of male interest. Something was up. Quincy immediately went into his alert mode. He watched as the policeman approached Jenna through the crowd. As the men surrounding Jenna became aware of his approach, they, obviously leery of the man, slowly peeled away, leaving Smythe-Caulley alone with her at the bar. He offered his hand, and introduced himself. As Jenna became aware of the suddenly empty space surrounding her and this man, she, mindful of Quincy's remark, responded cautiously to his greeting. At the same time she glanced around anxiously for Quincy. She steadied when she saw him looking at them. He gave her a reassuring smile.

"How are you enjoying our little slice of Paradise?" the policeman inquired. "Have you had an interesting time so far?"

"Yes, Barbados is lovely. I have been relaxing and learning how to water ski," Jenna replied. "It's just what the doctor ordered. I'll be able to get back to work with a fresh mind and a relaxed body."

"Rumor has it that you made an exciting find this afternoon," said Smythe-Caulley abruptly with a bit of a sinister leer.

Clearly taken aback, and somewhat alarmed, Jenna replied,

"What do you mean by that?"

Sensing a dramatic change in the atmosphere, demonstrated by an abrupt change in Jenna's body language, Quincy moved immediately to her side, interrupting the policeman's response.

"Smythe-Caulley," Quincy nodded. "What has brought you out from under your rock?"

Obviously taken aback at his old Major's abrupt appearance, the flustered Sergeant replied a little too quickly.

"Major McKenna Sir, I was just enjoying getting to know our lovely visitor here, when you so rather rudely interrupted."

"Bugger off Sergeant, and don't forget who you're talking to," said Quincy.

Appalled at the obvious animosity displayed by the two men, Jenna could only mutely stand by as the scene played itself out. Smythe-Caulley, bristling, but obviously outranked and outclassed had to give way. Turning abruptly from Quincy, he nodded to Jenna with a piercing glare, and stalked off through the crowd.

Glaring at Smythe-Caulley's retreating back, Quincy said, "I'm dreadfully sorry that you had to witness that. There's just no end to his ill breeding. What's so damned distressing is that he is still an officer in Her Majesty's service."

"What was that all about?" asked Jenna.

"That odious little turncoat is a shameful coward, and almost got me and my men killed in combat a few years ago," Quincy explained. "He was cashiered from the service, but, due to the fact that the mission in question was highly classified, the files were sealed. Because of that, he was able to worm his way into the constabulary here, retaining his military rank in the Colonial Service, with no one being aware of the incident, and the circumstances surrounding his severance from the service. The Governor seems aware that something is amiss, but cannot get to the bottom of the problem. There is no way I can enlighten Sir Robert. When I mustered out, I had so sign confidentiality documents pursuant to the Official Secrets Act. Rumor has it that Smythe-Caulley is enriching himself at the expense of the Colony and some of our better off tourists. More serious than some petty larceny and bribery, there have been allegations of highly inappropriate behavior with more than one woman tourist. To date, however, no charges have been brought."

"He referred to my exciting find this afternoon" Jenna said. "How could he know about the coin, and what does he have to do with it anyway?"

Alarmed, Quincy replied, "His division of the Constabulary would oversee any finding of artifacts on the island, but I doubt that his interest is official. I think he is trying to get his hands on anything we might find. I wonder who tipped him off. As long as you stay away from him, he can do nothing without making it official. Let's forget about him and enjoy the party. I'll deal with him later, with pleasure," he said with a certain amount of menace, "if and when the occasion arises."

The rest of the evening was spent moving from group to group, with Jenna the obvious center of male attention. The local ladies also seemed more than a little impressed with the Major and his newly displayed finery. Quincy was content to chat with passersby, and enjoy watching her. As the evening wore on, he realized that she was standing with her hand tucked into the crook of his bare elbow. He noticed because he became painfully aware of the touch of her warm hand, resting lightly on his arm. The pressure from her left breast on his bare elbow, and her thigh pressed against his leg was almost more than he could take. As time wore on he became anxious to cut the party short, and get her off somewhere alone with him. He did nothing however, contenting himself with her closeness, and her obvious enjoyment of the party. She was clearly unaware that she was pressed intimately against him. He loved the fact that her gesture was an unconscious one. She was also blissfully unaware of the effect that this bit of intimacy was having on him. Suddenly, Quincy noticed that he had not given Bobbie a thought since she led Ellis off into the party. Her lack of attention to him this evening, didn't seem to disturb him in the least. He had not sighted either of them in some time. No explanations would be needed later; Bobbie was clearly a woman who knew what she wanted, and it was with some relief that he realized her focus had suddenly switched from him, to the obviously enthusiastic Ellis Caulfield. Despite that fact that Bobbie was a beautiful and interesting woman, he had not particularly liked the idea that he could be considered a rich woman's playmate. Perhaps it was for the best.

Finally, with some reluctance, Jenna turned to Quincy and said, "I have come to realize why Bobbie was barefooted; my feet have had it with these high heels and this tile floor. I need to get out of them and sit somewhere quiet. Is it time yet to leave?"

"These gatherings seem to have a life of their own," said Quincy. "They sometimes last an hour or two if they are boring. Sometimes they last till morning, with the guests ending up naked, in the swimming pools. If you've had enough of this Major business for one night, we can slip away unnoticed. I haven't seen our hostess since she made off with Ellis."

"Great, let's go," said Jenna. She steered him toward the door and the balmy tropical darkness outside. Motivated by the firm breast rubbing on his bare elbow, Quincy eagerly fell into step beside her. The only one who noticed their departure was the Sergeant, still lurking by the potted palm in the dimly lit, back corner of the room. His burning eyes filled with hatred as he watched them step into the night.

Chapter 8 – Friday Night
After the Party

Jenna was flushed with excitement, awash in male pheromones. For three hours, a gaggle of eager and attractive males had jockeyed for her attention. As they walked out of Porters into the star lit night, she could hear the unfamiliar night sounds. She wondered what creatures made such an insistent noise. The grounds of the estate were dimly lit, and it seemed to her as if Quincy and she were strolling through a starlit paradise. Abruptly, they were at the front gate. The party noise faded entirely, to be replaced by the sound of an occasional car, passing between Porters and the Colony Club. Glancing right and left, Quincy gently disengaged Jenna's hand from his elbow and put his arm around her. He was ostensibly guiding her across the road, but, in reality, he was subtly pulling her firmly against his side. He led her into the lane past the Colony Club main entrance, then further into the shadows, toward the beach.

Conscious of their delicious intimacy, Jenna snuggled closer to him, listening to the night critters, and the breeze swishing through the stately casuarinas that lined the entry drive. The moonlight was sufficient to see by, but she felt protected from the world, invisible to all except this man, rock hard at her side, guiding her down the lane. She was intensely aware of the tension building in him as they progressed. They passed the entrance to the club, dim at this hour, for it was after midnight; all but the night porter had retired for the day. Even the guests tended to retire early, pleasantly pooped from a day of fun in the sun. As they passed the entrance, she looked up at Quincy, seeing for the first time the tension on his face and the deliberate direction he was leading them. As the light from the club's entrance faded away, they were enveloped in a gentle darkness, illuminated only by the rising half moon glimpsed fleetingly through the treetops. The tree lined, sandy path was deserted, and she instinctively knew that they were utterly alone. In the distance, she could just make out the water and the moon's path, lighting up the top of the waves. She was strangely excited and curious at the same time. Her female radar was buzzing madly, in anticipation of something different and wonderful. She was, she thought, exactly where she wanted to be. She was ready, receptive, and apprehensive all at the same time.

Abruptly Quincy stopped. She looked up at his face inquiringly. He seemed to have come to a decision. Slowly he turned toward her, his large, strong hands gently took hold of her bare shoulders and pulled her to him. He looked deeply into her eyes, as if searching for something, some signal, some sign. Jenna smiled tentatively, then demurely, as he drew her slowly to him. Crushing her to his chest, he leaned down and gently kissed her. For a moment, she was startled and hesitant. Then, knowing deep down inside that the culmination of their building passion was inevitable, she parted her lips and abandoned herself to the moment. Slowly and tenderly, as if he was afraid of scaring her or hurting her, Quincy explored her mouth with his tongue. Impatiently, Jenna pressed herself harder against his body, thrusting her hips into his groin. She intensified the kiss by drawing his tongue deeply into her mouth, sucking gently but firmly on it. His reaction was instant. His hands shifted from her shoulders to her waist. He lifted her off the ground, until they were face to face. His arms tightened around her and they melted into one another, kissing deeply.

The kiss went on and on. Neither seemed aware of the passing moments. They devoured each other, while pressing harder and more urgently together. Quincy maneuvered her to a nearby tree. By using it to prop her up, urged her with gentle body, language to wrap herself around him. Without any thought, Jenna responded eagerly, wrapping both legs around his slim waist, and squeezing as she savaged his mouth. He broke away from the kiss, and leaned back to look at her. She began unfastening the buttons of his jacket. He took this opportunity to start nibbling and sucking lightly at her neck. Quincy pulled the thin straps of her dress down over her shoulders, slightly exposing her right breast. He contemplated the results of his handy work for a moment, as Jenna was preoccupied with his buttons, pulling lightly on the hair of his chest. Then, leaning her back against the tree, with her legs tight around his waist, he bent down and firmly took her exposed, rosy tipped, rock hard, engorged nipple into his mouth.

The result was instant and electric. Jenna was now fully awake, energized, and wet with desire for this man she held locked between her legs. As he sucked her nipple, she moaned softly, her groin started to spasm and an orgasm ripped through her. She arched hard against him, and he became aware of a warm wetness, pressed against his stomach. This was too much for him. His hands acquired a life of their own. Bracing her gently against the huge casurena tree, he held her in place between himself and the tree. He slid his hands down along her waist to her legs, and lifting her dress. He slid his hands up her thighs and derriere to her waist; she was not wearing panties. Moaning softly, nodding her head, she sucked at his neck, crying happily, and encouraging him with every gesture and wiggle of her hips. He took one hand, and with a flick of his wrist unfastened his trousers, letting them fall around his feet to the sandy ground. Immediately, his erection sprang up against her sex, gently bobbing against her tight derriere. She continued to moan, louder, and squirmed against him so desperately, that her moisture was dribbling down into his bristly thatch, moistening his rock hard erection.

He looked down at her, she looked up, and with a gentle shifting of weight, and with a groan deep in his chest, he slowly entered her. Jenna was completely overcome. Slowly, inch by inch, he entered her, filling her completely, sliding into her. Relaxing her hips slowly, she flattened her groin against him, eagerly coaxing the last bit of him into her. Finally he reached her churning core. He held her impaled on his member as if she was pinned to the tree with a spear. She melted around him until neither could tell who was who. Slowly, she tightened her muscles around him, her vagina spasming spontaneously around his erection. He responded instinctively by gently pulling away, then thrusting hard into her once again. Their motion became spasmodic, urgent and involuntary. They could not stop, not even if shot dead on the spot. With an explosion of breath and a simultaneous groan, they climaxed together, shuddering with the impact of it. She could feel him spurt into her, hot and fully, once, twice, three times, and then, yet again. Each time she climaxed anew, until she was limp with expended emotion. Satiated as never before in her life, Jenna breathed deeply as if she had run a fast mile. So that's what I have been missing, she mused.

After a moment, he sank slowly to his knees, keeping Jenna firmly impaled. They squatted there kissing gently, her back to the tree and her legs tightly clasped around his waist, oblivious of the rough bark biting into her back. When his legs could no longer take their combined weight, Quincy gently reached out, pulled up her straps, and struggled erect. He gently set her on her feet. Shakily, her legs trembling with fatigue, Jenna leaned gratefully against the tree, while Quincy reached down, pulled up his pants, and deliberately fastened his fly. Taking the moment to collect himself, he turned to her.

.   "This isn't just a lark for me, Jenna. I want to spend much more time with you, in fact as long as you want to." With a warm smile, he continued, "let's go out to my boat and spend the rest of the night getting better acquainted?"

Nodding slowly, Jenna pushed herself off the tree, and taking his hand, she said with mock solemnity, "I think we should; this situation between us definitely deserves more time and much closer examination."

Together, hand in hand, they strolled down the lane to the beach, stopping only to slip off their shoes. He peeled off his socks, rolled up his pant legs and manhandled the dingy into the water. Lifting her effortlessly into the bow of the boat he spun the dingy around so that it was facing out to sea, tossed in his shoes and hopped in. Settling to the oars, he rowed steadily into the night toward the Billfish. When they reached the yacht, Jenna snagged the painter hanging from the stern and made it fast to the dingy. With an agility that surprised her, she clambered gracefully aboard. Quincy admired her maneuver, and followed quickly behind, relishing the view of her taut backside through the wafer thin, gauzy material of her dress.

In the grip of a warm glow of euphoria, and with an effort to dispel any awkwardness between them, Jenna turned, reached behind her back and unzipped her dress.

"How about a swim to cool off?" she said.

Shrugging out of the straps, she let the dress pool around her feet, she paused, letting him drink in the unobstructed view of her naked body, illuminated only by the strengthening moonlight. She then crossed to the rail and vaulted into the sea. Startled, entranced, and definitely interested, Quincy literally tore off his jacket and pants and followed her over the rail into the warm embrace of the water. They swam and frolicked until the combination of exhaustion, water, and the night air started to chill them. Regretfully, they climbed the ladder, gathered their discarded clothes from the deck, opened the door to the pilot house, and went inside. Jenna marveled at the warm wood inside, aglow with the dim, low voltage lighting. The pilot house windows afforded a surprisingly panoramic view of the surrounding moon speckled sea and the hotel with its lights twinkling on the shore.

Turning to follow him down the stairs, she entered what had to be the galley, and straight ahead, the master cabin. A huge V birth was the center attraction, surrounded by gleaming woodwork, hiding closets and cabinets. He opened one, tossed his thoroughly trashed dress whites and shoes to the bottom of the closet, and told her to hang up her dress, and join him in the shower to rinse off the salt. She did as he bid her, and nimbly joined him in the shower stall already steamed up from the hot water. It was a very tight fit. Nevertheless, they played with each other, without being able to do anything more intimate. Finally, he shampooed her hair, soaped her down thoroughly, neglecting not even one minute crease on her body. Squeaky clean, she was ejected hot and wet again from the shower, and told to dry off and turn down the bed. Quincy remained to finish up, nursing a painfully hard erection and looking forward to the rest of the evening / morning. Wrapping the towel around his waist, he dried off, and turned into the galley. He rummaged in the cupboard, and located two snifters and a bottle of Napoleon brandy. He poured two generous drinks, and returned the bottle to the shelf. Quincy entered the cabin. His breath caught in his throat. Jenna was spread out, naked on his bed, with her wet, long blond hair, fanned out around her head on the pillow.

Glancing up, she said, "Captain Sir, aren't you a tad overdressed for the occasion?"

With alacrity, he peeled off the towel, letting it drop to the deck, and climbed into the bunk beside her. He handed her a snifter, gently tapped it with his own, and said, "Here's to you my dear. You have brightened up my day and this humble cabin considerably."

"How very British of you; I noticed in, passing, that you weren't wearing underwear either," she chided.

"Sailors never overdress" he responded with a wry grin. "That way we're ready for anything at a moment's notice."

They chatted amicably, sipping their brandy, they lay snuggled together like spoons with his arm resting on her hip. With his fingers, Quincy lightly traced the silky white blond hair between her legs, marveling on its softness. His hand strayed occasionally, to run fully under her right breast, cupping it lovingly, and lightly pinching the nipple. Gradually, their talk faded, replaced by heavy breathing. Urgently, they turned again to one another. This time they starting slowly, exploring and touching each other tenderly, as new lovers do. Eager for the feel and taste of their new love, their explorations finally gave way to a renewed urgency. It seemed that they could not get enough of each other, penetrate deeply enough, taste each other enough, until, finally, totally exhausted, they fell asleep as the sun peeked through the cabin porthole. They slept as the world went on around them, unaware that events, beyond their control had taken a dark turn during the night.

Chapter 9 - Friday Night
The Colony Club Bar

After he was finished with the day's ski lessons, Norman was relaxing at the beach bar, having a sandwich and a drink with a slightly plump, but pleasingly attractive, middle aged woman from Venezuela, named Inez. She was drooling all over him. He figured as long as she was buying, he could live with the drool. Freebees were a perk of the job, and he was used to paying a price for them. In reality, he was still flattered by women's interest, even if it proved to be fleeting. It made him forget briefly, what a colossal wreck he had become. While half tuned out to Inez, and her incessant chatter, Norman happened to overhear that Bobbie Chastain was having a big party that night, and had asked several of the bar girls to help out at the bash. They were excited, as Bobbie paid well, and there was always plenty of food and drink left over for the help. Norman knew that Bobbie always asked Quincy to attend. She was busily trying to worm her way into his bed. Rumor had it that she was, perhaps, but not definitely, sporadically successful. She had obviously, however, not yet landed him as a permanent escort. He also knew that Bobbie liked to collect interesting visitors, and, depended on Quincy to bring along some of the more notable ones he encountered, in his daily routine of sailing captain and scuba diving guide.

This was the break Norman had waited for. He guessed that Quincy would, most likely, ask several of the Colony Club guests to join him for the evening. He had noticed some speculative glances between Quincy and Jenna after they returned from skiing. It seemed likely to him that Quincy would include Jenna in his evening plans. He decided that he would hang around the bar for a while, to see if he was right. With Jenna potentially gone for the evening, Norman knew he could break into her room and steal the coin. He was experienced in breaking into the guest rooms; from time to time, he had been supplementing his meager income with a little old fashioned larceny. He never took all he found, only enough, so that the bewildered guests could not remember exactly how much money was in his or her wallet after a boozy day at the beach, and in the island shops. His forays into crime were almost never reported, and, if they were, nothing ever came of it. Smythe-Caulley, who responded to the infrequent reports, always said he'd look into it. He always managed to cover for Norman. Eventually, the disgruntled tourist would leave the island and return home, forever ending the matter. Smythe-Caulley was particularly interested in getting his hands on the coin so that he could do a little historical research; Norman felt that it was worth the risk, and if he made the break-in look like a robbery, the crooked cop would cover for him anyway. Tonight, however, might prove to be a problem. Normally, the club was quiet by midnight. Tonight was calypso night, and there would be an influx of tourists from other hotels as well as a number of locals out for a good time. It was a popular show, and usually went to midnight, with the hard core of party people lingering to all hours. He'd have to be patient, pace himself, and see what developed.

Norman was still at the beach bar when Quincy beached his dingy, hopped ashore, and strolled by in his military finery. All the ladies, including Inez, were looking approvingly at the retreating figure, speculating idly, and wishing he were headed for a rendezvous with them. Norman, ignored by one and all at the bar, got up from his stool and left. "Be right back," he said to the bartender and Inez, and headed down the beach past his shack and into the lane leading out to the road.

Carefully positioning himself behind one of the large Casurena trees, he waited for the group to appear. He was close enough to the entrance of the club, to see clearly that the departing group, headed for Bobbie's home, included both Jenna and Ellis. The coast is clear, he thought. All I have to do, is to wait until most of the guests have turned in and the calypso evening crowd has gone home; then I can get the job done. Chuckling to himself, he scurried back to the beach bar for another drink. Careful to remain sober enough to do the job, he would then retire to his shack and wait for the appointed hour. By midnight or one AM, he reasoned, the time would be perfect for a little burglary. Who knows, maybe the lady from Venezuela would still be at the bar, and she could buy him another drink, perhaps dinner. He could enjoy the calypso show with her, maybe pass a little time afterward. He intended to remain sober, so who knows, it might prove to be fun. Norman was a happy man, things were working out, and his partner in crime, Smythe-Caulley, he hoped, would be pleased with his initiative.

Having disposed of Inez earlier with a promise of a continued escapade the following night, Norman had retired to his shack to wait out the calypso evening. Now, past midnight, the band had departed, and couples were leaving for home or retiring to their rooms. Norman roused himself from the stoop of his shack. He had been sitting there it seemed, forever, gazing sightlessly out to sea. He was hoping that Quincy and Jenna would remain at the party, for good while longer. As he was about to go inside, he heard some people walking down the lane. Ever cautious, he moved into the shadows. He was pleased to see Quincy and Jenna walk down to the dingy and cast off. He watched them until they reached the Billfish, then, satisfied that they would be occupied there for the rest of the evening; he went inside to prepare for his burglary. He lit his one lantern and surveyed his meager wardrobe. He had very little to wear, certainly no black clothing appropriate for a sneaky break-in operation. Sighing, he chose his darkest swimsuit, a faded blue Speedo, and his darkest hula shirt, a faded grey number, with a hole under the left armpit and a slightly torn pocket. Hardly the appropriate outfit for a master thief, he thought. Well, if all goes well in the next few days, he could be on easy street before he knew it. He realized that he was kidding himself, but he needed the pep talk to get himself going. He was realistic enough to know that, if all went well, and he and Smythe-Caulley were able to steal the treasure, assuming there was one in the first place; Smythe-Caulley would find a way to screw Norman out of a decent share.

Undeterred, Norman took a deep breath, and left the shack. He walked down to the water line to make sure there were no fresh footprints in the sand running along the beach leading from his shack to the guest wing. Once in the water, he followed the lapping waves to a spot directly in front of the guest wing. As he walked, he looked carefully at the terrace and the beach chairs spotted here and there along the beachfront of the terrace.

He quickly located Jenna's room, and noted with satisfaction that there was a dim light left on. It was probably the bathroom light so that she would not have to stumble around in the dark when she came from the party. This was a real break. The night watchman must have noticed by now that the guest was out, and had left the light on. He would not have to turn on a light, possibly alerting the night watchman to new activity. It was one risk eliminated. He crouched down by the water, and waited until the night watchman had gone by. He knew that his circuit of the club would take him about twenty minutes, and Norman was comfortable with the timing. As he approached the building, he moved cautiously, still checking around for a lingering guest. Just before he reached the terrace of Jenna's room, he noticed a shape in the sand near one of the coconut palm. He stopped to listen. He heard snoring, and edged closer. It was a man, curled on his side in the sand smelling strongly of rum. He was apparently out like a light, and therefore no threat. He could not see who it was, and he did not want to risk waking the man, so he continued on to Jenna's patio door. He carefully crept up to the sliding glass door, and using a trick he had learned years ago, leaned on the sliding portion until the safety glass and the sliding frame bowed out from the stationary potion of the door, disengaging the lock. With a swift push to slide the door open, Norman slipped inside, carefully pulling the door almost closed behind him. He made sure the door did not reengage the lock. Normally he would reverse the maneuver upon exiting the room to conceal the break in. This time, when he exited the crime scene, he would leave the door ajar signaling that someone had been in the room.

Pulling the curtains aside, he moved fully into the room. He was now completely screened from the night watchman, and could take his time. If need be, he could let the man go around one more time before he left her room. Looking around he was struck by its orderly appearance. There was none of the usual female clutter, no clothes flung over the furniture, no towels lying around. She must be expecting company tonight, he thought wistfully, regretting that he had blown his own chance with her the day before. Is she in for a surprise when she gets back!

He quickly went to work, and, within minutes, he had located her purse, her passport, and the coin left innocently in the top dresser drawer. Too easy he thought; this only took five minutes. Chuckling to himself, he carefully replaced the passport. He did not want her retained on the island due to lack of documentation after this adventure was over. Never steal the passport, he thought, it's a bad business decision. He took all the money from the wallet, and flung it on the floor, stuffing the coin and the money into his shirt pocket. He moved to the sliding glass door. He pulled the curtains aside, peered out into the darkness and, satisfied that he was alone, slid the door open and stepped outside. He turned, slid the door partially closed, then reversed direction to head back to the surf line. Mindful of the drunk near the palm, Norman was proceeding carefully, looking around, alert to any presence.

In two steps, he stopped dead. There in front of him, partially concealed by the tree trunk, was Trent Carver, sitting with his back leaning against the coconut tree, looking out to sea. The drunk was now awake. He must have heard Norman or sensed him, because he abruptly turned, struggling to regain his feet. It was instantly obvious to both men that Norman had just come out of one of the guest rooms. Without thinking, Norman snatched up a freshly fallen, green coconut. As Trent was struggling to get off his knees in the sand, Norman brought the coconut down hard on the top of Trent's head. He dropped like a stone and lay still. Norman, gripped by mindless panic, looking neither left nor right, sprinted down to the water and dove in. Surfacing ten yards out from shore, he glanced quickly back at the building and dimly lit grounds. Seeing no one, Norman turned, and swam quickly along the beach, to a point directly opposite his own shack. He tore off the shirt, stood up in the waist deep water, and boldly walked though the slight surf, onto the sand. He proceeded directly to his shack, leaving a second set of footprints in the sand. Norman entered his shack and closed the door.

Unobserved by Norman and the night watchman, Lyle Farmer had been asleep, stretched out on a pile of life preservers in a small sailing dingy, chained to the water sport kiosk, about fifty yards from Jenna's room. He was there sleeping off a drunk, brought on by Eileen's threatening to break up with him unless he stepped up and married her. For some time, he had been reluctant to do so he kept telling himself, because he felt that his skiing business was not yet firmly established. He was reluctant to add to his overhead. Wives were expensive; hell, girlfriends were expensive, and a pain in the ass, to boot. Roused by the commotion nearby, Lyle looked over the gunwale of the skiff just in time to see Norman brain Trent with the coconut. Keeping silent, he watched

Norman scamper to the water, swim down the beach, and stroll up to his shack. Stunned, he sat there for several minutes, and then, prompted by the sight of a woman walking along the path toward the scene. He lowered himself over the side of the skiff, away from sight of the club, and bolted for the car park.

Norman looked through his one window, checking to see if anyone was around. Relieved, he suddenly remembered the money and the coin that he had stuffed into his shirt pocket. Hastily, he unwadded his shirt and fumbled for the pocket. The cash was gone, but thankfully, the coin remained. Relieved and exhausted, Norman plopped down in his only chair and tried to regain his composure. Instinctively, he reached for his gallon bottle of Eclipse rum, pulled the cork, and took a deep swig.

Unconscious of the passing time, Norman sat on his sagging chair and drank until he was numb, not insensible; just numb. He was beyond caring what came next. His mind was awash with regret, fantasizing on Trent coming to and screaming, "stop thief, murderer!"

Gradually sounds started to filter through the alcoholic fog shrouding his brain. He became aware; a woman was screaming bloody murder, accompanied by a growing background noise. Confused, he set the bottle down on the floor, and stumbled out his door. He saw people in various stages of undress, running in the direction of the guest wing facing the beach. Instinctively, he stepped out of his shack, and followed along. When he got there, the night watchman was standing over a sobbing Janice Carver, who was clutching her husband Trent to her chest. Rocking back and forth, she was screaming between sobs,

"He's dead, he's dead, help us, help us!"

Finally, Chloe Whiting, acquainted with the Carvers, was able to lead the hysterical and sobbing Janice away from the body to a chair on the terrace. Her husband Tedd managed to get her a glass of water. The authorities were called, and the guests, the night staff, and Norman milled around, speculating as to what could possibly have happened. One of the staff requisitioned a large beach towel and covered up most of the body. The faded red towel lay on the sand with Trent's feet sticking out one end; blood was seeping through the Colony Club logo covering his head.

Within forty five minutes, a short, wiry, khaki clad white man, followed by the night watchman, the desk clerk, and two uniformed constables came bustling into the hotel. His arrival drew the crowd together again, serving to re-focus them on Janice and the corpse. They lapsed into silence to hear what was going on. The man was Sergeant Smythe-Caulley. He strolled through the terrace toward the beach, trailing the desk clerk and the night watchman. He was asking questions in a rapid staccato, impatiently listening to the brief answers provided by his escorts.

Noticing Norman in the crowd in his usual bleary eyed condition, the Sergeant pointedly ignored him. He stopped briefly to comfort the widow, and told her he would return shortly. He walked down to the beach, noting that the sand around the shrouded corpse was churned up with countless footprints. No one had thought to keep the crowd back. No evidence there, he thought, as he knelt down by the body and drew back the now blood stained, beach towel.

"Keep these people back," he said over his shoulder, as he bent to examine the dead man. He quickly noticed the blood dripping to the sand from a gash in the man's head. On closer examination, he saw that the gash was centered in a large dent in the man's skull. Obviously, this was the cause of death, he thought. He also noticed, about two feet away from the dead man's head, lying on its side in the sand, a fresh green coconut, with a large, sandy, dark spot on the pointy end. Smythe-Caulley carefully re-covered the dead man and, standing up, picked up the coconut, and walked to one of the lights illuminating the terrace. The bottom of the coconut, where it came to a point, was covered with blood with a few hairs sticking to the knot. He carefully set it down on a nearby table and instructed the uniformed constable, who had come huffing up to join him, "See that this is bagged and sent to the lab, I believe we shall find that the victim's blood is all over it."

"Yassir, right away, Sir," responded the constable coming to attention. "The odder men be on their way wid de doctor. Dey be here directly."

Smythe-Caulley returned to the corpse, looked up into the coconut tree near the body. Stepping aside smartly, he dodged a fresh coconut falling from the large bunch at the top of the tree, twenty feet above him. It hit the ground next to him with a tremendous thud. People standing nearby could feel the impact through their feet.

It was instantly obvious to him what could have happened. The constabulary would, of course, go through the motions of autopsy and further examination of the scene of death, but he was confident that it was death by accident. He returned to the widow and carefully explained to her what he surmised had happened. Unconsoled, Janice resumed her sobbing, until she was led away by Chloe Whiting, trailed uselessly, by her husband Tedd.

Smythe-Caulley briskly instructed his men to have the doctor pronounce the victim officially dead, block off and secure the death scene, and remove the corpse and the coconut to the laboratory. He then turned to the crowd and briefly told them that this seemed to be an accidental, if not freakish occurrence, and asked if anyone present had witnessed anything. There was a unanimous consensus. No one had seen anything. They had all been drawn from their beds by the commotion, when Janice Carver had stumbled onto her husband's corpse, and started screaming at the top of her lungs. He then asked them to disburse. He would call on them in the morning if need be.

As the crowd faded away, he noticed Norman looking intently at him before he turned and walked down the beach towards his shack. Smythe-Caulley felt instinctively that something was awry, and that Norman was at the center of it. He would have to wait until Norman contacted him tomorrow for the answers he wanted.

Chapter 10 – Saturday
The Conspiracy Grows

Next morning, Norman awakened to find himself in his usual sodden condition, spectacularly hung over, and filled with dread and remorse. God, he thought to himself, what a mess! What will I do? Aware that Smythe-Caulley has labeled the death an accident, he was still apprehensive about the investigation. Shaken, he went about his morning routine, a swim, cleaning the shack, and then wandering off to the kitchen for coffee. As he circled through the car park, he saw Lyle drive in. He paused to let Lyle lock the car and join him. Together they walked to the kitchen. Norman, wary about Lyle, who seemed to be scrutinizing him closely this morning, could see that there was something on his boss's mind. They finished their coffee and strolled past the front entrance, starting down the lane towards the beach.

Lyle stopped, and Norman turned to him enquiringly, expecting some instructions for the day's skiing business. Watching Norman intently, Lyle said simply, "Norman I saw you last night on the beach."

The blood drained out of Norman's face, and, too shocked to say anything, he sagged against a nearby tree. Hyperventilating, he finally gasped out, "What did you see?"

"I saw you brain Trent with a coconut," Lyle replied. "Then you ran down the beach and dove into the sea."

"Christ on a crutch," sputtered Norman. "What are you going to do? Are you going to the coppers with this?"

"I don't know. Why should I keep quiet? Murder is murder. Why did you do it?" Lyle asked.

Faced with the inevitable, Norman came clean. He was deathly afraid of the policeman, nut Lyle had him dead to rights. He explained to Lyle about his relationship with Smythe-Caulley, and the fact that he was always having to do the dirty work for the man. He was afraid that if he crossed him, he would be deported back to Australia to face a court marshal for desertion. He went on to tell about Smythe-Caulley's instruction to steal the coin and their tentative scheme to appropriate anything found by the group seeking the actual treasure "Killing Trent was an accident," Norman whined. "He saw me coming out of Jenna's room and I just reacted before he could cry out. When Smythe-Caulley arrived, he looked at the coconut and the ripe bunch on the tree, and concluded that Trent was just brained by a falling coconut. It appears, at least for the moment, that no one suspects anything."

"What about Jenna? What do you think she'll do when she finds out she was robbed and a dead man was found outside her patio door?" demanded Lyle.

"I don't know" said Norman miserably. "I guess we'll have to wait and see. Smythe-Caulley has always covered for me; perhaps he can cover this up as well."

"Does he know that it was you who killed Trent?" asked Lyle.

"Not yet," replied Norman. "I was afraid to tell him. There's no telling what he'll do. Now that you know, and assuming that you are willing to keep quiet about this, I had better give him a ring immediately. He should be in his office by now."

"Let's do it together," said Lyle. "I want to know what's going on myself, as it seems that I am now in on the scheme with the two of you. You know, of course, that if that crooked bastard finds out the truth, he'll hold it over your head forever. If need be, he'll throw you to the wolves just to save his own skin."

"I know," said Norman miserably. "But what can I do? He can't protect me and the scheme if he is left in the dark. If he knows the truth, he can at least steer the investigation away from me and cover for us."

Lyle was very aware of the "us" in the statement, and it sobered him. He was loath to get involved with the two, but a sudden and overwhelming surge of greed had made him realize that this could be the solution to his personal and business problems. Reflecting on the likelihood that there might actually be a treasure to steal, he realized that, for the first time, a coin had been found on Sandy Lane Beach. That location had for many years been the only place on the Island consistently associated with the old rumor. This time, he reasoned, we might actually be on to something. If nothing was found, there would be no crime.

The conversation with Smythe-Caulley was brief, as the Sergeant was at work and could say very little. Norman gave him a quick summary and rang off, agreeing to meet later that day at Maycock's Bay up the coast. It was an unpopulated and generally deserted spot where they could talk at leisure. Lyle and Norman would take the ski boat to the rendezvous, and Smythe-Caulley would drive up after he had finished interrogating some of the guests and the staff at the Colony Club. The rendezvous was on the same coast as the Colony Club, but well past the area known as the gold coast, just short of the northern part of the coast. It was relatively unpopulated, and a line of limestone cliffs and hills kept most people from the beaches in the area. People that frequented the area did so from mostly the sea side, fisherman and the occasional diver. Pedestrians usually parked on the road and hiked in. Most of the visitors were teenagers looking for some seclusion on the weekends. Smythe-Caulley's Land Rover with four wheel drive would allow him to get to the beach without incident. There were only a handful of these type vehicles on the island, so the conspirators would be virtually private from the road.

As Norman turned the boat into Maycock's Bay, he and Lyle spotted Smythe-Caulley's Land Rover pulled up on the seaside of a large clump of sea grape. The car was completely screened from the road, and so they beached the boat near the car. Now, both the boat and car were safe from inquisitive eyes on the road. The only risk of discovery lay in a chance passing, of a fisherman, coming home from a day's work, heading into Speightstown, to sell his fish. They felt comfortable, that if one did happen by, he would be well out to sea and would not recognize the vehicles, or the men.

The Sergeant got right to it in his usual menacing manner.

"Stupid business Norman. How could you cock it up so badly? You spoiled a perfect snatch by killing a tourist. Fortunately for you, many people saw me dodge the coconut falling from the tree, and it was within a few feet of Trent Carver's body. Everyone, including me, jumped to the same conclusion. The problem is that when Jenna White reports a robbery a few feet from the location of the dead body, things will go into high gear at the Constabulary. It will be impossible for me to control the investigation. A murdered tourist is bad business, and everyone, from Sir Robert on down, will be breathing on my neck." Turning to Lyle, he asked "Can you possible persuade Jenna White not to report the theft?"

"I don't know," said Lyle speculatively. "What could I say that would possibly persuade her? When she finds the room ransacked, she might think it was a simple burglary, but then she discovers that the coin is missing, she and Quincy will most definitely smell a rat. I might be able to persuade them that it will only bring the authorities into the coin business, thereby finishing any plans they might have for a treasure hunt. Since they were innocent of anything regarding Carver, they might keep it to themselves. They might not even want to tell the rest of the group."

No one had any other brilliant ideas.

"Just give it a go," said the policeman. "It might spell disaster if you do not. Norman, hand over the coin, and I'll get cracking on the research. There might be nothing to this after all. You might have created a mess for nothing."

Reluctantly, Norman handed over the coin. "Miss White was not in the crowd at the murder scene," said Norman. "Maybe she spent the entire night with Quincy aboard his blasted boat."

"I have an idea," said Lyle. "I'll keep a lookout for them coming ashore, and intercept them with the news of Trent's death. Perhaps it will scare her enough to keep her mouth shut. After all, how much money could she have lost?"

"It wasn't much," said Norman. "I didn't count it. I'll bet it was less than a hundred dollars. No doubt the rest of her money is in the hotel safe. The only reason her passport was in the room, is that most guests take their passports shopping, to take advantage of the duty free prices. They need to have it handy."

"Farmer, you're on it then," said Smythe-Caulley. "You're the only one of us, who is in on the find, and possibly, the treasure hunt. It's up to you to control the situation. See what you can do, and don't muddle it up. I'll find out about the origin of the coin if at all possible, and you keep an eye on the group. Keep me posted, and I'll guide you through this."

With that, the group broke up. Smythe-Caulley's backed the Land Rover toward the sea, turned it, drove up to the road, and turned right, motoring back toward Speightstown. The two remained, waiting until the car was out of sight, and then shoved off. As they cruised back to the Colony Club, they caught glimpses of the Land Rover, following along the coast road. Eventually, as it entered Speightstown, they lost sight of the car. Neither man felt like talking; both of them lost in their own speculations. The conspirators realized that they were going to be forced to trust others who were neither trustworthy nor honorable.

What they could do, what was to happen, and what part they would play in the unfolding drama they had no way of knowing. Lyle was busy speculating about Eileen's possible involvement in this plan. She would obviously be included in the hunt, so he reasoned that, sooner or later, he would have to rope her into the plan to save his own skin. She might prove useful in manipulating Jenna. One thing was certain; they both knew that each man involved, vehemently mistrusted the other two. Sooner or later, there would be trouble. Someone, maybe more than one, was going to get hurt. Arriving back at the Colony Club, the two spotted Quincy and Jenna aboard the Billfish, lounging in the cockpit, sipping something hot from a couple of enameled mugs. Quincy was shirtless, sporting his customary pair of old faded khaki shorts, and Jenna was wearing what must have been one of Quincy's old army T shirts. They seemed relaxed, happy, and content to be together. As they throttled back and prepared to beach the boat, the duo waved at the pair, but neither Jenna nor Quincy noticed them.

"Perfect," said Lyle. "Norman, you go about your business, and I'll go over to the water sports shack and wait for them to come ashore."

After beaching the boat above the waves, they went their separate ways, Norman apprehensive, and Lyle determined to pull this off.

Chapter 11 – Saturday
The Coin is Gone

Oblivious to what had happened ashore the night before, and ignoring everyone on the beach, Quincy, fully relaxed, and satisfyingly tired, contentedly contemplated Jenna over his cup of coffee. What he saw was a stunningly beautiful sight; Jenna, her face aglow in the late morning sun, her knees pulled up to her chest, had stretched his old army T shit over her knees to her ankles. Her hair was tousled, her lips swollen to a dark pink. The expression on her face made his heart sing. She looked well and thoroughly bedded, and quite obviously smug about it.

"What are you smirking about Quincy McKenna?" she grinned. "You look like the cat that ate the canary."

"I was just letting my mind play over the events of the last twelve or so hours, particularly the latter part of the evening; thinking that I could get used to more of this, on a regular basis," he replied.

"You were, were you? Well don't go getting the idea that you are so damn irresistible. I could be just indulging myself in a little holiday fling," she teased.

"If you are," he countered, "then you are giving a pretty convincing display to the contrary. I have never had an experience in my life to top last night, and I admit that I'm quite shaken. I'm not as immune to romance as I thought. You are damned irresistible, yourself. Now you are going to have to deal with what you started. I'm not going away quietly. You have more than a week left on the Island; that should allow us time enough to explore our situation to see if it's just an island romance, or if there is more to it. We'll see what develops, and deal with it as it comes. This potential treasure hunt is another bloody complication; I'm almost temped to ignore it, and concentrate on you. I think, however, that with where you found the coin, and the persistent rumors about Bluebeard, coupled to the historical fact that he actually did frequent this Island, we have to at least make an attempt to find something. We should re-convene the original group and make a plan."

"I agree," said Jenna. She slipped her legs out of the T shirt, affording him a quick peek at her unclad, rounded bottom. "Let me use your bathroom to pull myself together. Then we can go ashore and get started. Do you have anything more respectable than this T shirt that I can slip on? My dress is ruined, and I'd rather not parade our little interlude in front of the whole club."

"I think there may be something in the lost and found that you can use. Tourists are always leaving odds and ends aboard after day trips. I always toss them in the locker, so that the items can be re-claimed by their owners. Surprisingly enough, few items are ever picked up. You can pick through the lot, after you pull yourself together," he replied. "I'll get ready to go ashore. The locker is in the galley under the starboard seat cushion."

Jenna slipped through the pilot house, and headed down the steps, toward the master cabin with its private head. She stopped briefly, rummaged through the lost and found, and located a faded pair of pink shorts that would suffice, and a musty, blue blouse that was obviously too large. She could tie the tails together under her breasts and make do. Happily, she stepped into the head and closed the door. Thirty minutes later, she reappeared with her hair combed, her legs shaved, and a smile on her face, dressed in her new found finery. She sauntered onto the deck and announced, "I'm ready to go. I hope you don't mind that I used your toothbrush and your razor. I decided that after last night that it would not matter. If either of us has anything unsavory, the other surely is already infected. I also took the liberty of swiping a paper bag to take my ruined clothes home in." Wincing slightly, Quincy agreed.

"The paper bag and the toothbrush are fine, but I can never use the razor blade again. The hair on women's legs just tears up the blade. No matter," he finished. "I have a full pack of blades, and you're welcome to them all, as long as you're here with me. If you decide to stay on, I'll lay in a lifetime supply."

Walking over to her, he pulled her close and kissed her upturned face. She sighed and responded.

"Now that's a good morning kiss to be proud of," she breathed throatily. "Let's go ashore before this goes any further."

Quincy hauled in the dingy and handed her down into the bow, then, untying the painter, he stepped lightly onto the seat and sat down. The man had obviously had a lot of practice, as the dingy did not even rock when he gracefully sat, and shipped the oars. With one counterstroke, he rotated the dingy one hundred and eighty degrees, and started pulling strongly for the beach.

Jenna contented herself watching the play of muscles across his legs, chest, and arms, as he rowed briskly ashore. She loved watching him move. She realized with a start that, while Quincy was not a conventionally handsome man, he was the best looking one she had ever seen. She hugged herself, grinning inside, and realized that he might be hers forever, if she wanted him; and right now, at this very moment, she had never wanted anything so much in her whole life. Notwithstanding the fiasco with Norman, so far, this was turning out to be her best week ever. Certainly no other time she could remember, could hold a candle to it. Her Manhattan flat and her demanding job seemed only a distant memory. Quincy efficiently beached the boat, driving it up onto the sand with a few powerful strokes, stepped over the side, and handed Jenna to the beach without getting her feet wet.

"Thank you, gallant Sir," she quipped, as they walked up the beach toward the terrace.

To the right, toward the water sports kiosk, they noticed a small group of people clustered around a roped off patch of sand, just opposite the patio of Jenna's room. Curious, they walked over, and, recognizing Chloe and Tedd Whiting, Jenna asked, "What's going on?"

Chloe turned abruptly and said, "Oh Jenna, something terrible has happened. Trent Carver was killed here last night. A coconut fell from this tree and caved his head in."

Stunned, both Jenna and Quincy were speechless. Finally Jenna asked, "What about his wife? I think her name is Janice. Is she Ok? Where is she?"

Tedd replied, "Chloe took her to her room after the police left last night, and the doctor gave her a sedative. We haven't seen her since. The front desk sent a maid to check on her periodically this morning, and reported that she appeared to be in a deep sleep. I'll hate to be around when she wakes up, but Chloe will have to help out. We are the only people Janice really knows here, and she'll need comforting, and some help with the police. Whatever arrangements need to be made, when this is all over, she will, no doubt, want to take her husband's body home for burial."

"Terrible tragedy," mumbled Quincy, strangely upset by the death of a man he had never met. He felt that there was something missing here, but said nothing about his instant reaction. He was no stranger to violent death, but always before, he could instinctively understand the context surrounding a tragic event. Something was strangely amiss here. He glanced up and noted the ripe bunch of coconuts hanging from the tree, and looked briefly around. The roped off patch of sand seemed oddly too far from the tree, for the explanation of the accident to ring true.

"Do let me know if I can be of help," he offered to Tedd, as he efficiently steered a speechless Jenna back to the concrete path leading to the beach wing, heading toward her room.

"Which one is yours?" he asked.

"Number 104."

She pointed down the path on the right. She stumbled to the door and fumbled with the key, in the bottom of the paper bag containing her dress, shoes, and miniscule clutch. Quincy gently took the bag from her, opened it, found the key, and ushered her through the door. Jenna took one look at the opened drawer, and the wallet on the floor, and exclaimed, "Oh my God, Quincy, I've been robbed. I'll have to call the police."

Thinking quickly, Quincy put his arm around her, and led her over to the easy chair, and sat her down.

"Let's look around a bit first, and see what is missing before we call them. This looks bad; you robbed, and a dead body found just outside your patio door. I've seen a lot of death, and the explanation seems a little too neat to me."

With that, he started looking carefully around the room. He examined the bathroom, looking in the two drawers by the sink. Nothing seemed awry. It was a little too neat for a woman's bathroom, but most likely nothing unusual for a smart, organized, and successful attorney. He looked in the bedroom, strode over to the dresser, and looked inside the open drawer. It was full of tiny, lacy things bunched hastily to one side. "Was there anything important in here with your underwear?" he asked.

Shaking her head, no, she suddenly raised her fist to her mouth, her eyes sprang wide open.

"The coin," she gasped.

Quincy put two and two together.

"That's what the thief was after, I'll wager. How much money was in your purse?"

"About thirty dollars," she replied. "I put all my jewelry and cash in the hotel safe, when I realized that jewelry was out of place at the beach. I sign for anything I want. I just kept a little mad money for emergencies."

"The only thing of any value that's missing, is the coin," reasoned Quincy. "I daresay that your friend Trent just happened along at the wrong moment and paid dearly for it. Odd," he mused, "hardly anyone knew about the coin. Warrell was not at the bar, and unless you told him before you mentioned it to the rest of us, he is in the dark. Ellis was with us last night. At least he went over with us. I didn't lay eyes on him again. Probably Bobbie got him off somewhere in private for the evening. That's easily checked. That leaves Lyle, Eileen, and Norman. I doubt Eileen would kill a man, or rob a room for that matter. That leaves Lyle and Norman. Lyle, I can't really judge. He seems legitimate, but Norman is a complete derelict.

Guiltily, Jenna nodded agreement. Fresh on her mind was the disastrous hour on the beach she had spent with Norman. She was ashamed by her impulsive behavior, and she fervently hoped that Quincy never had to know about that incident.

"I think we had better say nothing of this theft," said Quincy. "You are only out a few dollars, and we do not want to explain the coin to the authorities. That might prove very sticky for all of us. The thing for us to do is to round up the group as soon as possible to decide what, if anything, we are going to do about your find."

"I agree. Let's put together a dinner party away from the Colony Club where we can talk quietly, and come to a decision."

"Good Idea," said Quincy. "I know a place we can meet. It's near Black Rock. It's called the Coconut Grove, and it serves food until about eight o'clock when the music starts. It's not much of a place, merely a concrete slab cantilevered out over the sea, with a cook shack and a bar. There's no parking at all but on the road out front. You'll love the food and the view, and the price is right. No one really gets there much before eight, but they start cooking around five and the bar is open at four thirty. I'll set it up, and come and collect you at four this afternoon."

Before he could say goodbye, there was a soft knock at the door. Quincy crossed quickly to the door, and opened it, only to find Lyle standing there.

"Good timing," said Quincy. "I was just coming to look for you. Why are you here?"

"I was just checking on Jenna. There was a death right outside her patio door last night, and I was afraid that she'd be upset. I see that she's in good hands, so I need not be concerned anymore. What did you need me for?" Lyle asked.

Quickly Quincy filled him in, and Lyle agreed to notify Eileen and Ellis, but when the discussion turned to Norman, Quincy pointedly asked that he not be included.

Curious about Quincy's reaction to Norman, Lyle asked him point blank, "Why not include Norman, he knows about the coin?"

I don't trust the man," replied Quincy bluntly. "The fewer the people who know our plans, the better off we'll be."

Readily agreeing, Lyle chuckled inwardly. Of course Norman would be in the loop, but excluded from the hunt. He would be free to team up with Smythe-Caulley, to execute their plan. Events are meshing nicely, thought Lyle, as he left the room. "See you both at five."

When Smythe-Caulley returned to the constabulary office at the Savannah, he went immediately to the Admiralty division of the records office. The coin was burning a hole in his pocket. Due to his high rank in the Colonial Service, he literally had free run of the whole department. No one took particular notice of him, as he browsed through the records. It was not an uncommon sight, though it was unusual for him to be browsing in the Admiralty section. He quickly located the appropriate section on piracy in the Caribbean, and the Lesser Antilles, in particular. He was soon absorbed in his research. The records made fascinating reading. It was a wild story of ships plundered, colonies set ablaze, slaves stolen, and finally, pirates run to ground, and either killed in battle, or transported to England for hanging.

Throughout the narrative there were many references to cargos stolen, particularly Spanish ships raided, and the Spanish Crown's treasure from the New World plundered. No significant amount of booty was ever recovered; at least, there was no written record of any loot taken, or returned to the rightful owners. Many slaves were retrieved and returned, but that was the most of it. What loot was found when the pirate ships were taken, was sent to the British Crown, to help defray the cost of enforcing British law in this part of her colonies. No trace of treasure, stolen from the Spanish galleons, was ever recorded. There were many observations of Bluebeard's ship sighted in and around Barbados, Trinidad and Tobago. The British fleet, when they finally cornered him, failed to recover anything. He died unrepentant without revealing where he had stashed his loot.

The Sergeant sat back in his chair thinking. Once Lyle found out what was going on, and if Miss White was persuaded not to report the theft, he and his cronies would be able to keep a close eye on the activity. They could strike as soon as opportunity presented itself. He was excited; this might be his ticket out of the service. He would resign his commission, and live out his life on one of the islands, indulging his every fantasy.

Chuckling, he stood up, returned the books to the file clerk, and headed to his office to await a call from either Lyle or Norman.

Lyle called at two o'clock. Smythe-Caulley quickly filled him in on the research and offer the opinion that the prospects seemed good that something might come of all this. Lyle delivered the news that Jenna had decided to let the theft go unreported, and that Quincy and he had were proceeding with some planning. He revealed that the group, minus Norman, would be meeting that evening at the Coconut Grove.

Smythe-Caulley said, "As long as the theft is not going to be reported, I'll say that the enquiry is closed after the autopsy is finished. I can then release the body for transportation back to the United States, and that will get the Carvers permanently out of our hair. You can tell Norman, that within twenty four hours, he'll likely be completely in the clear."

"He'll be very relieved," responded Lyle. "He has been a total wreck since it happened. I don't think he's been sober since."

"You tell him to be bloody grateful and sober up. We cannot have him lurching about like a drunken clown. If you can't square him away, I'll have to reconsider his participation. I can easily get rid of him if needs be."

"Don't worry, I can handle Norman, He'll be alright," reassured Lyle.

With that exchange, the pair rang off, and Lyle went in search of Norman. He arrived at the water sports shack to find Warrell stacking equipment and the ski boat, with Norman at the tiller, making the rounds in front of the club.

"That's the last lot for today," said Warrell. "Norman should be done in about twenty minutes."

"Right, I'll finish up here, you can shove off for the day. I'll see you early tomorrow for the show, and we can set up next week's business."

"Right, Boss; thanks. See you tomorrow." Warrell walked off whistling.

Lyle busied himself arranging the equipment, keeping an eye on the ski boat, and planning his lecture to Norman. When Norman delivered his skiers to the beach, Lyle helped him unload the boat and told him to take it to the mooring and come back to the shack. Norman was soon rowing the old dinghy ashore. When the two men had finished the chores, Lyle turned to Norman and said, "I've been on the phone with Smythe-Caulley, and he tells me that you'll be officially in the clear within twenty four hours. He is very upset that you are drinking so much and has decided that if you cannot get hold of yourself, you will be out of the deal."

"He can't do that, I'm the one that has done all the work and taken all the risk," replied Norman.

"He can't?" responded Lyle.

"Of course he can," replied Norman with resignation. "We both know that he can do anything he wants with me."

"That's right, and I know he means business. He told me he has researched the coin, and this looks like a good possibility that the group is on to something. Of course, they still have to find it, but I'm confident that with Quincy in charge, they have as good a chance as anyone would. He's a very competent type; oddly enough, Smythe-Caulley seems very wary of him. I think they have some history with each other."

"OK," said Norman, I'll be all squared away by morning. I just need some time to get used to the idea. You can tell that bastard he can count on me."

"Tomorrow then; early." Lyle headed off to find his car and Eileen.

Chapter 12 - Saturday Night
The plan is Hatched

Promptly at four, Quincy called for Jenna, as promised. This time, he was dressed in a comfortably worn pair of khaki slacks, and an open necked, white, short sleeved shirt, and a pair of comfortable sandals. When Jenna appeared at the door, Quincy's heart caught in his chest. She was dressed simply in a lavender summer frock and a pair of flat sandals. She carried a small colorful straw purse. He could see that she wore only the barest hint of lipstick. She glowed like a flame in his eyes, and he realized that, for the first time in his life, he might be in love. Nothing in his life had prepared him for this moment, and he stood there, mute and staring, rooted firmly to the doorstep. He was, by nature, a cautious man, parsimonious with his emotions, and totally unprepared for the depth of the feelings washing over him. He had known her for only a few days, and despite their romantic encounter, he had never before been assailed with these intense feelings. He was, uncharacteristically bewildered, and out of his depth. It was a bit unnerving, but exciting at the same time. Regardless of his reservations, he could not help himself; he plunged ahead.

After opening the door, Jenna flashed him one of her best smiles, seeing that he was momentarily stymied, she stepped close, and kissed him gently on the mouth.

"I have been waiting for you, all of my life Quincy McKenna," she said. "Let's get started on the rest of it immediately."

Quincy blinked, smiled, and came out of his trance. He encircled her waist with his strong arms, and kissed her deeply.

"I agree, my love," he said. "I am as eager as you to get on with it."

Hand in hand, they headed for the car park where his battered Austin pick up waited to take them to the rendezvous with their partners in adventure. They motored down the coast road, chatting happily about nothing in particular. They were loath to disturb their mood, wanting to savor the happiness they shared. There would be time enough to get down to business, when the group convened. They arrived at four thirty, parked on the street, and walked down the steep hill to the hut on the left of the driveway. Before them, stretched a plain, gray, concrete platform, with tables and umbrellas on it. A million dollar view of the sea, and a glorious tropical sky approaching sunset, was taking shape before their eyes.

The waiter showed them to a table for four, pulled up an extra chair to accommodate a fifth person, and departed with their drink order. After he served them, they sat quietly, touching frequently, looking out to sea, sipping their drinks, until the others arrived a little after five.

Lyle and Eileen had picked up Ellis at the hotel because his Vauxhall had plenty of room. Ellis could never have squeezed into Quincy's tiny Ute. In fact, Quincy always felt he was more wearing the little truck, than driving in it. Once the waiter had delivered the drinks all around, they started into the business of the meeting.

"I've been giving this considerable thought," said Quincy. "All previous attempts to find any treasure on this island, seem to have been concentrated on digging up the sandy beaches, and the surrounding palm and casurena woods. I feel that we can't neglect these areas, but I also want us to look in the sea, between the reef and the shore. Over a hundred years, what with the storms and tides, something might have been washed out to sea, or buried by the sand, as it naturally shifted with the currents and the frequent tropical blows. We need a two-pronged attack, and we need to go about our business unobserved. We do not want to be observed searching, that might come to the attention of the authorities. What do you all think?"

"I concur," said Lyle.

Ellis nodded his assent vigorously, "Good plan. How do we go about accomplishing this without attracting attention?"

"I think people at the club have noticed that Jenna and I have been spending time together lately, so it would not be too odd if I invited her aboard the Billfish, to do a little scuba diving for one or two days. Right now, most of the attention is centered on the Carvers. I doubt if anyone would pay much attention to the Billfish leaving for a few days," offered Quincy. "We can make a great show of topping up tanks and laying in supplies for a little romantic cruise. We will anchor inside the reef off Sandy

Lane, and the Billfish can serve as our base of operations for the duration."

He continued, "You lot could spend several days skiing. The beach crowd is used to seeing Lyle come and go, and they know Eileen periodically helps out both of us. Ellis could keep you booked up, and busy skiing up and down the coast, honing his skills. You would have to make sure he was skiing, both going and coming from the Club, that's all."

"I think it might work," Ellis said. "By coming and going every day, Lyle and I could bring in any needed extra equipment or supplies that we may have overlooked. If Lyle uses the fourteen, he could hide the equipment in the boat, away from prying eyes, when he takes it out each night. No one checks the boat in the morning, when he launches it."

"I guess we're agreed," said Eileen, her face aglow with anticipation as glancing around the group. "This is exciting! Imagine if we really found something fabulous. It would be simply smashing."

Lyle looked at her and realized that it was high time he brought her into the conspiracy so that she did not do something inadvertent to expose the conniving would be highjackers. She was essentially guileless, probably due to her youth, but Lyle knew her stubborn streak, and he would have to approach her very carefully. She was not one to be told what to do. Very independent, she was jealous of her independence. He considered using the potential of marriage with their new found wealth as a lever. He would play that card only as a last resort.

Satisfied with the broad outlines of their plan, the group paid attention to the menus, placed their order with the attentive waiter, and, sipping more drinks, continued chatting in detail about the supplies they might need. Quincy offered his list, and the others chimed in and added their input. Lyle offered to round up anything Quincy did not have on hand, and Ellis chimed in that he would pitch in to help. It was decided that anything bulky would be delivered to the Billfish by Lyle and Ellis the Sunday, using the fourteen, after dark. The growing crowd started to intrude on their privacy, so they called a halt to the planning. Lyle kept the list and said he would get in touch with Ellis in the morning.

Soon, the tables started to fill. Jenna and Ellis particularly noticed that it was a mixed crowd of locals; they were obviously the only tourists in the happy crowd. Lyle and Eileen seemed to know many of the people, and after dinner, with the business of the gathering concluded, they grabbed their drinks, excused themselves, and rose from the table to greet their friends.

Ellis, obviously abandoned, said, "I guess I'll stroll over to the bar and see what's happening. If I don't connect with someone obliging and find a ride home, I'll call a cab, or better yet, I'll give Bobbie a ring and see if she wants to join me. You, two, have a good time, and call me tomorrow if you or Lyle need my help. Also, if we need any new equipment, you can count on me to pay my way, as part of this enterprise."

With that, he stood up, picked up his empty glass, and headed for the bar. By the time he had a refill in his hand, he was busily chatting up two girls he had just met. Both

Jenna and Quincy smiled at Ellis's smooth approach. He might not be Jenna's cup of tea, she mused, but he was obviously in demand with most of the ladies. There was always room for a handsome, free spending, single man.

"He seems to be well occupied," said Jenna. "We can just go on about our business. What would you like to do?" She asked.

"Have you ever heard steel band music?" asked Quincy. "They start playing around eight, and I know you'll love it; we could also see how well we do together on the dance floor."

"I've never listened to a steel band, but I have heard of it. Dancing with you sounds like a perfect way to get my hands on you again," replied Jenna, as she scooted her chair closer to Quincy. She took hold of his hand, and, dragging it into her lap, she pinned it firmly between her thighs. They sipped their drinks and split their attention between people watching, and the rapidly developing multicolored sunset. They were waiting for the green flash, and, by paying close attention, were not disappointed.

At eight o'clock, the band was set up, and a car arrived, dropping off Norma Stout. The crowd applauded as she walked down to the club. She was a perennial island favorite and made it a habit of showing up occasionally, at randomly selected clubs, for impromptu jam sessions. The bands and the clubs loved her for it, because revenues soared when she was around. She stopped at several tables, greeting friends. She waived at Quincy and Jenna, and took to the microphone.

For the next three hours, Jenna was transported. She underwent a total immersion course in island music, calypso songs, and dance. She was happy, enervated, and very much in love.

Finally, at eleven, Quincy, replete with ulterior motives, pleaded exhaustion, and dragged her away from the growing party. The coin, their plans, Lyle, Eileen, and Ellis were totally forgotten for the rest of the night.

On the drive back to the Colony Club from Black Rock, Quincy pulled her close, and put his arm around her. They stayed that way for the rest of the drive, with her head on his shoulder, and her left hand idly playing across the fly of his pants. Luckily there was very little traffic at that time of night, as soon became obvious that she would be forced to deal with Quincy's rapidly growing condition. As he pulled into the car park, she playfully asked him if he would care to come to her room and view her etchings.

"I would love to," he said "However, I think we'll have more privacy if we go aboard the Billfish. Why don't we stop by your room and collect whatever you need, change if you wish, and we can row out to the boat? Why don't you pack enough gear for a few days, that way you'll be all set for Sandy Lane?"

They did just that. Quincy was a little overwhelmed by the amount of gear Jenna considered essential for a few night's stay.

Eagerly contemplating the rest of the night, the pair rowed out to the boat, unaware that Norman was watching them from the door of his shack. When they boarded the Billfish, it was too dim for Norman to observe them further, so he re-entered his shack, and resumed draining his bottle of Eclipse rum.

Not in a rush tonight, both Quincy and Jenna knew what was in store for them. They deliberately proceeded slowly, paying particular attention to each other, determined to make the most of their second night together.

"I want to linger over every moment," said Jenna, as she strolled through the pilot house. "Let's really enjoy this; tomorrow is going to be a busy day, and we will likely be working late when Lyle and Ellis pull up with the extra equipment."

"Right," said Quincy. "I'll organize some nightcaps, and you can stow your gear. There are empty drawers in the cabin and in the bath."

Jenna turned serenely to her task, mulling over which bits of nothings she should wear for this auspicious evening. She hummed as she stowed her gear. Finally, primped to her satisfaction, and hardly wearing anything but her dazzling smile, she stepped back into the master cabin.

Quincy was stretched out on the bed wearing nothing but a big grin, two half-filled snifters propped judiciously within reach, on the chests of drawers on either side of the bed. Laughing happily, Jenna quickly shed her nothings, leaving them in an untidy pile on the floor. Inexperience as she was at real intimacy, she instinctively understood that she could trust Quincy and his growing regard for her. Her sexual experiences to date had been very conventional, even with Quincy. Now she was standing sat the foot of the berth, which was waist high on her, contemplating the smorgasbord of lovely male animal at her fingertips; she decided to play.

Reach out slowly, she took one foot in each hand and started to massage his feet as she slowly drew his legs apart. Momentarily startled, Quincy spotted the mischievous look in her eye and decided to relax, and go with the flow. He eased over onto his back, trying subtly to see what she was up to. She seemed delighted with her find.

"Well, well, well," she said, "let's see what we have here. Perhaps I should take a closer look."

She ran her hands up his legs, kneading the muscles on his inner thighs as she progressed. She was gratified at the response. He was stretching his whole body, obviously enjoying her attentions. His erection was growing longer and harder as her hands approached it. She eased herself up onto the bunk between his legs, and slid up onto her knees. Gently running her hands over his groin, she cupped his testicles in one hand and wrapped the other firmly around his erection. Quincy groaned and arched his back. Delighted with his reaction, she leaned down and planted an soft kiss on the head of his penis. The result was instant. Quincy went dead still, and stopped breathing. She took an experimental lick, and he twitched a little, still holding his breath. Gaining confidence, she slowly encircled his member with her lips and slowly slid her mouth down over him. He groaned and started to twitch spasmodically. She was getting excited herself. She had never had such control over a man in her life, and it was an immense turn on. She was instantly wet and swollen. She knew that he would not date to move a muscle; he did not want her to stop. Tentatively, she ran her tongue up the length of his erection and sucked gently on the head. Quincy was breathing hard, clenching and unclenching his fists at his side. She started slowly running up and down his member with her mouth, sucking gently on it. It tasted good, and she wanted more. Suddenly, unable to stand the unbearable tension, he reached down and grabbed her by the waist, lifter her bodily into the air, and in one fluid and uninterrupted move, planted her firmly on his member. She was instantly impaled to the core. They came together in one shuddering orgasm. It went on and on. It was sudden, violent and deep inside her; she had the reaction she had been seeking. Quincy was shattered. He had been drained completely. Slowly he pulled her down to him and started kissing her. They kissed more deeply, and he stirred inside her. Before they knew it, he was stroking in and out, and she was arching her back, driving forward onto him in a frenzy of passion. Their excitement reached another frenzy, and her drove into her hard, and stayed still. She clenched involuntarily around him and started shuddering uncontrollably. They came together again; it went on and on. Finally, she sank down onto the bed beside him, put her head on his shoulder, and just held him close. Quincy was speechless, replete with emotion and overcome with sensation. They fell asleep and slept soundly until the sun came in the porthole.

Chapter 13 – Sunday
The Search is Organized

The timing was not good. Most of the stores were closed. Nevertheless, the treasure seekers decided to do what they could, to supplement their supplies when the stores re-opened. Quincy and Jenna were up early; well, early, for two people who had been making love 'till three in the morning. By eight o'clock, Jenna was as ready as possible. Decked out in shorts, T shirt, and practical sneakers, she took the dingy ashore to meet Eileen. The two girls' assignment was to raid Goddard's Supermarket in Speightstown, and lay in enough supplies for the entire group, for four or five days. At eight thirty, Jenna strolled up the lane toward the entrance of the club, just as Lyle and Eileen turned off the coast road in Lyle's Vauxhall. Lyle stopped the car, hopped out, Eileen slid over, and Jenna hopped in. Lyle waived the women off, and turned down the lane, walking towards Norman's shack.

Lyle had spent the drive, from Paradise Beach to the Colony Club, bringing Eileen up to speed on the plan, and had run into unexpected opposition. She was vehemently opposed to participating in any theft, and refused to cooperate with the plan. Lyle was upset. I'll deal with her later, he thought, I have to work something out or she's going to blow the whole thing up in our faces. Finally she agreed to not say anything for the moment, and they drove the rest of the way in silence; each searching their own thoughts.

Eileen was going to be a problem. She wanted nothing to do with stealing anything, and she especially wanted nothing to with that bastard Smythe-Caulley. She feared and detested the man. He had cornered her one night when she was driving home, slightly the worse for wear. He had pulled her over, with his light flashing. She had made the mistake of pulling her car far off the road into the boat launching area of Oistins' modest fishing port. The light was very dim, and the two cars were not visible from the road. Instinctively, both drivers had extinguished their lights when the cars came to a halt. He had followed her with this car, blocking hers from leaving, and turned off the flashing light. He did not want to draw any attention from passersby. At that time of night, there was no one around the boats, and the nets were hung between the fish-cleaning sheds and the coconut trees. He was an old hand at this sort of situation, and had been keeping an eye out for her for some time.

The incident started harmlessly enough. She thought she knew why she had been stopped, but, unaware of anything specific, when she recognized the Sergeant, she instinctively became worried about her isolation. Eileen did, however, roll down her window and greet him when he walked up to the right hand side of the car.

"Good evening, Constable. What is the matter?" She asked.

"Have you been drinking, miss?" He inquired.

"A little wine, with dinner," she replied. "Not to any great extent."

"You were weaving all over the road," he said. "Where are you going?" "My boyfriend and I had dinner at Sam Lord's Castle. Since we had separate cars, he has gone on to the airport, to pick up a freight shipment. I was driving home to my cottage in St. Lawrence Gap." She replied. Although alarmed at his rather menacing attitude, she tried to appear normal and cooperative.

"Please step out of the car," he ordered. "Bring your driver's license and registration with you."

"Isn't it a bit unusual for a high ranking officer in the constabulary to be making traffic stops?" She asked. She did not move to get out of the car.

Annoyed, he repeated himself loudly, "Get out of the car."

Frightened now, she started rolling up the window. He reacted swiftly by wrenching open the door. She had neglected to lock the door when she had driven off from the restaurant. She started to scream, but he reached in and grabbed her by her shirt front, yanked her out of the car, and flung her up against the hood. Winded, she could only gasp, stare at the now enraged man, and cower. By now he knew he was clearly over the line. Eileen was genuinely terrified. Frustrated and enraged, he grabbed her by the shoulders and shook her, pushing her horizontally over the hood of the car, until she was almost prone. Only the tips of the toes of one foot were touching the ground. When he bent her over the car, he purposely positioned his body between her legs. One sandal had come off her foot and now lay a few feet away, thrown there by her momentum, when he plucked her out of the car.

"Who do you think you are? Do you not know that I know who you are? Your fancy planter family cannot help you now. You're in real trouble for not cooperating with an arresting officer."

"I'm sorry, I'm so sorry," she sobbed. "I did not mean anything by it. I was frightened. It is so dark, please don't hurt me."

Staring intently into her face, he said, "Perhaps we can work something out."

The sheer malevolence of that statement caused her bowels to loosen. Clenching her muscles, she was just able to control herself; she did not want to telegraph her growing terror.

"Anything," she gasped.

He stared at her for a moment, then, shifting his left hand to her neck, grasping it firmly, he moved his right hand to her shirt front, grabbed the neckline and tore it open, exposing her small pert breasts. They shone dimly in the meager starlight. He fondled them roughly, pinching the nipples hard. He was getting very aroused. She started weeping and struggling feebly. She was bent over backwards, flat on the hood of the car. She grasped desperately at his face, trying to scratch his eyes out. At the same time, her legs flailed wildly, trying to kick him. In a very cold voice he said,

"Stop that, or I'll throttle you." He squeezed her neck hard and shut off her breathing.

She instantly stopped struggling, and he eased up the pressure. He ran his right hand up her right leg. Reaching her panties, Smythe-Caulley moved his hand under the elastic, over her stomach, hooked his fingers through the crotch of her panties, the back of his hand rubbing hard against her pubic hair, and, in one violent motion, ripped them off and flung them behind him. He pushed her dress up over her waist. She lay totally exposed to his searing gaze. He took her in completely, relishing his control. He loved it this way. Control was almost more important than sex; almost, but not quite. He had waited for her for a long time. Never before had he had an opportunity to get close to her.

He started groping her pubic area, reaching for her vagina. In spite of her panic, she was getting wet. Humiliated, she was unsure whether it was arousal, or that she had wet herself. He did not seem to care. He located what he was looking for, and roughly thrust three fingers inside rubbing her clitoris with his thumb. In pain and humiliation, she writhed under his grip. She was unable to tear his hand from her neck. Every time she grabbed at his wrist, he choked off her breathing. Finally, overcome by lust, with his right hand, he started to unfasten the buttons of his fly. He fumbled around in his shorts, and found his semi-flaccid penis. Stroking and squeezing it vigorously, to get suitably hard. He almost succeeded. Prematurely, when he moved to penetrate her, he suddenly ejaculated all over her naked stomach. Simultaneously, she threw up all over him.

Stunned at the turn of events, he let loose of her neck and stepped back. Eileen fell forward onto her knees. Without hesitation, she leapt to her feet, and shoved against his chest with all her might. Unbalanced, he landed hard on his backside. She turned and fled into the night, between two beached flying fish boats, and vanished from view. Infuriated, he staggered to his feet, brushed the sand from his hands, buttoned his fly, and started after her. Abruptly, he came to a halt. He was confused about what he was about to do. Was he going to kill her? What if someone was on the beach? What if someone came along and saw the two parked cars? He came to his senses. In a panic he ran to his Land Rover, started it up and backed around. When he reached the road, he looked in both directions, pulled out onto the highway, and headed toward Bridgetown. Once he was underway, he turned on the lights. He was not done with her. It would be harder now, but he would be patient. Who would she tell? Not the police; and Lyle might not believe her. He thought he would be safe from the assault. As usual, he had left his victim with nowhere to turn.

While he had stopped short of raping her, he had hurt her badly. He had given her the scare of her life, and there was nothing she could do about it. It was her word against that of a high ranking policeman in the island's constabulary. She never told a single soul. Lyle was baffled by the vehemence of her reaction to the planned heist. After arguing back and forth for thirty minutes, they left it that she would participate in the treasure hunt, and, if the treasure was found, she would bow out of the events that followed. Lyle did not know that she would never cooperate with the policeman. She would die first. Meanwhile, Lyle proceeded with his agenda thinking, "I'll deal with her later."

It was a normal part of Lyle's daily routine to spend time with Norman each morning. They had business to discuss, schedules, bookings, and a decision as to who was going to man the two regular boats. Willy and Ted always took boat two, and serviced the busy Paradise Beach Club area and anyone else, that came up between their base at The Paradise Beach Club, and The Aquatic Club near Bridgetown. They never went further east, because on that side of the island, the water was always rougher, and tourists preferred to ski on the gold coast. In fact, if there was a little blow, those two would bring their clients north toward the Colony Club and calmer water. As the two conspirators walked and talked and sipped their morning coffee, Lyle briefed Norman on the plan for the treasure hunt, instructing him to ring Smythe-Caulley with the update, and report back to him in the evening, with their plan for the surveillance of the treasure hunt. He suggested using Warrell to run the ski boat in the afternoons this week, because he was totally unaware of the coin or either scheme for the treasure. Norman would then be free to team up with the crooked policeman to execute their planned surveillance. Once Lyle was updated this evening, he would be prepared to help the other two conspirators when the time was right. That accomplished, he walked down to the beach, launched Quincy's dingy from where Jenna had beached it, and rowed out to the Billfish.

Quincy saw him coming, strolled to the stern, fished a piece of paper from his shorts, leaned down, and handed it to Lyle, and said,

"I thought of a few things that were not on the first list I gave you, here's the completed list of the gear we need; some dive spares, some tools, and a metal detector, if you can find one. You had better collect Ellis if you can. You're going to need help handling it all."

"Safer, I think, if I round it up myself, and pick up Ellis later. He can then help me load it into the fourteen, and we'll see you about midnight."

"Fine," said Quincy, "I'll see you both then."

Lyle shoved off and rowed back to the beach. He waived to Ellis who was standing on the terrace watching the exchange, walked over and told him to sit tight for the moment. He'd pick him up at six, ostensibly to take him out for a drink at one of the Island bars. They would then load the fourteen, cover the gear, and take the boat to the launch ramp.

Quincy returned to work, charging the dive cylinders, and servicing the auxiliary engine. On a boat the size of the Billfish, the maintenance list was endless, and he'd be busy all day, until the ladies returned with the supplies. Once he and Jenna got rid of Eileen, who knows what might happen? It would be hours before the other two men pulled up with the needed gear. They could use the time to good advantage, getting better acquainted. The memory of last night was still etched into his mind. Smiling to himself, and whistling a slow tune, he set to work.

Norman, still sipping his coffee, called Smythe-Caulley at home; he filled him in on Lyle's briefing.

"Splendid" he said. "You and I will rendezvous and go over to Sandy Lane in the afternoon tomorrow. They will not have accomplished anything the first morning. Call me later at home when you are with Lyle and we'll firm things up.

Humming to himself, the Sergeant carefully locked his front door and climbed into the Land Rover for the drive to his office at the Savannah.

The ladies returned about four in the afternoon. Not in any particular rush, Eileen had taken Jenna into Holetown, first to browse some of the boutiques that were open. Jenna purchased a few things and was anxious to try them out on Quincy. The ladies stopped for an early lunch at Le Bistro, before finally moving on to Speightstown and Goddard's.

When the dingy was unloaded, Quincy suggested that Eileen get hold of Ellis, to see if he needed anything for tomorrow. He was unaware that Eileen now knew about both the plans for the treasure hunt, and those for the subsequent heist. He and Jenna eagerly prepared a cold dinner in the galley, and opened a chilled bottle of white wine. They both knew that they had plenty of time to kill before midnight. Oddly enough, instead of jumping into bed, they found themselves nestled into the cockpit talking about their past. As usual, they really knew nothing about each other. The overpowering mutual attraction had blown the mundane curiosity out of their heads. They talked through the sunset and long into the evening, pausing briefly to freshen their drinks, and once a quick swim to cool off and rinse off the day. By late evening, they had recapped their history, professional and personal to the point that their growing attraction started to make sense to them. Quincy represented adventure to Jenna. His rather glamorous life, while fraught with dangers, had made him into a confident and adventurous man. He was at home anywhere, and was thoroughly confident with his abilities. Jenna was an educated urbanite, longing to be free of the city. They fit together like a pair of gloves. It was apparent to them both that they were in the middle of the beginning of a wonderful relationship. They did not want to talk about the future as yet, content to take it as it comes. They were both looking forward to what was to be. The treasure hunt had been driven from their thoughts for many hours. Finally, they went down to the galley, poured themselves a cup of tea, and settled into the bunk for a rest before the others showed up.

Chapter 14 – Monday
The Search Begins

Just after midnight, Quincy heard the sound of an outboard motor running at very low throttle. He hopped off the bunk, pulled on a pair of khaki shorts. He left Jenna in the master cabin, and went quickly and silently, on bare feet, onto deck. The light from the pilot house, barely enough to cast some light on the deck, was not enough to illuminate the area around the Billfish. That was good, he thought. There was enough moonlight to just make out a boat approaching the stern from the south. Quincy figured that they had launched at the Holetown fish market to avoid anyone at Colony Club being aware of what was going on. He moved to the back of the Billfish, and opened the transom, standing by to catch a rope. The fourteen appeared out of the gloom, and, Ellis, standing in the bow, tossed him a rope. Quincy made it fast to his stern cleat, and told Ellis to tie off his end to the center cleat of the fourteen; the small boat would then be at right angles to the yacht. That way, both men in the skiff could manhandle anything together, and pass it over to Quincy without losing it overboard.

Without much conversation, the three men worked quickly with a minimum of wasted motion. Soon the deck of the Billfish was cluttered with an assortment of items.

"I even found an old metal detector," said Ellis. "I'm not too sure exactly how it works. I could not locate any directions."

"No matter," said Quincy. "I'll be able to figure it out. We worked with them in the army, and they're all about the same. You lot had better shove off before anyone notices you out here. I'll stow this gear and see you tomorrow, late morning at Sandy Lane."

With that, he untied the fourteen, and tossed the rope to Ellis, who offered a brief wave. Lyle started the motor again, and slowly headed back toward Holetown. The boat vanished in the dark. It was running without lights. There was nothing to hit, and the harbor patrol confined their activities to the Bridgetown areas, unless specifically requested to help out elsewhere. The two men were mostly silent on the trip back to Holetown. When they arrived, it was only a few minutes work to back the trailed down the beach and load the boat. Before they drove away, Lyle noticed that the bar at the fish market was still open, and suggested a nightcap. Ellis readily agreed. Even though the two men had been together on a few occasions, skiing and planning, they had never exchanged any personal information. Somehow, they both had the urge to get to know the other. After all, they were embarking on an exciting enterprise together. The bartender brought them a drink, and they sat companionably in the corner, chatting for over an hour. Finally, they noticed that they were the only customers left, and finished their drinks. While they had not formed any lifelong attachment to each other, they had swapped enough information to be more comfortable with each other. In fact, Lyle was now starting to feel a twinge of conscience about the conspiracy growing against the group. He'd deal with that later. They drove the boat back to the storage lot, and Lyle dropped Ellis at the entrance to the Colony Club and drove off home.

After the boat left, Quincy opened a few hatches in the stern cockpit, and lowered most of the gear into the storage compartments. The metal detector he lugged into the pilot house for scrutiny later in the morning. Looking around the deck, and checking the lie of the boat, he satisfied himself that all was shipshape. He stepped back into the pilot house, turned off all but a single dim light, and went below to bed. He was tired from the evening with Jenna. He was not used to such vigorous lovemaking, especially back to back, and, their five year age difference was beginning to tell on him. I'd better get my beauty rest, he mused. It seems that between Jenna, and the treasure hunt, I'm going to have a few demanding days ahead of me.

When he stepped into the master cabin, he smiled at the sight of Jenna, curled on her side, with the sheet pulled up to her waist, snoring softly. Apparently she was equally tired, he thought, with a certain satisfaction. She's not used to the vigorous workouts, either. I think things will work themselves out, at least in that regard. With that happy thought, he dropped his shorts to the deck, and crawled into the bunk beside her. He snuggled up to her warm, naked bottom, put his arm around her waist, and lowered his head to the pillow. With his face resting in the tangle of hair, at the nape of her neck, he relaxed, ready for a good night's sleep. She stirred slightly, pushed her bottom more firmly into his lap, and resumed snoring. Quincy inhaled the heady fragrance of a well-loved woman, smiled, trying to ignore his instant erection, and closed his eyes.

They were up at dawn, and, after a quick cuddle, they got busy. There was too much excitement in the air to delay getting under way. Jenna quickly finished her toilet, and fired up the galley. Quincy went on deck, dropped a bucket on a line over the side, and, hauling up a bucket full of sea water, dumped it over his head. That, and a quick tooth brushing, while checking the day's weather seaward, and he was ready for the day. The weather was, as usual, perfect; a few rain clouds were drifting by, interspersed with plenty of high dry cirrus clouds, and bright sunshine. There was a six knot breeze blowing. Good, he thought, We can motor or sail; probably better to motor down, less time, and easier with a novice aboard.

Attracted by the smell of coffee and frying bacon, he spat the mouth full of toothpaste over the side, rinsed his mouth out again, and spat again. Satisfied with his morning ablutions, he tucked the toothbrush into his short's pocket, ran his hands through his wet hair, and headed into the pilothouse, and down the stair to the galley, where Jenna was just dishing up scrambled eggs, bacon, and a piece of fried bread. He smiled hugely, patted her derriere lecherously, sat down and pitched in. Jenna laughed happily, admiring the sight of the man she loved, tucking into a meal she had prepared. She could not remember the last time she had cooked for a man. It felt good.

She quickly joined him at the table, playfully thumped him in the ribs and said, "Move over, you big galoot. You'll have to get used to having company at meals from now on."

Quincy grinned, scooted over, but said nothing. His mouth was full of food, and he was very hungry. Fuel, he thought, I need more fuel.

While Jenna policed the breakfast dishes, Quincy busied himself getting the Billfish underway. He stopped in the pilot house, and turned on the ship to shore, opened a few portholes to let the air circulate, slipped under the stair, opened the bulkhead, and gave the engine compartment the once over. He flipped a couple of switches, making sure the battery was up, the water maker running smoothly, the diesel tank full; satisfied, he shut the door, and went back up on deck. In the cockpit, he started the small auxiliary diesel engine, and let it warm up. He double checked the dingy painter to make sure it was securely fastened, and then walked forward to the bow. He paused to open the hatch to the master cabin, stuck his head down, and yelled,

"Hey, galley slave, on deck. We're getting under way, and I need you to steer us out of here."

There was a thump, a muted curse, and the sound of bare feet slapping on the deck as Jenna headed up. Satisfied, he went to the bow, reached down for the mooring line, unfastened it and held on tight. The Billfish was a large boat, and, as strong as Quincy was, the steady breeze pushing the boat toward shore was making him strain to hold it in place. While waiting for Jenna to emerge, he belayed the line around the cleat and waited patiently. When Jenna appeared on deck, Quincy told her to throw the clutch lever into forward, and steer the boat out to sea. As the boat started to move, he released the line from the cleat.

Gingerly, Jenna did as she was instructed; the Billfish started to move. Delighted, she stepped to the wheel, and pointed the bow straight out to sea. Quincy laughed at her serious attitude, but nodded encouragingly. He walked the mooring line aft along the leeward rail. When they were past the mooring, he dropped the line into the sea.

"Why did you walk the line down?" She asked. She knew nothing about boats and wanted to learn anything she could.

"By keeping the mooring and the buoy along side until we passed the buoy," he said. "I was able to make sure we would not run over the line, and foul the prop."

"Makes sense. I'll remember that," she said.

Jenna concentrated on steering, as he leaned over her and pushed the throttle forward to a two thirds position. At optimum cruising speed, the little auxiliary diesel could push the Billfish along at about six knots in calm weather. There was no advantage, this morning, to hoisting their sails for the short trip to Sandy Lane Beach.

Quincy took over the helm, patted the seat cushion next to him, and said, "Relax and enjoy the view. We have about an hour before we get there. First, we have to clear the reef, and then we can head south. Once we're running parallel to the beach, you can take over again, and I'll drag that old metal detector out on deck, and look it over."

The hour passed quickly. She loved handling the boat. She experimented with the large stainless helm, while he was absorbed in dismantling the detector. He pretended not to notice her zigzag pattern, and was secretly pleased that she wanted to get the feel of the boat. He was hoping that she would be aboard for a long time.

"Sandy Lane coming up on the port side," said Jenna proudly. She had remembered the right words.

Quincy grunted, looked up, nodded, and snapped the cover back on the machine. He put it aside, pushing it across the deck to the pilot house bulkhead, making sure it was out of the way. He stood up, eyeballed the reef and sandy areas, and said, pointing to a spot on shore,

"Turn in here and head straight for that inlet opening."

He reached over, cut the throttle back to one quarter speed.

"I'm going forward to rig the anchor. You see the dark green below the boat and the light brown between the dark and the beach?"

"Yes, she said."

"Well, that's where the reef stops, and the sandy bottom begins. When you're almost to the sandy area, I'll signal you with my hand. Cut the throttle back completely, pull the clutch lever back to neutral, and point the bow upwind, toward the south."

"Aye, Aye, Sir," she said seriously. She anxiously peered over the bow, with a frown of concentration on her face.

She watched him, his dark hair ruffled by the wind, his muscles moving smoothly under his deeply tanned skin, as he manhandled the large Danforth anchor, to a ready position. He made sure the chain would run freely over the winch, and, out of the mouth of the chain locker. She was mesmerized by the sight, until suddenly she realized, he was waving vigorously at her, and shouting, "Now, Now."

Smoothly, she turned the boat into the wind, cut the throttle, and brought the clutch to neutral. It was as if she had been doing it all her life. Satisfied when the boat swung back out to sea, he waited for it to lose momentum. When the breeze started to push the boat backwards to the shore, he flung the anchor out from the bow, and watched it sink to the bottom. He noted how much chain was used to hit bottom, and thought, about forty feet under the bow. Then he let the chain run out another seventy five feet, and hit the winch brake. That would allow the boat plenty of rode, to keep it in place, unless there was a serious blow. He waited for the anchor to dig in, and catch. When the boat was abruptly pulled to a halt, he looked over the side, and estimated about thirty feet of water under the keel. He grunted with satisfaction and headed aft.

"Well done, Matey. We can set a stern anchor after dark when we check the wind for the night watch. Anchoring is trickier than tying off to a mooring. If the wind shifts only sixty degrees, we could slip the anchor and be blown aground," he said, reaching for her. He pulled her close, and kissed her thoroughly, running his hands all over her bikini clad body.

"Do you treat all your sailors that way?" she asked, smiling.

"No, only the half nude, sexy, ravishing ones," he said, sliding one hand inside the bottom of her suit, and pushing the other one up under her skimpy top. He freed one fat, plump breast, and got busy caressing her nipple. Not entirely satisfied, he leaned down, and sucked the nipple into his mouth, running the smooth bottom of his tongue, over the instantly rock hard nipple. Shamelessly, she arched against him, savoring the rush of sensations in her loins, then, shaking her head, and pushing him away, she said, "Not so fast buster, you're supposed to be finding me a treasure today."

Laughing, he stepped back, while she tucked her breast back inside the small scrap of material she called a suit. She pulled up the equally skimpy bottom, and he said, regretfully, "OK, let's get cracking."

Meanwhile, back at the Colony Club, it looked like business as usual for the water sports outfit. Warrell was loading four people into the twenty footer for a half-day skiing. Lyle was backing the fourteen down the beach to launch it. Ellis showed up, and made a big thing about pitching in to help. Eileen sauntered down the beach, carrying towels and a pair of skis.

They got the boat situated, and Ellis said, loud enough for several nearby guests to hear, "I've asked the kitchen to pack a lunch for us. I want to spend the day skiing, and cruising up the coast, if that's OK with you."

Lyle smiled and said, "You've booked the whole day, so it's up to you. We're here for your pleasure."

Eileen piped up and said, "I'll go along to the kitchen, then, and fetch the picnic basket."

The men returned to organizing the gear, and, after ten minutes, Eileen reappeared with the hamper, and a waiter in tow, carrying a bright blue cooler. The two men arranged the items in the boat, thanked the waiter, helped Eileen into the boat, and pushed off. Both men hopped in. Lyle dropped the motor, fired it up, and started out to sea. Ellis settled into the middle seat next to Eileen.

About two hundred yards from shore, Lyle stopped that boat, and said to Ellis, "You'll have to ski until we're out of sight. Hop to it, and we'll be under way."

Ellis slipped off his shirt, grabbed the skis, and positioned himself on the side of the boat. He slid over the side, clutching the skis. While he was putting them on, Lyle circled the boat, bringing the tow rope to Ellis. Satisfied that Ellis had the handle, Lyle eased the slack out of the line. Ellis squared himself with the boat, adjusting to the gentle pull, and waived his hand at Lyle to start. With a muted roar from the engine, and a puff of smoke, they were off. Ellis rose smoothly from the water, and, steadying himself, he pulled outside the wake. Within minutes, the boat and skier were out of sight of the Colony Club beach. Lyle throttled back, Ellis let go of the rope. Eileen busily hauled in the line, while Lyle circled back, to pull Ellis out of the water. Handing the skis up to Eileen, Ellis boosted himself out of the water, and climbed into the boat. He crawled to the seat, grabbed a towel, and said, "Let's go!"

Lyle turned the throttle up full, and the boat sped off toward the south. At their speed, it was only a ten minute run to Sandy Lane beach, where the Billfish lay at anchor.

Lyle spotted Quincy and Jenna loading the dingy, and pulled alongside. "Need any help?" he asked.

"Right." said Quincy, handing over the metal detector. "You take this. We've got everything else. See you on shore."

Back at the Colony Club, Norman had finished checking the bookings. The day was all organized, and when Warrell returned with his first four guests, he helped him gas up the ski boat, and said,

"Your afternoon party is all set; seven singles to ski. I suggested that they swim out to the raft and you can ski them from there."

"Yes, Boss," said Warrell. "Where will you be?"

"I'm going into town for some spares, and some errands for Lyle. I'll see you in the morning."

"Good enough," replied Warrell. "I'll get going." The two men parted, and Norman strolled back to his shack to put on shorts, a shirt, and some shoes. He had agreed to meet Smythe-Caulley at one o'clock in Speightstown, near the fish market. He'd hop a north bound bus on the coast road out front, and just make it in time. If he was early, he'd perhaps have time to have a drink at the small bar at the fish market. Smythe-Caulley was late. Norman had three rums under his belt by the time he spotted the policeman. He hardly recognized him. He appeared, walking in from the road, in seersucker trousers, and a white shirt. Norman had never seen him out of his khaki uniform; he looker smaller and much less menacing, thought Norman. Appearances can be deceiving.

"Where's your car? He asked.

"I did not bring it. I'm on my motor bike" he replied. He was clearly annoyed that Norman had been drinking. "I thought we would be less conspicuous this way, and it is easy to hide the motorbike in the trees when we get there. Very few people know I have the machine, so we can remain anonymous. Let's get cracking. We're late already. You start walking back south along the road, and I'll go collect my machine."

He turned away, and Norman gulped the last of the drink, and headed out. By the time Smythe-Caulley caught up with Norman, he was a half mile south of the fish market. The policeman, riding a much worn, scratched, and dented, BSA C10, pulled over. Norman clamored on, and the pair sped off.

"I trust you're not thoroughly pissed." said the policeman, irritated.

"No, I only had one drink," Norman lied.

They rode in silence back past the Colony Club through Holetown, and on down the coast road, until Smythe-Caulley spotted the small bridge over the Sandy lane inlet. Making sure they were unobserved, he pulled the motorcycle off the road. Norman got off, and, together, they pushed the machine into the woods. The sandy soil made it rough going, but in ten minutes, they were satisfied that the old BSA could not be seen from the road.

"Let's go," said the policeman. He led off in the direction of the beach. It soon became obvious, when they spotted the Billfish at anchor, that they could not approach the party on the beach too closely without being spotted. Annoyed, they back-tracked, crossed the inlet again, and trekked north along the beach until they could crawl out to the tree line bordering the beach, and look back across the inlet at the activity.

The gang on the beach was busy. Jenna and Eileen set up the picnic in case anyone came along. Quincy was busy instructing Lyle in the proper use of the metal detector. It became apparent that it would be a two man job. Lyle and Eileen would work the detector with Jenna spelling Eileen periodically, and helping out with the boats, and miscellaneous chores. Quincy and Ellis were to return to the Billfish, and set up for diving. The beach party decided, so that they would be unseen, to run the metal detector up the inlet, during the afternoon. Then, later in the evening, Quincy and Jenna would sweep the beach, along the shoreline. They got busy. It was hot and thirsty work. The two watchers were, by now, equally hot, itchy, very thirsty, and hungry. Neither man had planned anything to eat or drink. When the search party broke for lunch, the two gazed disconsolately at the picnic scene. Finally, Smythe-Caulley said, "I cannot take another minute of this. I'm going back to the machine, and drive to Holetown for some supplies. You hold the fort here."

Unhappily, Norman agreed. Surprisingly enough, the policeman was back in less than an hour. Norman remarked, as he twisted the cap off a lukewarm Orange Crush, "That was quick; I'm dying of thirst." He hid his revulsion at the sweet soda; he was grateful to have anything at all to drink. He could at least have brought a beer, he thought. He kept the opinion to himself.

"I was able to drive the bike down a path about a hundred yards north of the inlet, into the trees, without pushing it," he replied. "Its quicker, and it's still invisible from the road. The machine is now less than one hundred yards from us. We can beat a hasty retreat if we need to."

Refreshed, they resumed their surveillance of the search party. They worked steadily in the inlet until dusk. The divers, Quincy and Ellis, were up and down all afternoon, working the inside of the reef, along the sandy edge. When the divers stowed their gear, and hopped into the dingy to come ashore, Lyle, Eileen, and Jenna, started packing up the picnic and ski gear in preparation for the return to the Colony Club. Disgusted at the lack of results, the two watchers waited until the ski boat departed for the Colony Club, then, they also packed it in. They had trouble finding the bike, but finally they wrestled it back onto the road, and, when the coast was clear, the duo sped back toward Holetown. Smythe-Caulley dropped

Norman in Holetown with instructions to take the bus to Sandy Lane the next day. He would rendezvous with him as soon as he could break away from his office. Both men were mad, hot, sticky, and discouraged. Norman really needed a drink.

No one witnessed Quincy and Jenna walking in the gathering dusk along the waterline with the metal detector. Suddenly the machine pinged. Excitedly, they dug in the wet sand with their hands, completely forgetting the shovel in the dingy. There was another coin! In ten minutes, they had three more; then, for over an hour, nothing more. All the coins were found in shallow water. Excited, and satisfied with the day's accomplishments, they put the gear in the dinghy, and rowed back to the Billfish. To say they were excited would be an understatement. Even Quincy, normally stoic, was grinning from ear to ear. "Let's fix some supper and open a good bottle of wine," he offered. "If you start dinner, I'll drop a line over the side and catch us a fish or two for the grill. While we're working, perhaps a gin and tonic would be nice." They arrived back at the Billfish, and Quincy handed up the gear to Jenna and they quickly stowed it away. He took a quick look around to check the lie of the boat and glanced out to sea, verifying that the weather would remain calm. A short hail to the harbormaster on the ship to shore confirmed that there were no squalls on their way tonight; satisfied, he turned off the set.

By the time he had finished, Jenna appeared with a frosted glass full of gin and tonic. They toasted each other and took a big swig. After a long day, it was like nectar of the gods. Sun, sand, and salt water had rendered them thirsty, tired and hungry. After a brief kiss and a fondle, he retreated to the cockpit and baited a line; Jenna headed down and started rummaging through the fridge for the makings of a salad, and something to go along with the fish. Ever practical, she also checked to see what was available if the fish were not biting tonight. Before she had the potatoes and onions pealed, Quincy appeared with two mackerel flapping in his bucket. Surprised at the quick results, she commented, "that was quick work, you're some fisherman."

"Nothing to it," he replied. "With a boat anchored, and a light shining down into the water, fish always are attracted to the light. It is simple to bait a hook and haul them in. Usually there are so many different types that you can sometimes even be choosey."

She laughed and said, "I learn something new every day. That's good to know, at least we won't starve. Do you want me to clean them?"

"Thanks, but that's man's work," he joked, "just stick to your pots and pans."

Laughing, she attacked him and started swatting him with the dishrag. His only defense, was to envelope her in his arms and smother her mouth with kisses. They were laughing so hard that nothing serious developed. When the onions started to burn, Jenna reluctantly returned to the stove, and Quincy retired to the sink to deal with the fish. Twenty minutes later, they sat down to a feast with an ice cold bottle of Riesling to top it all off. During dinner, their talk turned to more serious matters. Acknowledging that the finding of more coins was a good indicator that they were really on to something, they speculated that it might take some time to actually find the source of the coins. That led to the length of vacation she had left, and what to do about it. Soberly, they explored their options. Both acknowledged that their relationship appeared to be getting more serious, but at the same time, they both declined to bring up the possibility of a long term relationship. It seemed enough that things were going well between them at the moment. Jenna volunteered that she could stay on; no one at her office knew where she was, or how long she had intended being gone, so she reasoned that some extra time could do no more damage to her career than she had already inflicted. She privately thought, do I really care? Surprised, she realized that she did not care.

When the wine was gone, Quincy said that it was time to set the stern anchor for the night. They went on deck, and he dug out another Danforth from the stern locker and handed her the end of the rope as he stepped down into the dinghy. "Hang onto the rope, and I'll set the anchor." He untied the dinghy and rowed toward the beach. When he was in about ten feet of water, he dropped the anchor overboard and rowed back to the Billfish. Tying off the dinghy, he took the rope from Jenna and stared pulling in the slack. When the anchor was firmly bedded in the sand, he let out about twenty feet of slack and tied it off to the stern cleat. "That should hold us just fine for the night," he announced. "Let's turn in. I want to wash the salt off me. Would you care to join me?"

Laughing at the leer on his face, she solemnly replied, "Absolutely, and this time, I'll wash you down." She scampered down the stair shedding her suit as she went, leaving him to close up the pilot house before descending to join her. By the time he arrived, she had soaped herself thoroughly and was ready for him. He joined her slippery self in the small shower, and luxuriated in her attention to detail, as she soaped him down, every crevice and protuberance. Finally, frustrated by the lack of room in the shower, they stepped out, died each other off, and fell into bed. They were very ready, and they joined immediately, kissing deeply. It didn't last long, and they were soon exhausted. They lay back in each other's arms and immediately fell into a deep sleep.

Chapter 15 – Tuesday
The Wreck

Jenna rolled over, wincing at the symphony of sore muscles. She had worked hard yesterday, and her body was complaining at the unaccustomed activity. She rolled onto her back, reached out for Quincy, and came up with nothing but a pillow with a dent in it. He had apparently awakened earlier, and left her sleeping. She glanced at the clock on the bulkhead, and saw that it was seven in the morning. She sat up, and realized that the dull thumping coming from the deck overhead had probably awakened her. Slowly, she threw her legs over the side of the bunk, and stood up. Her muscles protested, but the movement made her body feel better. She rummaged in one of Quincy's drawers, selected an old T shirt, and pulled it on over her naked body. Feeling somewhat respectable, she wandered into the galley where she prepared a pot of coffee, set it on the alcohol burner, then, ventured up the stairs into the pilothouse. She could see Quincy working near the stern of the boat, and, suddenly, the generator started up, quickly followed by a loud pump. Jenna ventured on deck and walked over to Quincy who was inspecting a row of scuba bottles sitting in a tank of water on the deck.

Not attempting to be heard over the racket, she tapped him on the shoulder. Startled, he turned swiftly, spotted her, and broke out in a huge grin. He turned, and pulled her into a crushing hug, exposing her naked bottom to the world. Oblivious to her concerns about propriety, he leaned down, and kissed her deeply. She ignored the breeze on her bare bottom, and returned the kiss, enthusiastically. Finally, with a pat on her bare backside, he released her, turned, and looked at a gauge on the tank manifold. He turned off the air feed, and shut down the pump. The noise subsided instantly, and he said, "Good morning, sleepyhead. I thought the noise would bring you around. We have work to do today."

"I know, I know," she replied excitedly. "Let's grab a cup of coffee and plan the day."

They took a look around, enjoying the beauty of the day, and went through the pilothouse, and down to the galley. Jenna poured two mugs of coffee, and turned off the burner. Quincy had taken an old battered coffee can from the shelf, and spilled the contents on the table. There lay the four coins they had dug up the evening before. They sat and stared at the coins for a moment.

"Are they the same as the first coin you found?" asked Quincy.

"I'm not positive, because I didn't study it very closely, but if you notice, these coins are not all the same," She replied.

"Now that you mention it," said Quincy, fingering two of the coins, "one has a ship on the back, and one has a mounted soldier, or warrior, on the back. Both are stamped 'Espania' on the face side. If you hold them, you can feel that the warrior coins are slightly thinner, and smaller. No matter, they are definitely Spanish in origin, and very old."

"What do you suppose they are worth?" asked Jenna.

"Who knows?" offered Quincy, "I expect that they are worth more as artifacts, than they are as silver or bullion."

"I can't wait to show the others. This means that we're not wasting our time," said Jenna, clapping her hands together. "Where are the rest? Do you think there are many more?"

Laughing, Quincy said, "Calm down before you get too excited. We shall have to think this through, and set up a systematic search, based on the location of our last find. Due to the fact that the coins were found at the water's edge, I suspect we'll find some more, either in the water nearby, or in the sand far above the waterline."

At that moment, they became aware of the sound of an approaching boat. Quincy went topside to investigate, and Jenna scurried into the master cabin to pull on some clothes.

It was the other three searchers arriving from the Colony Club. As Jenna emerged from the cabin, hastily pulling her hair into a loose ponytail, the four trooped down the stairs and into the galley. Suddenly the galley seemed very crowded. Ellis and Eileen slid into the bench, while Lyle excitedly snatched up two of the coins from the table.

"You found some!" he exclaimed with excitement. "Where were they?"

"Right near where Jenna found the original coin," replied Quincy. "They were all just below the waterline in less than six inches of water. The metal detector ceased to be effective when the water got over six inches deep, so we could not follow the trail out into the water. It was quite dark by that time, so we knocked off for the day. We left a shovel stuck in the sand, marking the find, so we have a place to start looking today."

Ellis spoke up, "How should we proceed? Do we assume that any other finds will be under water, or do we continue to look onshore?"

Sipping his coffee, Quincy replied firmly, "We cannot ignore either possibility. I suggest that Lyle and Eileen sweep the beach with the metal detector between the tree line, and the point where we found the coins. The rest of us can don some masks and fins, and do some shallow diving, sifting through the sand with our fingers, just off the beach. We should start from the same point. If we locate any more coins or artifacts, we can concentrate our search around the new find. How does that strike you all?"

Everyone nodded enthusiastically.

Lyle said, "Eileen and I will take the metal detector and start immediately. See the rest of you on the beach."

With that settled, the pair got up from the table, climbed the stairs, and left.

Ellis spoke up, "I'm a pretty decent free diver, and I expect you are, too, Quincy. What about you, Jenna? Do you have any under water time?"

"None at all," she replied. "But, I'm game to try. After all, the water is pretty shallow close to shore. You two can take the deeper part, and that way, we can cover more ground."

"That should work," said Quincy. "Let's sort through the gear, and get cracking."

The three abandoned the coffee, leaving the coins on the table, trooped up to the deck, and opened the stern lockers in the cockpit. Within ten minutes, each had a properly fitting mask, a snorkel, and a pair of fins. Jenna went below, to put on her swim suit. Ellis and Quincy loaded the dinghy with the gear, and added a few bottles of water. When Jenna returned topside, they took turns smearing their bodies with lotion, for protection from the sun. Quincy especially enjoyed his task, and, it seemed to Ellis, that Quincy was especially thorough with Jenna.

"You can get badly burned," said Quincy, "so check yourself often, and before you get too red, pull on a T shirt. If I'm going to snorkel all day, I use a shirt, and long pants."

"You're not serious!" exclaimed Ellis. "That's making too much of it."

"Tell me that again after you have burned the back of your knees," cautioned Quincy. "We should be ok for an hour or two, but if we do any more snorkeling, we'll have to suit up."

With that exchange, they climbed into the dingy, and headed to shore. Half way there, Quincy said, "I'll start here; Ellis, you too. I'll work from here to the reef, and you work from here, toward Jenna, and the shore."

The two men donned the gear and jumped overboard. Jenna took up the oars, and headed for the beach. When she arrived, Lyle helped her pull the dinghy up onto the sand.

"Let's get to work," he said.

He then took the shovel, and scribed a line from the water to the trees. He said to Eileen, "We can pass back and forth along the line to the trees. It should not take too long. If we find nothing, we can join the others in the water."

"Great, let's get on with it," said Eileen.

The pair picked up the detector, and started traversing the line in twenty foot swaths on either side of the line. Jenna sat on the dinghy's port gunnel, put on her fins, grabbed the mask and snorkel, and walked backwards into the water. She had seen people try to walk forward into the water, wearing fins, and had laughed herself silly at their clumsy progress. She had realized that by walking backward with the fins on, it was no problem. Smugly, when she reached a depth of water waist high, she donned the mask and snorkel, and fell backwards into the sea. For a few minutes, she floated on the surface, getting used to the sensation. Ducking her head under water, she experimented with the snorkel. Eventually, she was able to submerge, and resurface, clearing the snorkel without drowning herself. Satisfied that she was ok, she swam to the shore, and, in about a foot of water, pulling herself along with her hands, she used her hands to sift through the sand from the water line outwards toward the other swimmers. Immediately, she found another coin. She slipped it into her suit bottom and continued, working herself slowly out from the beach, all the time, keeping track of the location of the shovel, stuck in the sand, at the water's edge. In about two feet of water, she found another, and then, for the next hour she found nothing.

Norman was excited. He had returned early that morning to their lookout spot, and had noticed the decidedly different approach taken by the searchers today. They seemed much more energized, very directed. It was a complete change in attitude from the previous day. He watched the pair with the metal detector as they diligently searched their grid, glancing out to sea occasionally to make sure there were no passersby. Once when a boat sailed by, headed north, they sat down and pretended to be enjoying the sun; concealing the metal detector from the view of the boaters. The passengers on the passing sailboat did not seem to pay any attention to the group on the beach, or the divers; they sailed on by without incident. Eventually, Norman watched as Jenna headed to shore, stripped off her fins, and walked over to the dinghy. After depositing her gear in the boat, she grabbed a towel, and dug something out of her suit bottom. She then walked quickly over to the others who had almost reached the tree line. They stopped when they saw her coming, and, gathered around Jenna as she held something out to show them. Norman was completely beside himself. They had found something! He watched as the trio walked down to the water, and started signaling the pair of divers. After waiving vigorously for about five minutes, Ellis finally noticed them. When Quincy surfaced, he yelled to him, and the two men started swimming to shore. When the group was gathered on the beach, they talked excitedly, comparing notes.

"Let's go aboard the Billfish, fix some lunch, and think this through," said Quincy.

The rest nodded, and headed for the boats. In ten minutes, they were aboard, the chores assigned. Within fifteen minutes, they were seated around the chart table on the pilothouse benches, munching on sandwiches, and swilling water like parched camels.

"Diving is thirsty work," said Quincy. "It dehydrates you, and you need to pay attention or you can get into trouble."

The group nodded and devoted a few more minutes to polishing off the lunch.

Finally, happily full, Ellis said, "Quincy and I found nothing. We covered most of the territory from the beach to where we were scuba diving yesterday. Lyle and Eileen were also empty handed. Where do you suppose we should look next?"

For a few minutes, no one spoke up, until Quincy, said thoughtfully, "Suppose a ship was driven onto the outer edge of the reef, in a storm, broke up, and settled to the bottom. There's a small, fairly new, fiberglass boat on the face of the reef right now. It sits about one hundred yards from here in sixty feet of water up against the seaward face of the reef. I am sure that's what happened to it. If that did happen to one of the old wooden boats, it would eventually rot apart, and whatever contents were there, would be scattered all over the reef, and the sandy bottom toward the shore."

"Yes," said Lyle. "Periodic storms would scatter stuff toward the beach. How could we actually locate a wreck, and if we did, how would we go about finding something in the coral?"

Turning to Lyle, Quincy asked, "Do you have a glass box on the ski boat?"

"We do. We use it all the time to locate lost anchors and such. In fact, the tourists love to look at the fish when they're not skiing," he replied.

"I've got one on the Billfish, too," said Quincy. "What if we take the two small boats, drift out over the reef to the sea side, and see what there is to see? I'll make up some markers to drop if we spot anything promising; then we can come back with the tanks, and take a proper look."

The all agreed; the women gathered the debris from the lunch, and headed for the galley. The men went aft to raid the spares locker for line, and anything that might float, as well as extra scuba weights, to serve as anchors for the markers. When they were ready, they left Jenna on board to keep an eye out for possible visitors, and to prepare something for an early dinner. The rest of the searchers started for the reef.

About the time that the search party was having lunch, Smythe-Caulley came bellying up to Norman, looked out at the beach, and said, "What's going on. Where are they?"

"Keep your knickers on, Sergeant; they went aboard the Billfish about a half hour ago. I think they found something. Everyone seems very excited, and they are scurrying around with more purpose today."

"They must have found something after we left yesterday. I wonder where they found it?" mused the Sergeant.

'It looked to me like Miss White found something in the water this morning near the shoreline. The two on the beach found nothing, and, unless I'm mistaken, the two men diving farther out found nothing either."

"We'll have to wait and see. Did you bring anything to drink today?" asked Smythe-Cauly.

"Yes, here, take what you want." He passed over a string bag with some warm beer and two wrapped sandwiches. They settled down to wait, unenthusiastically eating the sandwiches, and sipping warm beer. Trust Norman to bring something alcoholic, thought the policemen.

Apparently, lunch on the Billfish was over. The watchers observed four people load some gear into the dinghy and the fourteen, and launch the two small boats from the Billfish. They commenced a slow transit from the anchored yacht to the outer edge of the reef. Lyle, in the ski boat, and Quincy, in the dinghy, were leaning over the side of the boats holding what appeared to be glass boxes. Occasionally, someone in one of the boats would throw something overboard. Something was seen bobbing in the wake.

"Markers," breathed Norman. "They're marking spots on the reef."

The two boats reached the outer edge of the reef, and circled the same area. More markers were thrown, and the boats came together for a few moments.

"They're spotting something, and marking locations on the reef," said Norman.

"Bloody right," replied Smythe-Caulley. "We can't see a bleeding thing from here. Let us see if we can move closer. They seem to have abandoned the beach for now. We can run round to the inlet, and crawl along it, until we are opposite the Billfish. That will bring us at least two hundred yards closer to the activity. If they land on the beach again, we can scarper back to the road."

"Right you are, Sergeant, let's go," said Norman, with alacrity.

With that remark, he scuttled backwards into the tree line until he was out of sight of the boats, stood up, turned, and started to jog back to the road. Catching the lumbering derelict was easy.

Smythe-Caulley said as he passed him by, "We'll leave the machine here, follow me."

He trotted off toward the road. Norman trailed along behind, cursing his lack of conditioning. By the time the pair of conspirators reached the tree-lined beach, opposite the Billfish, both boats were, once again, tied to the stern, and a conference was underway in the Billfish's cockpit.

While they were talking, Quincy and Ellis kept busy sorting out the scuba gear. It seemed that a decision had been reached. Both men donned the scuba gear. One man got into each boat. Quincy was joined by Eileen, and Ellis by Lyle. Jenna, once again, remained aboard the Billfish. Suddenly, Jenna stared hard at the shore, as if she had seen something. She disappeared, momentarily, into the pilothouse and returned to the stern of the Billfish with a rather large pair of binoculars. She commenced scanning the beach in the direction of the watchers. Both men froze in horror. Startled, they reacted by burying their heads in the sand, and remaining motionless. They stayed that way for five minutes, until, finally, Smythe-Caulley said, "I'll take a look. You stay down." Cautiously he raised his head, and looked out to the Billfish. Jenna had walked to the bow, and was now busily observing the activity in the boats.

"It seems ok now," said the Sergeant, "but, we had better be more careful. If we're twigged, we're done for. Let's put a bit of bush between us and the boat."

Both men crawled along the edge of the woods until they were partially concealed by a small stand of sea grape. They resumed their watching.

The two boats split up. Lyle and Ellis, in the ski boat, went over to a mid point on the reef where there was a marker bobbing. Quincy and Eileen, in the dingy, proceeded, with Eileen rowing, to the outer marker at the edge of the reef. Both men prepared to dive, waved at the other boat, and fell backwards, into the sea. The two remaining in the boats tied off the marker lines, to the bow of their boats, took up the glass boxes, leaned over the sterns and proceeded watching the divers. Jenna kept her vigil from the bow of the Billfish.

The conspirators followed the activity from behind the small stand of sea grape.

Chapter 16 – Tuesday Afternoon
The Find

For a while, nothing much happened. The divers left two trails of bubbles, surfacing slowly, further and further away from the two boats. The two boat tenders peered into the depths through the glass boxes at the divers. The two on the beach sweated in the sun, swatting occasionally at flies and sand fleas, growing increasing bored, and irritated. Suddenly, Eileen sat up, looked around hastily, waving at Jenna and Lyle on the other boats. She put the glass box down, shipped the oars, and started following the trail of bubbles surfacing briskly in a straight line toward the center of the reef, directly in line with the location of Jenna's original find. Abruptly, Eileen stopped rowing, and realizing she was drifting close to one of the other markers, she grabbed the line, took the glass box, and peered over the side of the boat. She could see nothing, as the glass box was flooded with bubbles from Quincy's exhausted air. He surfaced right beside her, so suddenly, that she let loose the box, and leaned back, startled at his sudden appearance. He pushed up his mask, rescued the glass box, and grabbed the transom of the dinghy.

"What's happened?" asked Eileen. "Did you find something?"

"Perhaps," replied Quincy. "Signal Lyle and Ellis to come over here."

Eileen shouted at Lyle, who saw her gesturing. He reacted by taking a wrench, pounding on the shaft of the outboard, signaling Ellis under the water. Ellis glanced up, caught Lyle's come-on-up gesture, and headed for the surface. Once Lyle had retrieved the diver, he fired up the motor, and headed for the dinghy. On the bow of the Billfish, totally frustrated, Jenna was jumping up and down with excitement. The two on the beach were in agony. They had not thought to bring a pair of binoculars, and could only look on, in despair. What had happened?

When the ski boat came along side, Quincy said, "Lyle, take the painter, and tow us back to the Billfish. Eileen, let that marker be. I will want to come back to it directly. We're going to get fresh tanks, and you, Lyle, are going to join Ellis and me on the bottom. Come, let's not muck around. Go!"

He handed the painter to Lyle who throttled up, and, with Ellis holding the dinghy's rope, they returned promptly to the Billfish.

Jenna met them at the stern, tied off both boats, and, when the four had clambered aboard, said, "Quincy McKenna, if you don't tell me immediately what's going on, you're going to be fish food."

"Calm down Jenna," he grinned. "Give us something to drink. We're parched, and we'll discuss what I think I found."

Even more frustrated, she rushed to the galley for a jug of water and some glasses. She re-appeared in the cockpit, having stubbed her toe on the stairs in her haste.

Hopping on one foot, she poured out the water, spilling some deliberately on Quincy in the process. Finished, she sat down in the cockpit and said, "Give!"

Grinning, Quincy started to narrate his dive. He had gone down directly over the sunken boat, and cruised slowly around it. Finding nothing in particular, he followed the chain from the bow of the wreck until he found the anchor, firmly imbedded in the face of the reef. He surmised that when the boat was driven toward the shore in a storm, the power had failed somehow, and the crew had launched the anchor in a vain attempt to keep the boat from being driven ashore. The anchor had skidded along the sandy bottom until the boat was driven onto the reef. When it caught, it had only served to hold the boat in place, while the waves battered a big hole in the bottom. It had then, he surmised, drifted back along the top of the reef, heading out to sea. Holed, and sinking rapidly, it had floated down the face of the coral, and settled onto the bottom. It looked as if it had been bounced around for years, on the bottom and into the coral face of the reef. It was a shattered, but largely intact, wreck. Someone had been at it. It appeared that some salvage had been attempted. The engine was still in the hull. Whoever had tried, had not realized any profit from the salvage.

Intrigued, he again gave the boat the once over, and turned back toward the coral face, finning toward the shore. As he started up the face of the reef, he spied a partially buried, coral encrusted chain, hanging down along the reef face. It was a heavy, old iron chain, rusted through in spots, and, obviously, too heavy to be used by the wrecked and sunken, thirty foot cruiser behind him.

Intrigued, he swam over to the reef, and examined the chain more closely. Following it down to the base of the reef, he came across an old fashioned, iron anchor, with one claw deeply embedded in the reef. He had passed over it, in his search, several times, not recognizing the shape from above. The coral infestation was so complete, it hardly resembled an anchor anymore. It was, definitely, an anchor, and about one hundred fifty years old, if a day, he thought. He turned around, and swam upward, along the face of the reef, following the chain to the top of the face, then along the coral, as it headed toward shore. Swimming slowly, he lost sight of it twice, but, both times, he circled and picked it up again. It led him to a hole in the reef, about fifty or sixty feet in diameter, with a sandy bottom. The chain fell over the lip of the wall, ran down the face, and disappeared into the sand at the bottom of the seaward wall. Swimming down to the bottom, he checked his depth gauge, and saw he was at forty feet, plus or minus, at the sand. He traced the chain gingerly with his hands, cautious to avoid any cuts from the coral encrustation. He stopped when it disappeared into the sand, and started to dig with his hands. Immediately, he hit something. Swishing the sand away from the object, he let the cloud settle, and then looked carefully at the object. It was an old fashioned, iron deck cleat, firmly fastened, to a piece of intact decking. He looked around, and spotted one of their markers. Quincy swam over to the lead weight, and towed the line back to the chain, and tied it off. Looking up to the surface, he spied the dinghy with the oars resting in the water, and headed up. Careful of his ascent rate, maintaining it at less than twenty feet per minute, he decided that he had not been deep enough, long enough, to necessitate a safety stop. He surfaced right next to the light box held by Eileen.

"That was it," he said. "I think we've found it. By my estimate, the old ship had the same problem as the cabin cruiser. From the looks of things, they had let out more chain, probably with a sea anchor attached, as well, and, when the hook lagged into the face of the reef, the old ship was held in place, and pounded to pieces. What was left of it sank into the hole. The subsequent tidal movements and squalls covered most of it with sand over the years. When it broke up, the cargo was, no doubt, scattered along the top of the reef. Some of the coins eventually made it ashore."

The group collectively let out a sigh. They were unaware they had been holding their breath while Quincy was speaking.

Jenna leapt to her feet, threw herself at Quincy, and kissed him firmly on the mouth.

"We're going to be rich!" she exclaimed. The group broke into laughter. Abashed at her outburst, she sank into Quincy's lap, and, with one arm around his neck, she said firmly, "Well, we are!" She smiled happily at the rest of the group.

"It's not quite as simple as all that," said Lyle. "We still have to retrieve the booty. First of all, we have to find something that identifies the wreck as the one the coins escaped from; then, we have to find the rest of the cargo, and retrieve it."

"That should not be a big problem," said Ellis. "We're in relatively shallow water, and if we carefully monitor our bottom times, we could in theory, dive all day, and all night for that matter, without injury."

"After a bit of a rest," offered Quincy. "Why don't the three of us suit up, and go down for a reccy? If we turn up something specific, all the better. When we are finished, we should all have a good feel for the site, and then, we can make detailed plans. I hope the job does not call for a lot of equipment, because I do not have the wherewithal to fund a big operation."

"Neither do I," said Lyle.

"No matter," retorted, Ellis. "I do."

Laughing excitedly, the group started shuffling the dive gear around, and replaced the spent bottles with fresh ones. Lyle dug out a rig for himself, and Jenna and Eileen went below to prepare a snack.

"They're going to need their energy," said Eileen.

The pair happily dug in, and started piling up a platter of tasty snacks, and some iced soft drinks.

An hour later, Quincy glanced at his watch and said, "The dive interval looks fine. Ellis and I could easily have an hour or more on the bottom, and you, Lyle, could last about ninety minutes, at forty feet. Let's suit up."

The group fell to with a will, wrestling the extra gear into the boat with the new tanks. They were soon, all of them, in the ski boat, headed for the hole. Jenna refused to be left behind this time.

The two women would follow the action from above with the glass boxes, and be available if the divers needed anything. The two ashore were, by now, almost insane with curiosity. It was all they could do to remain concealed, and keep an eye on the search. When the boat reached the marker, Eileen snagged the line, and made it fast to the forward cleat. The three men, armed with gloves and pry bars, fell back off the gunnels, splashing into the sea. Quincy led the way down to the sand and directly to the chain where it disappeared into the sand. They had agreed that Ellis would scour the top of the reef around the hole, Lyle would circle the inside of the hole at the base of the reef, and Quincy would try to dig up as much of the hull as he could. With a signal from Quincy, the men fanned out, and began their search. Each diver carried, in addition to a four foot pry bar, a small canvas bag, and a dive knife on his weight belt. They were fully prepared to dig and pry up anything interesting. The only witnesses to the search were a few nosy Barracuda, some slim, silver Mackerel, and a large cloud of Sergeants, flitting along the top of the reef.

Jenna fussed about the Barracuda, but Eileen assured her that they were harmless; they just looked sinister. The big risk, she said, was that the two men poking around the reef could disturb a cranky Moray, and get bitten for their trouble. She added that both men were very experienced divers, and would, no doubt, be keenly aware of the large, bad tempered, green eels.

Quincy labored long and hard at the base of the chain, and succeeded in creating a sand cloud so dense, he had to back off for a while, and let the swirling sand cloud settle. There seemed to be no end to the piece of hull he had unearthed. He began to suspect that the section of the boat attached to the anchor was nearly intact. He had cleared enough of it to determine that it was not deeply buried, and seemed to lead off in the direction of the wall closest to the beach. By his estimate, he figured that distance to be about fifty feet. Knowing that sailing ships in those old days seldom exceeded sixty feet in length, he calculated that the stern of the wreck could be lodged snug up against the coral wall of the hole on shore side. He eyeballed the possible location, then swam over to Lyle, and tapped him on the tank with his pry bar. Lyle turned, and Quincy made a motion for him to follow.

They proceeded over to the spot where Quincy estimated the stern might be. He started digging, and Lyle followed suit, hoping that Quincy was on to something. He had found nothing, and was getting discouraged already. Suddenly, Lyle's bar struck something solid. He immediately dropped it, and started digging with his hands. Quincy followed suit. Soon, the cloud of sand was so dense that they had to back off, and let it settle. Lyle quickly retrieved the pry bar before it became buried in the sand. When they could see clearly again, they could make out another piece of decking. Working carefully they started in opposite directions, clearing away as much sand as they could. Drawn by the activity below, Ellis joined them, and with hand signals, Quincy had him digging, as well. Periodically, they paused to let the sand settle, and, within twenty minutes, they had cleared a twelve-foot long section of deck, showing the stumps of splintered railing posts still imbedded in the wood. Quincy consulted his dive watch, and signaled the other two to surface. He then started up. Reluctantly, still looking at their discovery, the other two followed. By now, they had unconsciously deferred to Quincy for so long, that they now reacted to him as their leader. They did not think to question his judgment.

Surfacing, the divers pushed up their masks, and grabbed a hold of the side of the boat. The two women eagerly crowded to the side to hear what they had found.

"It looks as if the ship sank completely inside the hole, and has remained largely intact," said Quincy. "The question is, did the cargo remain aboard when the bottom tore out, or did it scatter on the top of the reef before it went under?"

"If it scattered on the reef," responded Ellis, "it will, by now, be totally absorbed by the coral, unless it remained encased in wooden chests. If it is in the sand, we'll have to dredge for it."

"Either way, it sounds like a lot of work, and expense," said Lyle, discouraged.

"Let us not start getting too pessimistic," said Quincy. "We have about thirty more minutes of bottom time. We should put it to good use. Ellis, you get back to the top of the reef right above the wreck, and Lyle and I will dig along the bottom. If we find anything, we can use that canvas sack in the bottom of the boat, and the flotation bag, to raise it up."

Once again, the men secured their masks, and started floating back down toward the bottom, looking for the site where they had unearthed the stern of the small ship. Already, the sand had covered most of it up. Great, thought Quincy. By morning, there won't be a trace of evidence to show we were here. That explains why the wreck had remained undiscovered over all the years, it may also help us to conceal our find until we are ready to salvage it.

Ellis poked and prodded at the reef, all the time keeping an eye on the activity below him. He spotted a funny shaped lump of coral on the edge of the reef, and swam over to it. It turned out to be a slightly oval shape, about three feet long, with a flat end on one side. Curious, he took the end of the bar, and started scraping at the coral on the flat side. Within minutes, he was surrounded by a cloud of bait fish feeding on the coral fragments. He saw something smooth in the coral. Dropping the bar, he pulled his dive knife from his belt, and, with the flat tip started scraping carefully at the spot. It was clearly a piece of wood. Jamming his bar into the reef to mark the spot, he slipped over the edge of the coral face, and swam down to the other two divers. Gesturing excitedly, he motioned them to follow him up. They followed. Locating the pry bar, he motioned to the other two. They approached and examined Ellis's find. Excited, Quincy gave them the thumbs up, and gestured for the two to wait a minute. He then headed slowly to the surface. Within five minutes, he returned with the lift rig tied to his belt.

He gestured to the two men to spread out, and the trio started attacking the base of the lump with their pry bars. Amid a cloud of coral debris and baitfish, they hammered at the coral for ten minutes. With a lurch, the lump broke away from the reef, and slid soundlessly over the edge. The three divers followed it quickly to the sandy bottom. It had come to rest next to the piece of exposed deck buried in the sand. The three men exchanged looks, and Quincy quickly pulled the lift rig from his belt. Grunting, and slipping along the bottom, the three men managed to manhandle the very, heavy lump of coral into the lift sack. Quincy then attached the lifting balloon, removed his regulator from his mouth, and started to fill the lift bag with air. When he was forced to replace his regulator to breathe, Lyle quickly pulled his out, and continued to fill the bag. Finally, the three men had placed enough air into the lift bag, to float the coral lump just off the bottom of the sand. It barely had neutral buoyancy, but it was floating off the bottom. Quincy waived them away, and lifted the lump slowly off the sand. As it rose, he pushed it upward some more. The lift bag expanded as the depth grew shallower, and soon the three were rising carefully, not too fast, following the bag to the surface. It broke through to the air about ten feet from the fourteen.

Excited, Eileen and Jenna skulled the boat over to it, and grabbed the lift bag by an edge. Quincy, surfacing directly along side of the lift bag, pulled out his regulator, and said quickly, "Don't pull on it; the bag might deflate, and it will sink right back to the bottom. Pass me the ropes from the bottom of the boat, and get the other two men aboard, right away."

While Lyle and Ellis passed their gear up to the women, Quincy tied the ropes firmly to the net bag containing the coral, bypassing entirely the lifting bag. He then called Eileen over to the side, and told her to make the ropes fast to the center cleat. Satisfied that the ropes were securely fastened, he swam to the stern, unclipped his weight belt, and tossed it into the boat. He then unshipped his tank, and passed it up to Jenna. He removed his fins, then his mask, passing each item up to Jenna. While he was disposing of his dive gear, the other two men stowed all three sets of dive gear in the bow of the boat, giving them room to hoist the coral aboard.

Quincy clambered aboard, and with his voice tight with suppressed excitement, said, "Alight you lot, let's see what we've got here."

With that, the three men grasped the ropes, and, careful not to foul the coral piece with the lift bag, dragged the thing aboard. It fell to the bottom of the ski boat with a crash, splintering part of the center seat, and gouging a chunk out of the bottom of the boat.

"Bloody hell," said Lyle. "That thing weighs a ton. What do you suppose is in it?

"We'd better get it back to the Billfish before it sinks this little boat," said Ellis. "We can pry it open there."

Lyle nodded his head, anxious to spare his boat any further damage, started the engine, and headed carefully back to the Billfish. Unobserved by the others, after triangulating their position with some outstanding landmarks on shore, Quincy unobtrusively reeled in the marker line, and placed it with the others in the bottom of the boat.

On shore, behind the sea grape, the two men were pounding themselves on the back and laughing as quietly as possible.

"They've got it," chortled Norman. "They've got it."

"Yes, but what is it?" asked Smythe-Caulley. "We have to wait until Lyle returns tonight, to find out exactly what it is. We can't do any more here. It looks to me like they're done for the day, so we should pack it in and head back. I'll drop you, and head to the bar in Holetown. When Lyle comes ashore later, get with him, and join me there."

"Right," said Norman. "Let's push off."

The two men scuttled backwards on their hands and knees into the woods, rose to their feet, and walked off. It mattered little about their caution. All eyes aboard the Billfish were firmly fixed on the lump of coral in the cockpit. For once, Quincy was not concerned with the growing mess and disarray on his beloved boat. He would clean it up later.

It looked to him like they had, in fact, found something very interesting.

Chapter 17 – Tuesday Evening Treasure!

The five treasure hunters stood in the cockpit, silent, staring at the huge lump of coral resting on the deck between their feet. Finally, Quincy said, "This calls for a drink. I'll fetch the necessary."

Jenna piped up, "I'll grab some shrimp and crackers."

In a matter of minutes, the pair returned. The other three had settled down in the cockpit propped on the cushions, their feet nonchalantly resting on the lump of coral. They were grinning, mostly to themselves, already fantasying about what might be at the heart of the lump of coral. The possibilities seemed both endless and exotic. Lyle felt equal parts excitement, and trepidation. Now that they had indeed found something, he would have to deal, not only with the reluctant Eileen, but Norman, and that bastard Smythe-Caulley, as well. He reluctantly admitted to himself, that he was very afraid of the policeman. Now that a find had been established, Smythe-Caulley would want to move on the searchers.

Quincy poured them each a glass of Gordon's gin over ice, with a slice of lime. "A proper drink for a bonzer crew," he intoned solemnly. He then raised his glass and drained it in one gulp. They all followed suit. Jenna choked on hers, but swallowed it gamely. She wasn't used to a straight drink like that, but she was determined not to be left behind.

"What shall we do now?" asked Ellis. "Break it open here, or haul it ashore, and do it there?"

Reluctant to expose anything yet to the policeman, Lyle volunteered. "We dare not take it ashore; too many questions! We need to keep this under wraps, or we'll lose it. Let's crack it open here and see what we've found."

Everyone nodded enthusiastically, and Quincy motioned for Eileen to get up. He pulled up a cushion, opened the tool locker, selected a large cold chisel and a ball peened hammer, and closed it again.

They sat there, staring at their find for a few minutes, sipping their drinks, until Ellis said, "OK, I'll do it. Give me the hammer and chisel."

He set down his drink, took the tools from Quincy, and kneeled next to the block of coral. Positioning the chisel in the center of the lump, he struck it with a hard swing of the hammer. The chisel sank into the coral about an inch. He levered it out, moved it over a few inches, and repeated the process. Five times he did this. Suddenly, a crack appeared completely across the coral mass. He set down the chisel, and hit one side of the lump, right next to the crack with the hammer. The lump split apart, breaking open the box encrusted inside the lump, as well. The contents spilled onto the deck.

Speechless, everyone stared at the contents of the box, scattered at their feet. The items glowed in the fading light. The colors of the sunset imparted a magical glow to the objects. Before them lay gold, a ruby encrusted chalice, an emerald studded crucifix, and mounds and mounds of Louis D'Or. There was not one silver doubloon in evidence.

"Crikey" said Lyle.

"Mother of God," said Ellis.

"Bloody hell," said Quincy, sitting down with a plop. "Will you look at that?"

Jenna and Eileen, instinctively, reached out, and took a handful of the coins. "They're heavy," they said in unison. They laughed delightedly.

"This is a whole new ballgame," said Ellis. "We have a major find on our hands. The doubloons Jenna found are probably the least of it. It appears that, in addition to scouring the reef between the hole and the shore, we'll have to dredge the hole to recover the rest of the booty. How in hell do we do that, without being discovered by the government?"

Silence reigned as the partners tried to assimilate their new situation, and the potential magnitude of their find. Not one among them had anticipated anything remotely like this. This was now a very serious business. They were looking at well over a hundred thousand pounds in gold and jewels; much more, if the items were treated as artifacts, rather than as bullion. In 1956, it was a lot of money. They had no idea what the salvage operation would uncover. Contemplating the potential salvage job, Quincy was becoming more skeptical each moment about their chances of pulling this off without alerting the authorities. In addition, the activity would attract every character on the island.

"This is definitely not what I expected," said Quincy. "This is not a Spanish treasure, most likely French. It could be that there are two wrecks down there; or it might be that there is two sets of booty on the same wreck. We'll have to dredge the entire sandy bottom inside that hole in the reef to find out. If there is more of the French treasure, I wonder where it might have come from."

"I guess the pirates raided one of the French islands, or a French ship up around Martinique or Guadeloupe," replied Ellis. "There was no love lost between the British, the Spanish, the French, and the pirates. They attacked any target that they could overwhelm easily."

"Sounds about right," said Quincy. "We need to stash the find somewhere safe, and decide exactly what to do; any ideas?"

For a moment, nobody spoke up.

Finally, Lyle ventured, "I don't think we should take it ashore. You should keep it aboard the Billfish. You could hide it in the bilge; the water down there should keep it covered up, and we can meet back at the Colony Club tomorrow, and decide what to do then. Eileen and I have to get Ellis back soon, or the hotel staff will start to worry. We were supposed to be back by dusk, and it's way past that. Quincy, when we leave, we can load the coral lump onto the ski boat. On the way back, Ellis and I will chuck it overboard in deep water. No one will ever find it there."

"That's as good an idea as any," said Quincy. "Give us a hand, and we'll get this lump aboard the fourteen, and I'll clean up this mess. Later I'll root out an old canvas sack to put the gold in and see where it's possible to conceal it."

Everyone nodded their agreement. They got busy, and, in minutes, the coral pieces were in the dingy, balancing each other in the bow. Quincy had located his old army duffle, and, with a lingering last look at the gold, the partners shoveled it into the bag, and clipped it shut. The light in the cockpit seemed to have diminished considerably when the gold vanished into the bag. It didn't really, it just seemed so to them. Not one person aboard had noticed the magnificent sunset fading away in the background. The fabled green flash had been trumped by gold.

Lyle, Ellis, and Eileen boarded the ski boat. Lyle started it up, and with a wave to Jenna and Quincy said, "See you tomorrow."

"We'll be back at the mooring by mid morning," said Quincy. "I'll talk to you then."

He waived them off. He and Jenna watched the boat vanish in the gathering dark. When they could not see it anymore, Quincy turned, grabbed the duffle, and struggled with it into the pilothouse.

"It's too bloody heavy for this bag," he said. "I'll have to hunt up a better sack, or split it into two lots."

"I'll help you," said Jenna, heading for the locker.

"It will keep for morning," said Quincy. "I'm hungry, thirsty, and horny, in that order."

"I think I may be of assistance," retorted Jenna, smiling enthusiastically at him over the gold. "I have considerable experience in these matters."

He nodded sagely, and followed her down the stairs into the galley.

They drank and chatted as they worked together preparing dinner. Despite his stated intentions, Quincy fell asleep over the dessert. She shook him awake, and led him to his bed. He crawled in, still protesting. She closed the door, and returned to the galley to clean up. By the time she had finished, she re-entered the master cabin to find him asleep on his back, snoring softly. Without hesitation, she joined him, and, within minutes, she too, was fast asleep.

In the ski boat, there was little conversation. Ellis was deciding how best to organize a salvage operation under the government's nose, and speculating on the odds of its success. Eileen was worried about Lyle and the coming heist. Lyle was struggling with what, exactly, to tell Norman and Smythe-Caulley. He had serious reservations about telling the crooked cop about the gold. Lyle headed the boat out to sea, and when he reckoned he was in about three hundred feet of water, a mile or so offshore, he throttled back. He and Ellis muscled the coral pieces and the shattered box overboard, sluiced down the deck, and sped off into the night. The searchers would all touch base again, when the Billfish returned in the morning.

They were back at the Colony Club beach in a matter of minutes. Ellis stayed to help Lyle load the fourteen onto the trailer, then left for his room, and a hot shower before dinner. He had much to think about, and only one evening to do it. Lyle and Eileen drove away, towing the boat, headed for the meeting with Norman and the policeman. In the car, Lyle was trying to reason with Eileen. She was adamant. She would not meet with Smythe-Caulley, under any circumstances!

Enraged by her attitude, and unaware of her reasons, Lyle said, "I don't have time to drop you home before I meet the men, so you'll have to come along."

"Forget it." She spat. "Drop me at the bus. I'll get home by myself."

"Fine," he said, stopping abruptly in the middle of Holetown. She got out quickly, and slammed the door. Lyle sped off to the meeting.

During their fight, he had come to a decision. He instinctively did not trust the Sergeant, and he was totally ambivalent about Norman. He considered him a joke, an alcoholic joke, and a definite liability. He would report that their find contained more pieces of eight, and nothing else. They would be excited enough about that news. Feeling better about his decision, he pulled into the parking lot at the fish market, parked the car and boat, and walked over to the little bar.

The fish market bar was all but deserted. Lyle found the men at a corner table. Norman was as usual a little drunk, and Smythe-Caulley was mad as usual, glowering at Norman who was blissfully aware of the strained atmosphere. The stooped, gray haired bartender looked mournfully at the three white men, knowing he had to stay open as long as they wished to sit and drink. He brought Lyle his drink and retreated to the bar.

When Lyle informed the two men that Quincy's group had uncovered a chest of doubloons, they were filled with excitement and anticipation. They could taste the money. The two pumped Lyle for details about the rest of the search, but Lyle, knowing nothing more, pleaded that he had done enough for one day. Smythe-Caulley was getting frustrated; he wanted action, and Norman just stared, bleary eyed, at the other two men. Finally, frustrated by the lack of further news, the policemen stormed off into the night. In reality, he was thinking furiously. He had to plan his next move. He did not want to share the proceeds of this enterprise with anyone, especially Norman. Timing was the important thing. Knowing Quincy as he did, he reasoned that it was only a matter of time before he decided to contact the governor about the find. He had to decide how to make the next few days come out to his advantage. He needed to get to Quincy, and neutralize Lyle and Eileen. Norman was a different problem, he was totally unreliable. He needed a plan by morning.

The remaining two men ordered another round of drinks, and for another hour, belabored the meager information available and Smythe-Caulley's nasty disposition. Unaware that Norman was really paying attention, Lyle, with a few rums under his belt, drunkenly let slip a hint about the gold. Norman did not bat an eye. Actually, he was pretty numb by this time, but it was a semi-normal state for him, and he was able to function quite well in that condition. He picked up on the slip immediately. A glimmer of an idea formed in his sodden mind. He was going to cook up a plan to team up with Smythe-Caulley, and screw Lyle and Eileen out of their share of the booty. What exactly he could do, he did not have a clue, but he was sure the Sergeant would come up with something. Dirty trick, he thought, but all's fair in love and war.

Norman had no idea what a bad decision he had just made. They drank up and left. The door closed right behind them, as the relieved bartender locked up, and prepared to head home. Lyle offered Norman a lift back to the Colony Club, dropped him off, and sped home with the fourteen still attached to the Vauxhall. He had to deal with Eileen and help plan the group's next move. He too had serious concerns about keeping their find from the government. It was a small island, and everyone seemed to know everyone else's business.

Chapter 18 – Wednesday
Quincy Hides the Loot

Norman's morning was better than most. He had not drunk himself to sleep, as usual. He had tried, in his befuddled condition the night before, to formulate a plan in his head. He had nothing specific so far, but he instinctively knew, and hoped, that Smythe-Caulley would be able to plan a way to confiscate the treasure and eliminate Lyle and Eileen from the equation. The policeman was an evil bastard; he could count on that, at least. With nothing much to offer, but a snippet of information about gold, he hurried through his customary ablutions, and headed for the kitchen. He retrieved his usual coffee, but, instead of hanging around to gossip, he scurried off to use the phone. He reached Smythe-Caulley at home. When Norman told him that something dramatic had come up after he had stormed off last night, the policeman was instantly alert and curious. He pressed Norman for details, but Norman would tell him nothing over the phone.

"Look," said Norman. "I don't want anyone else to know what's going on. We can meet at Animal Flower Cave this afternoon. Our bookings are light today, and I can take off the afternoon. There's a tour going out early this afternoon. I can tag along as far as St Lucy Parish Church. You can pick me up just north, along the road to Crab Hill. No one will be the wiser; the tour goes straight on to River Bay"

Reluctantly, the Sergeant agreed. "Very well, Norman, it had better be important. We need to control this situation or it will get away from us." Now that he knew there was something to steal, he was impatient to get on with his plan. He had no intentions of sharing the treasure with anyone. A plan had formed in his mind. He would use the men's weakness for their women against them. He would also enjoy himself in the process. He had a score to settle; some long awaited, unfinished business. At Animal Flower Cave, he could eliminate Norman from the enterprise completely. His decision made, he rooted in his service trunk and came up with his old service revolver. Checking to see that it was cleaned and oiled, he wrapped it in a towel and set it aside, ready to take with him later.

When he rang off, Norman went back to the kitchen for another coffee. He wished it was a stiff belt of rum, but he didn't dare face the policeman with rum on his breath again.

Aboard the Billfish, Jenna and Quincy were having a very leisurely morning. They had awakened, and enjoyed a lusty interlude before arising leisurely to begin preparing to weigh anchor. While Jenna prepared the breakfast, Quincy went up to the pilothouse and opened his charts. On the back of the Chart for the Florida Keys, he made a light pencil notation of the landmarks he had memorized yesterday when he had surreptitiously removed the marker buoy from the wreck's chain. He was confident that, with these landmarks noted down, he could find the hole, and the wreck, again. More than likely, in the midst of all the excitement, no one else had paid any attention to the location. They probably thought the hole was still marked. After breakfast Quincy intended to retrieve all the markers. He was starting to have some serious reservations about what to do next. It was a dicey business to skirt government regulations, and he was not positive that it was the correct thing for him to do. He was, after all, an officer, a reserve officer, but an officer, none the less, in the Queen's service. His oath of service bound him completely to a duty to Queen and country. He'd have to decide exactly where he stood in the matter. Mindful that he was dealing with four other people, he decided to take a cautious approach. He instinctively knew that Jenna would agree with any decision he would make, after all, she was an officer of the court, and not inclined to be crooked. Ellis was already rich and he was, Quincy was sure, really into this for the excitement. That left Lyle and Eileen as the wild cards. In the back of his mind, he had a nagging suspicion that Norman and Smythe-Caulley, who knew about the original find, could be trouble.

Replacing the Florida Keys Chart in its cubby hole, he grabbed the chart of the waters around Barbados, and went down to breakfast. While eating, he ignored Jenna, spending the time, instead, studying the chart in detail, his mind churning with thoughts of how to proceed.

Due to his scuba expeditions, he was fairly familiar with the shallow waters around the Island, especially the Gold Coast. He picked the sites, and led the dives, so he knew, first hand, most of the interesting dive sites. While there were few other dive operations active on the island, he was looking for a spot that would remain undiscovered, at least for the foreseeable future. Curious, and a little miffed at his lack of attention during breakfast, Jenna interrupted his study of the chart.

"OK, Romeo, what gives?"

Startled, Quincy replied, "Sorry Love, I was looking for a hidey hole."

"A what?" asked Jenna.

"I'm looking for an out-of-the-way spot to stash the gold. I'm not too keen on having it sloshing around in the hold of my boat. Too many people know about it, and, sooner or later, there's bound to be a bit of mischief. It will be much safer for all concerned if it's out of the way, and out of reach. Once we decide on a plan of action, there will be time enough to deal with it then. There's also the question of the authorities. I'm sure Smythe-Caulley is lurking about somewhere, and while, technically, the treasure would be classified as salvage, it is definitely inside the Crown's territorial waters. We need to consider what we're going to do. Until then, it's best that the gold be kept out of the wrong hands. If we report the find, I'm certain that there would be a reward, and that would be the honest and straightforward thing to do. We do have to consult with the others."

"Probably a good idea," Jenna agreed. "We have time to mull it over before we get together with the others."

Quincy stood up and said, "While you police the breakfast dishes, I'll pop over in the dinghy, and pull up all the rest of the marker buoys. Then, the site will be safe from discovery. There won't be any remaining sign that anything is out of the ordinary. The chunk of missing coral will never be noticed, even by a casual scuba diver. This is not a particularly good dive site, so it is unlikely one will happen by."

Jenna nodded; Quincy leaned over and kissed her deeply. "Right, I'm off."

As Jenna worked at the sink, she could hear him bump the dingy alongside, and when the Billfish rocked gently, she knew that he had pushed off and headed over to the reef. Giving in to temptation, she slipped up to the pilothouse, opened the bag, and took out one of the gold pieces.

Just one, she thought. We might need it for proof later. I'll keep it secret for the moment. She refastened the bag, and went back down to the galley. Remembering, suddenly, that she had been robbed at the hotel, she resolved to put it in the hotel safe with the rest of her valuables; her decision made, she put the coin in her beach bag. Happy with her decision, humming to herself, she returned to the dishes.

When Quincy returned, they busied themselves stowing the loose gear. He took the time to scrub down the cockpit, and remove any traces of the coral that remained. He wanted his Billfish to look as good as usual. He hated clutter, and he always felt better when his true love was fully shipshape. When they were finally finished, Quincy decided to sail back. Jenna was excited.

"Can I steer?" she entreated, giving him a big hug.

"Why not? This will be your first official sailing lesson," agreed Quincy. "First, let's check the wind. If it's bearing right, we can hoist the jib, and get underway. When the course is set, and we have cleared the reef, you can hold her steady while I hoist the main. The two sails should do for a start; we're not in a big hurry today."

The wind was bearing slightly from the southwest, so he stationed Jenna at the wheel, checked the dinghy's painter, went forward, and hoisted the jib. When the sail filled with wind, and the Billfish started to move, he cranked up the winch, and hauled in the anchor.

"Keep her steady on this heading," he called out to her. "We'll clear the reef with plenty of room."

Jenna was concentrating so intently, she just nodded, and gripped the wheel as if her life depended on it. Once the anchor was washed off, and stowed, Quincy went over to the main mast, and untied the sail. Once the sail was free to unfurl, and, when he had checked that the boom was securely snugged down, he hauled the sail to the top of the mast. Unprepared for the impact of the wind, Jenna let out a screech when the sail filled with a loud pop, and Billfish heeled over and picked up speed.

"Whee!" she squealed with delight. She was sailing.

Quincy laughed at her pleasure. He mused to himself, I am well and truly hooked on this woman. I'm going to have to consider how I'm going to have to handle her and my growing attachment. It is sudden, but it feels like the real thing. Am I ready for that? Is she ready for a commitment?

Keeping an eye on the lie of the boat, he went forward, ran the jib out a bit more, and snugged off the line. Returning aft, he freed the boom line, and pulled it with him back to the cockpit. Once he sat down, he let the line out until he was satisfied with the trim of the sail, and then tied it off to the cleat.

"Right you are, Captain," he said. "Take us home."

"My God, can I really?" she asked.

"Sure you can," he said, pointing north along the coast. "The wind's right. Just wait until we are into dark green water, and head that way. Keep an eye on the sails, and the pennant on the top of the mast. If it's streaming at an angle to the sail, we'll maintain good headway. We're going to make one stop, and then we'll continue on home."

She warmed to the task, keeping an eye on the pennant, the sail, the coast, and occasionally batting away Quincy's hand, as it toyed with her breasts. He was also, occasionally, lightly pinching her nipples through her thin T shirt. Jenna was having the time of her life. Abruptly, she realized that she was, for the first time in her life, deeply in love, and deliriously happy. She snuggled closer to Quincy, letting his hand wander at will. Hell, she thought, he won't let me run us aground. Happily, she abandoned herself to the moment.

In an hour, Quincy stirred and said, "We're here."

"Where's here? Jenna asked.

"Billfish reef, I call it. I haven't a clue what the locals call it," he answered. "Pull us into the wind for a moment. Look up at the pennant, and turn the boat, so that it lines up with the sail."

He unfastened the boom, and when the speed had fallen off, moved amidships, and snugged it down. He quickly lowered the main, and, leaving it loose, he went forward and lowered the jib. He also left it loose and untidy, piled carelessly on the deck.

"Hold it steady," he said.

He ducked into the pilot house, checked the engine compartment, returned to the cockpit, and fired off the diesel.

"Let me have it for a moment," he said.

Carefully, he lined up several landmarks on shore. They were far enough out to sea that he was confident that no one watching from shore could see exactly what they were doing. Satisfied with their location, he levered the engine into neutral, dug into his locker, and pulled out the glass box. He then went to the stern, opened the transom, bent down to the water, and looked down into the deep.

"Great." He said.

"What are you doing?" asked Jenna, as he went to the pilothouse and dragged the bag of gold on the deck.

"We're hiding the treasure here. I know this reef like the back of my hand. The current here is a little tricky, so no one dives here. I do sometimes, because there are many big fish that hang around this bit of coral, and they're good eating. They are not hard to spear, because they are not chased around all the time. The gold will be safe here, at least for a while."

With that, he dragged the bag to the stern, and checking once more for watchers, he dropped it overboard. As the bag plummeted to the bottom, he followed its progress, looking through the glass box.

"Damn." He said.

"What's wrong now?" she asked.

"It's too far from the wall, in plain sight to any passerby who happens to be looking down. There are numerous glass bottomed boats running around this side of the island, I'll have to move it. Not to worry, I'll be back in a jiff."

He rummaged through the locker, located his mask, spit in it, leaned over and sloshed it out in the sea. He pulled it on over his head, and jumped overboard. Startled and dismayed, Jenna rushed to the stern. Here she was, alone on a drifting boat, with no clue as to what she should do. She grabbed the glass box, leaned over and looked down. She saw Quincy swimming down to the sandy bottom. When he reached the bag, she saw him drag it to the wall, and leave it just under a slight overhang. He turned, and pushed off from the sandy bottom, rising to the surface as fast as he could go. He surfaced about ten feet from the boat, grabbed a lungful of air, and said.

"Thanks for waiting, Love."

"You're a bastard, Quincy McKenna; you scared me half to death, abandoning me like that," she yelled at him.

"I'm sorry, Jenna. I didn't think. I do this all the time. The boat was not going to drift far, and I can always catch up to it. If the wind is too brisk, I always anchor first. You were in no danger. I promise. I'll make it up to you."

"Damn right you will," she smiled reluctantly.

She watched him swim to the stern, and hoist himself onboard. He closed the transom, leaned over, and kissed her deeply.

"Let's go," he said. He then walked forward, saying over his shoulder, "Mind the pennant now," as he hoisted the jib and tied it off. The gold had returned to the deep.

He watched as she steered the boat back on course, then he hoisted the main, returned to the cockpit, and tied off the boom.

Turning to her, and grinning, he said, "You mind the shop, I'm going to get some dry shorts."

With that, he stripped off the wet khakis, and hung them on the cockpit rail. Grinning at her, in all his naked glory, he sauntered to the pilot house, and disappeared inside.

Flustered, flushed and amused, she muttered to herself,

"You're a beautiful bastard, McKenna. I'll give you that."

She resumed her navigation, eyeballing the pennant and the shoreline. She soon was so absorbed in the pleasure of sailing the boat that she forgot about him momentarily. In ten minutes or so, he re-appeared carrying two frosted beers, handed her one, and sat down beside her.

"Are we home yet?" he quipped, as he sipped his beer.

She laughed, tapped his beer with hers, and said simply, "I think I love you, Quincy McKenna."

"I love you, too, Jenna. I want you to stay here with me. We can really get to know one another. I am feeling that we might have a real future together. You cannot go back to New York yet, we must see this through."

She was beaming, and nodded her head, unable to speak for a moment. He leaned over, enfolded her in his arms, and, ignoring the boat, kissed her deeply. The kiss lasted a long time. Finally, they both became aware that the sails were flapping in the breeze, and they parted reluctantly. He regained control of the boat and she said.

"We'll talk more about this tonight."

With a long sigh, she leaned back and stretched out on the cushion. Quincy smiled, sat back, and steered a course for the Colony Club. He kept one hand on the wheel, and the other played lightly on the inner part of Jenna's thigh.

His beer was forgotten.

Chapter 19 – Wednesday
The Animal Flower Cave

Having totally forgotten his resolve to stay completely sober for his meeting with Smythe-Caulley after his usual liquid lunch with a cute tourist at the beach bar, Norman returned to his shack, and donned one of his more presentable hula shirts. He looked around, wistfully, for his missing sandal, but had to settle for a pair of seedy looking sneakers. They were originally white, but now their color was somewhere between gray, and splotchy green, with dabs of dried, red paint mixed in. The last time he had worn them, he had painted the red stripe on the ski boat. Satisfied that he met the minimum requirements for sartorial decency, he ambled up to the front entrance, where a tall, handsome, black man, dressed in a pair of black pants, and a white shirt, was standing next to a white van sporting a sign which read, "Island Tours." He looked up as Norman approached, and smiled.

Norman said quickly, "How are you today, Winston? I was hoping to cage a lift with you, out near St Lucy Church. I have to see someone this afternoon, and she can run me back when we're finished."

With a huge grin, Winston said, "Yas, mon, I know who you be seeing. I tought she be done wid you, long time now."

"Not yet," grinned Norman, with his best leer. "At least, I hope not." He was using his old girl friend Cora Hunt, as a plausible excuse for the trip. In fact, she was done with him, a few months back. Norman, embarrassed by yet another romantic failure, had deliberately not mentioned it to anyone at the time.

"Well," said Winston, "we got plenty room. Jus tree people today, Mon. We goin stop at Speightstown, St Lucy Church, River Bay and Cherry Tree Hill. Den we goin back past Farley Hill to see de monkeys."

"Great," said Norman. "When you leaving?"

"Bout fifteen minutes. You be here, you can go. Jes don go boderin the ladies, now. This is my bidness, Mon."

"OK, thanks, no worries," replied Norman. "I'll be right back."

When the bus pulled out, Norman was discrete; he did not want to call attention to his presence. He sat all the way in the back of the van by himself. The tourists crowded in the front to pay attention to Winston's colorful travelogue. In Speightstown, Winston stopped at the colorful fish market and the line of small stores opposite. He allowed them time to sample the wares displayed by the various vendors. There were island fruits, bananas, ackies, sowersop, and sugar apples. There were baskets, and other items made from oak seed pods, palm fronds, and various other local items. In season, there were pieces of sugar cane to chew on. The tourists always loved this stop, and he had to be patient and round them up for the rest of the tour.

In less than an hour, the van pulled up to the famous, moss covered, old limestone church. Winston parked the bus under a huge old tamarind tree, ushered his guests out of the van, and on to the crushed limestone pathway lined with colorful, blooming Hibiscus bushes. He led the way, and the tourists followed along snapping pictures, and asking about the old church and its legendary ancient slave graveyard out back.

Wanting to remain inconspicuous, waiting until the group had slipped inside the church, Norman finally left the bus. Taking the left fork in the road toward Crab Hill, he started walking north. He was thankful that he had worn shoes. His feet were tough, but he knew they were no match for the crushed limestone road. It was a pleasant walk, all things considered, and he used the time to fine tune exactly what to say to the ill tempered Smythe-Caulley. Just before he reached Crab Hill, and the turn to Conneltown and the Animal Flower Cave, he heard the policeman's BSA coming along the road behind him. He stopped, flagged the machine to a halt, and climbed aboard.

Scowling, the Sergeant said, "Hang on." They pulled away with a jerk.

Neither man said a word. Within ten minutes, they arrived at the Cave. Smythe-Caulley pulled the motorcycle over to some bushes, and parked. He took the time to place a rock under the kickstand so that the motorcycle would not fall over. The earth was soft here, and the bike was heavy. While the Animal Flower Cave was well known, it was not yet a real tourist attraction. It was an eerie, starkly scenic place, and very dangerous. The island ended here, in sixty foot high cliffs. The Atlantic Ocean pounded against the coral, so fiercely that the cliff face was a jagged mass of coral razors. One hundred yards from the edge of the cliff was a large oval opening in the solid rock. A rudely carved, coral stairway disappeared into the opening. It led down steeply over cracked, ill carved, mossy, coral steps into a large natural cave. It was over a hundred feet long. At the ocean's edge was a twenty foot wide, ten foot high opening, looking out at the wildly tossing, foam flecked, Atlantic Ocean. At high water, the waves crashed into the cave, and it was suicide just to go near the edge. Many people had been swept to their deaths. Rescue from the high cliffs was impossible, and it would take a fast boat two hours to get there from Speightstown. The battered bodies were seldom found. The Atlantic side boasted rougher, colder water, and contained many sharks which were always attracted to the taste of blood in the water. Halfway through the main cave on the right hand side, a smaller opening led down five feet, over a loose pile of mossy, smooth, coral rocks, into another cave. In this section was a trapped, crystal clear, twelve foot deep pool of fresh seawater. It was fed daily at high water by the waves, smashing their way through another opening, to the ocean. Adventurous teen agers flocked here during vacations to swim with, and attempt to deflower young, virginal tourist girls. They were largely unsuccessful, because the cave was a fearsome place. It did not, generally, appeal to young girls, local or foreign. At that age, they had more sense than the boys, and if they were inclined to surrender their virginity, it would, most likely, occur in a more romantic setting. Occasionally, some lucky kid would get to skinny dip, briefly, with his girlfriend, but they did not linger, and soon retreated to safer ground, up top, on the cliff. The grotto got its name, not from the simpering virgins, but from colorful little anemones, which looked like delicate flowers. When they sensed anything near them, they instantly retreated into their shells. They covered the coral in the tidal pools inside the cave.

On top of the cliff, the two men looked around. To their left, south along the cliff, was nothing but scrub coral cliffs and ocean. To the right, less than a mile in the distance, they could see a line of casurena trees leading down to the cliff edge. It was North Point, the northernmost tip of the Island. There, on a very scenic twenty five acres, perched over a private beach, complete with offshore standing sentinel rocks, and a famous blow hole, stood an old bird shooting lodge that was soon to be turned into a resort by some crazy American engineer. His wife, Ruth, had spent the last five years blowing holes in the coral, and planting a triple line of casurena trees to serve as a windbreak for the hotel and pool area to be built. She, and a local man named Darnley, were religiously watering the trees each week. When they were fully grown, the hotel construction would start. The locals thought that this was a mad scheme, but the people were nice, and they added to the local cast of characters. The prospect of some regular employment so close to home made the locals very friendly and helpful. The hour long bus ride to town was a chore when they wanted work.

The two conspirators looked at the ocean, and, hearing the waves pounding into the caves beneath their feet, agreed that they would talk topside, rather than risk the caves. There wasn't a soul for miles around to see them.

They sat down on coral lumps facing each other, and Smythe-Caulley snarled, "OK, Norman, give it up. What the hell is so important?"

"Lyle lied to you last night," he said. "Quincy and his lot found some gold. I don't know how much, but they found some."

"The hell you say!" retorted the policeman. "I don't believe a word of this. You're having me on."

"God's truth," stuttered Norman. He could see that Smythe-Caulley was already enraged. "Lyle let it slip in a casual remark later, after you left. I didn't call him on it, because I did not want him to think I had noticed the slip. The moment passed, and we left soon after."

"You mean to tell me, that, after you soaked up all that rum yesterday, you were awake enough, and had the presence of mind to let it go, and then call me?" he asked incredulously.

"Yes," said Norman forcefully. "I wasn't that drunk."

"What exactly did they find?" asked Smythe-Caulley.

"I don't know," replied Norman. "He didn't say. We say them haul that big lump of coral to the yacht, so I assume that it was part of that. What it was I can only speculate; probably something embedded in the coral."

"Did he say anything at all specific?" asked the policeman. "Did he say if it was big or small? Did they go back down after we left?"

"I don't know any more than I have already told you," responded Norman.

Smythe-Caulley sat and pondered this new revelation for a while. He was now, with this astounding turn of events, more determined than ever to act, and to keep the treasure for himself. Further delay would only serve to widen the circle of people, in the know, about the find. Norman looked on nervously, totally at a loss; he had nothing more to offer, except hope that things would somehow go his way. The policeman looked at Norman, he looked out to sea; he looked north and south. Finally, he shook his head, and muttered darkly, "This puts a new complexion on it, doesn't it, Mate?"

"What the hell do we do now?" pleaded Norman. He was out of ideas.

"What do you suggest?" queried the policeman, getting to his feet.

He started to pace up and down. Norman sat, dumbly, on his lump of coral, hopelessly out of ideas.

"I haven't the foggiest," he managed to stammer. "This is going to have to be your show now; I don't know what to do."

"You are a right sorry bastard, Norman, aren't you? You really are a useless little shit. I have turned a blind eye for years to your little misdeeds. I know you're an Aussie; an army deserter. I knew it a week after you swam ashore from that yacht you deserted, and started begging cash jobs along the coast. I've put up with you because of the occasional bit of good news, and the occasional bird you put my way. By the way, that bitch, Eileen, slipped through my fingers. I'll get to her soon enough now, but you are right about her. She's a real looker with a great little body."

"You can't talk to me like that, Sergeant. I know too much," said Norman, jumping quickly to his feet. "We're in this together."

"You know too much? You pathetic fool; you've murdered a man this week, and are looking to me to cover it up. It has slid by so far, because that Miss White has not yet reported your break-in. You can be sure she has put two and two together. She and her friends can report it if it suits them. You know the constables will quickly make the connection between your break in and a dead body found outside the room. So far, no one has thought to dust the coconut for prints. I'll bet yours are still on it, and definitely they are in her room. Then there's Lyle, and probably Eileen. I know he knows about the killing. You told him yourself. If he knows, most likely Eileen knows. What a bloody mess! You're a flaming disaster," shouted Smythe-Caulley.

Turning his back on Norman, he stalked over to his BSA, and opened the saddle bag. Reaching in, he drew out his old service revolver. It was a scuffed and worn caliber .455 Webley. Keeping his back to Norman, he broke it open, and verified that it was fully loaded. He had not used it since he was cashiered from the service.

While handguns were strictly banned on the island, he was allowed to have it, because he was an officer on active service. He was, however, not empowered to carry it off the barracks lot, unless there was a government-declared emergency.

Turning back to Norman, he leveled the gun at his stomach.

"What the devil should I do with you, useless sot?" he sneered.

Not believing his eyes, Norman shrank back from the slowly advancing policeman. He knew all about this handgun. They were standard issue for most of the British and Australian officer corps during the Second War. He was fully aware that one round in the stomach meant guaranteed death. He backed slowly toward the cliff edge, feeling his way carefully over the uneven, very sharp, coral ground.

He pleaded with Smythe-Caulley for his life. "You wouldn't, you can't," he said. "You're a copper. We're servicemen, mates, and partners. I'll do anything you want. You can have my bloody share. Just don't kill me."

"What use are you to me now?" sneered the policeman. "At least three people know about the murder, and if you're twigged, you'll surely give up the lot. You're a spineless drunk."

He raised the revolver; Norman knew in a flash that this was it. The madman was going to kill him. As Smythe-Caulley squeezed the trigger, Norman twisted around, and launched himself into the air, falling over the edge of the cliff, hoping blindly that he would not smash into the rocks at the bottom. Startled at this desperate move, the policeman rushed over to the edge, and looked down. At first, he saw nothing. Then, a retreating wave pulled Norman out from under the overhanging cliff. He was floating face down with a red stain seeping from his side, pulled out to sea by the backlash of the heavy surf. He was not moving. Cold bloodedly, Smythe-Caulley aimed carefully, and fired again. It was a long shot, and he was rusty. In a moment he was rewarded with a larger, spreading red stain around Norman's still floating, body. Satisfied, he looked around furtively. Had someone heard the shots? He wondered. Chagrinned, he realized he was alone with the wind, the birds, and the open ocean. There was not a soul for at least a mile. They had not passed anyone when they drove in, and they had seen no one since they had parked the motorcycle.

He walked back to the BSA, took an oil soaked towel out of the saddle bag, wrapped the pistol in it, and placed it back in the bag. He mounted the bike and kicked it into life. With a last glance around, he headed back, over the lumpy dirt and coral track, to the road to St. Peter.

He had serious plans to make; people to get rid of, and treasure to steal. What to do about Lyle and Eileen, even more importantly, what could he do to get his hands on the group's find?

Chapter 20 – Early Thursday Morning
Eileen's House

All the way back from the Animal flower Cave, Smythe-Caulley's brain was desperately turning over plans. Things were getting out of control; two deaths, and three people in the know about Trent Carver's murder and the treasure. Now, in a day or so, Norman would be missed, perhaps his body would be found with a gunshot would or two. Someone would surely remember that he was in St. Lucy's Parish today, and someone might have recognized the policeman, on his motorcycle. It was unlikely that anyone could connect the two events, but it was possible. He was not a stupid man, if he was to remain in charge, he must be decisive. He knew that he must act, and act now, or all would be lost. At worst, he knew could pin Trent's death on Norman, but then, where's Norman? Lyle and Eileen could panic, and tell all to the constables. He had no leverage at all over the American Ellis; he was an enigma. Jenna White was, at the moment, untouchable. Quincy McKenna was dangerous, and Smythe-Caulley was deathly afraid of him. Quincy had once threatened to kill him, but he had been cashiered while Quincy was in the hospital, and had promptly disappeared. The incident that had caused his disgrace and Quincy's enmity occurred on a clandestine patrol in Korea. He had panicked when a sentry had spotted him and turned to flee. It was only Quincy's swift action, disabling the sentry that had saved the squad from discovery. Had the base been alerted, they would all have perished. When he and Quincy ran into one another again on the Island, they both knew that their conflict was at a stalemate. Smythe-Caulley was, by then, firmly established in the colonial service constabulary, and

Quincy, now mustered out of the service, was a mere charter boat captain. His reserve commission held no sway on the island, only the Governor's favor.

By the time he returned home, he had his plan worked out. He showered and changed, retrieved the Webley, stripped, cleaned, and reloaded it, wrapped it up in the oily towel, and placed in the door pocket of his Land Rover. On his way out the door, he scooped up a handful of ammunition, and put it in his jacket pocket. He drove quickly back to the Savannah and arrived just as the office was closing for the day. He slipped into his office, went to his desk, where he spent several hours meticulously going through his files. He destroyed everything he had on Norman Evelyn, and Lyle Farmer. He had nothing on Quincy or Eileen. The other two were foreigners, Yanks. The only thing in the official records would be their entry permits. Admittedly, he had little or nothing on Lyle, but he wanted to be very careful. There was to be nothing that could connect him to any of the group he had targeted, no paper trail anywhere. To be sure, he spent another hour in records checking the master file. He found nothing further. Satisfied that all was in order, he locked his office door, and prepared to leave the building. It was late, about ten o'clock. Perfect timing, he thought.

On his way out, he stopped at the duty sergeant's desk, signed out, and informed him to make a note for his secretary that he would be out all day Friday on an investigation and would, most likely, be too busy to call in. He strutted down the steps, turned into the car park, got into the Land Rover, started it up, and switched on the headlights.

Now it begins, he said to himself.

He drove off in the direction of St. James. Twenty minutes later, as he passed Buccaneer's Bay, he turned right off the coast road, and drove up Holders Hill. He pulled left, before the crest of the hill, into a narrow, tree lined, lane and turned off the car's lights. From his vantage point, he could see several lighted windows in the small cottage tucked into the trees just off the main road. He settled down in the dark to wait for the lights to go out. He liked the darkness. It hid his actions, and provided anonymity. He was trained to move around in the dark, and used it to get away with almost anything he wanted. After all, most civilians were oblivious to most skullduggery.

Eileen felt the sun on her face. She stretched, rolled over, and yawned. She sat up, and reached out to the mosquito net, and pulled it aside. As she turned, and her feet hit the floor, she saw Smythe-Caulley sitting in a chair about five feet from her bed, pointing an evil looking pistol right at her. He smiled, and put one finger to his lips. "Ssh," he said. "Be very quiet, and I won't hurt you."

She opened her mouth to scream, but she saw him grow tense, and his finger tightened on the trigger of the gun. The air gushed out of her.

"Don't hurt me, please," she sobbed, covering her almost naked breasts with her hands.

"Do as I say, and you'll be all right for now," he said, standing up. "Go into the parlor, and sit in the chair, by the telephone."

Speechless, she walked in front of him while he prodded her roughly in the back with the barrel of the revolver. She could smell it; the scent of gun oil had permeated the room.

She sat down in the straight backed chair, looked at him and said, "What do you want me to do?"

He handed her a handful of linen, table napkins he had found during the night in the breakfront in the dining room.

"Tie your legs to the chair," he said. "Make the knots tight, or I'll hurt you." When she had finished, he shoved the gun into her stomach, and kneeled down to check her work.

"Good job," he said. "Remain still while I tie your arms to the armrests. Do anything funny, and I'll hurt you."

She stared mutely at the wall over his head, as he tied her arms securely. Satisfied, he took the remaining napkin, and shoved it into her mouth.

Shaking severely, and sobbing softly, she watched him mutely, dreading what he might do next. The memory of their encounter in Oistins was fresh in her mind, and she knew that this time, there was no escape.

Satisfied that she was completely immobilized, he leaned over, grabbed her gauzy pajamas, and tore them from her body. She was now naked in the chair. Grasping one breast in his hand, he squeezed it hard. Tears sprang into her eyes, and she started shaking all over. Satisfied that he had thoroughly terrified her, he looked her up and down, and grinned.

He said. "You know what I can do, don't you? Just nod your head if you understand."

She nodded, vigorously, several times. Tears streamed down her face. Mucus ran from her nose. She was clearly terrified. He grabbed the back of the chair and dragged it over to the phone table.

"Right," he said. "Here's what you're going to do. I'm going to remove your gag, and if you shout or scream, I'm going to beat you to death; but, before I do, I'll take one of your kitchen knives and cut you to pieces. You can then watch the blood flowing out of your body. Will you cooperate?"

Desperate and thoroughly intimidated, she nodded vigorously. He reached out, and gently pulled the gag from her mouth. She watched him like a snake. He tenderly wiped the tears from her eyes and face, the mucus from under her nose and lips, and then, placing his hand under her chin, he tilted her face up to him and said, "Here's what I want you to do."

In the water sports shack, the phone rang. Warrell picked it up, and listened. Cupping his hand over the receiver, he walked to the door and called out to Lyle, "It's for you. It's Eileen."

"Be right there," said Lyle, as he loaded some skis into the boat. Looking around to see if he had missed anything, he strode briskly to the shack, took the phone from Warrell, and said, "Hi girl, where are you? Norman did not show up today, and I really need your help."

There was a brief silence at the other end. Then, his heart dropped as Smythe-Caulley came on the phone.

"Don't do anything stupid. I am at Eileen's house; I've got your little chippe here, and if you don't do as I say, I'll kill her. Here, she wants to tell you something." With that, he held the phone to Eileen's face.

"Lyle, listen to me. He's got a gun, and he's threatened to kill me if you don't show up here within fifteen minutes. Please, I'm scared to death, come quickly."

"Right, don't worry. I'll be there as fast as I can. Put him back on," Lyle said.

When the Sergeant was back on the line, Lyle said quietly,

"All right, you bastard, I'll be there. If you've hurt her, I'll kill you."

He hung up with the policeman's laughter ringing in his ear.

Lyle turned to Warrell and said, "Eileen's got an emergency, so I have to go. I have no idea where Norman's got to. Do your best to manage the day, and I'll make it up to you."

"OK, boss, you go along now. I can manage. I hope everything works out all right."

"Thanks," he answered, rushing out the door.

He headed immediately to the car park, his mind going a mile a minute.

"What the hell is going on?" he mused out loud. "What's that crazy bastard doing with Eileen? She doesn't know anything." Even though he was unaware of her previous run in with the policeman, he instinctively knew that there was more going on than was originally planned. The situation was obviously totally out of his control.

For the first time in his life, Lyle was truly scared. He knew Smythe-Caulley was dangerous, but now, it appeared that he might be insane as well. He had turned ugly. He was frightened for Eileen; she had sounded terrified on the phone; her voice was close to hysterical.

Did Smythe-Caulley really have a gun? There were none permitted on the island. At least, he had never heard of one being used on the island in connection with a crime. It was a hanging offense. The only firearms he had seen were army rifles used when the constabulary paraded at the Savannah on ceremonial occasions. Not even officers carried sidearms. He drove like a lunatic.

Fortunately, he not only made it in time, but he had not killed anyone in the process. He slammed out of the car, ran up the steps, and flung open the door. He stopped dead in his tracks. There was Eileen, naked, tied to her chair, with the evil bastard standing behind her with a gun to her head.

"Shut the door, and sit down," Smythe-Caulley sneered. "You listen to me, and you listen well. Here's what you're going to do".

The policeman spoke without hesitation for twenty minutes. He did not repeat himself once. When he was finished, he grilled Lyle about the gold and was not satisfied that it had been left with Quincy. He'd have to deal with that right away. He was ecstatic at the detail of the find, and was getting excited about getting his hands on the treasure. He would think about salvaging the rest later; first things first.

When he was finished, he asked, "Do you understand me, and what you must do?"

"Yes," answered Lyle, shaken to the core. Never, in his wildest fits of fancy, had Lyle thought that the planned heist would take a turn like this. The man had slipped over the edge, and was dragging the rest of them with him. His admission that he had disposed of Norman terrified Lyle. Smythe-Caulley now had nothing more to lose; he could eliminate anyone who got in his way.

The maniac wanted him to kidnap Jenna White, take her to the old, abandoned Farley Hill Plantation House, and keep her there until he came for her.

"What if I can't find her? I know she's on the Billfish with Quincy. How will I get her to come ashore?"

"No problem," said Smythe-Caulley. "I'll telephone the front desk and tell them I need to speak to her about her visa. You hurry back to the club, take the message to her, and offer her a ride to the beach. In the boat, you can volunteer to help with her visa problem. Tell her that if she goes with you to the precinct house, you can get it straightened out for her, without any fuss. She'll go with you. You are one of her partners, aren't you? If she balks, spin her some tale about needing help for Eileen. If that doesn't work, force her somehow. Call me when you have her, and I'll meet you at Farley Hill. I'll bring Eileen with me. Do not let me down. Eileen's life depends on you."

Lyle sat there, stunned by the turn of events. Time was wasting, it was almost noon, and he had to do something, fast. Smythe-Caulley, sensing his indecision, leaned over Eileen, ran his hand down her body and stuck his hand roughly between her legs. She cried out and tried to wiggle away from his hand. He only smiled at Lyle and kept the Webly pointed at Eileen's head. Any doubts he still held about the policeman, and his cruel resolve, vanished from Lyle's head. He was serious, and people were going to get hurt. He didn't want it to be Eileen or himself.

"Ok," he said. "I'll do it. Give me ten minutes, and then make the call. When I get back to the club, I'll check at the front desk for messages, and tell them I'm going out to the Billfish. I'm sure they'll ask me to deliver it." He gave a last pained look at Eileen, and said, unconvincingly,

"Don't worry, sweetheart, everything will work out." She nodded numbly at him, her heart sinking. She knew what the policeman was capable of. She somehow still clung to the hope that it would come out all right in the end. Lyle left her there and drove off. After Lyle left Eileen's house, Smythe-Caulley turned to Eileen, and said, with a nasty look on his face, "Well, my dear, whatever shall we do to pass the time?"

She wet herself and cringed as he walked over to the chair. She thought, I'm going to die right here.

For the next three hours, the policeman systematically beat, and raped her into a state of catatonia. Fortunately for Eileen, she had passed out before he started raping her. This time he was successful; he was in total control, and, therefore, fully able to perform. When he was sated, not bothering to cover her smashed and naked body, he tied her up with the napkins again. She lay on the floor, unconscious and bleeding, while he gathered his things for the evening to come. As soon as it was dark again, he sprang into action. Closing her front door, he carried her and the chair out to the Land Rover, threw her in the back, and tossed the chair in on top of her. He planned to have her arranged, nicely re-tied in the chair, when Lyle arrived with Jenna. Because of the dim light at the old plantation house, he reasoned, Lyle might not realize that Eileen was half dead. The sight of the bleeding, battered woman, a friend of Jenna's, would also serve to warn the American girl to keep quiet, and cooperate. He hoped that Lyle would not be a problem; however, he was confident that he could handle him. By the time Quincy arrived, Lyle would be of no further use to him anyway. After all, he could just shoot him. What was one more dead body?

Unaware of what was going to happen to Eileen; Lyle hopped in the Vauxhall and sped down the hill. When he got to the club, it went smoothly at the front desk. He walked down to the beach, looking for his boat. Warrell was nowhere in sight, but the fourteen was where he had left it, earlier in the day. Quickly, he launched it, climbed in, started the motor, and sped out to the yacht. When he got there, he spied Quincy on the deck, coiling some lines.

"Is Jenna around?" he asked. "I've a message for her from the front desk."

"Hold on, I'll call her. By the way, we've got to get together this evening, and sort things out. I'll call you later. Just let Jenna know where you'll be."

"Right," he said, as Jenna came onto the deck. Holding up the slip of paper he said, "Message for you from the front desk."

He handed up the message. Jenna scanned it and frowned.

"Quincy, I've got to go ashore and make a call," she said. While I'm there, I'll pick up some things from my room. Lyle, if you'll wait a minute, I'll get my bag. Thanks for coming out to get me."

He nodded, and she dashed down to the master cabin. In five minutes she emerged, dressed in shorts, and a tank top, lugging her straw beach bag. She went over to Quincy and kissed him soundly.

"Miss me," she said. "I'll be back later."

She opened the transom and, taking Lyle's outstretched hand, climbed into the boat and sat down. They set off for the beach.

Quincy returned to the business at hand. He opened the locker in the cockpit, and removed a small block of wood sized to fit in the palm of his hand, and several sheets of medium sand paper. Humming to himself, he tore one piece of paper in two, folded it around the block of wood, and commenced sanding the rail around the cockpit. To most people, the varnish all over the boat looked pristine, but to him, he felt it could always be better. Several hours later, after he had sanded the entire rail, and applied two coats of marine varnish, he straightened up, rubbing the small of his back, and surveyed the results of his labor. Satisfied, he stowed the supplies in the locker, and went down to the galley. A few minutes later, he emerged with a gin and tonic in hand, sat down in the cockpit, and took a long sip. She's been gone a while, he thought; maybe I'd better go and fetch her. We can have dinner ashore, later tonight. It's Thursday, and they always have a good curry on. I'll just freshen my drink, get dressed and go ashore.

About twenty minutes later, he rose, chucked the rest of the ice overboard, and went below. He re-emerged just as the sun was setting, and climbed into the dingy.

Chapter 21 – Thursday Night
The Snatch

Lyle drove the boat slowly to the beach, his mind was racing. He liked Jenna, and she had been nothing but nice to him. Here he was contemplating violence toward her, and he was sick about it. He glanced at her, and she was busily fishing around in her purse. Finally, they approached the beach, and he said, "Hold on, I'll run us aground and then I'll help you out."

"Great," she replied with a grin. She was oblivious to his quandary. "I've got to stop by the room and the desk, and then I'll call a cab. Thanks for the lift."

"Actually, if you want, Jenna, I can run you over. I'm headed that way anyway and perhaps I might be able to help you out."

"That would be lovely; I'll meet you at the front desk." She hopped out of the boat and strode off up the beach toward the rooms.

Lyle pulled the boat further up on the sand and went over to the Water Sports Shack, looking for Warrell. He now knew that Norman was not returning. He was planning what to say to Warrell without spilling the beans; he was way out of his depth. One thing he knew, he had no choice in the matter. He did not want Eileen harmed, and he was afraid for his own life. When he found Quarrel, he asked, "Have you seen Norman?"

"No mon, he not back yet. Maybe he went to see Cora."

"Well," Lyle said, "if he does not come back, in time, you'll have to handle it. I've got to attend to some business for Eileen and Jenna, and I'll see you tomorrow. If there's any problem, ask Quincy for help, or call the boys at Paradise Beach; ok?"

"Sure mon, she'll be right. I gots everting under control. You go along now, I see ya tomorra."

"Right, thanks," said Lyle. He turned from the beach and walked toward the front desk. When he got there, Jenna had not yet arrived.

In her room, Jenna changed into a pair of slacks and a conservative blouse and put on a pair of light sneakers. She wanted to be presentable when she went to the police station. She snatched up her passport and put it into her beach bag. As she reached in, her hand brushed the gold coin. She had forgotten it in her rush to get going. I'd better put that in the safe when I get some money, she thought. She exited the room and headed for the front desk.

Arriving there she found Lyle passing the time with another guest and the front desk attendant. She said hello and asked to look at her safe deposit box. The desk clerk ushered her behind the desk and into the back room. She excused herself and returned a few moments later with Jenna's box. She placed it on the table and said, "Jus call me when you're through Miss."

"I'll just be a moment," replied Jenna, as the clerk left the room. Quickly, she opened the box, took out the wallet and removed fifty dollars. She placed the coin in the box and closed the lid. "I'm all set she called out."

The attendant returned and took the box back to the vault. Jenna thanked her and stepped outside and into the lobby. Lyle turned to her and said, "You all set?"

"You bet, let's go. I've got to see the constables about my visa. Do you know where they are located?"

"Yes, no problem, he replied. He led the way to the car park, opened the Vauxhall and helped her in. Going around to the right side, he was trying to smother his misgivings. He hopped in, and started the car. He backed out and turned to the gate. As he exited the property, he turned left. Jenna frowned, and said, "Aren't we going to Bridgetown? I thought that is where the office is? Asked Jenna.

"I have to first make a stop at Fraley Hill," replied Lyle as he got into the car and closed the door.

As they drove off, Lyle hesitated for a moment, and, making up his mind in a flash, he said, "We're not going to the police station. Something has come up, and I need your help. We need to talk, and I will explain everything. Is that ok?"

"What about my visa problem?" She asked.

"There is no problem; it was a ruse to get you off the boat. Eileen's got a real bad problem, and I need your help. Will you hear me out?"

Confused, but not yet alarmed, she replied, "Ok."

"Good," he said, "I'll find us a place to talk." They drove on in silence, each trying to make sense of the situation. Finally, he pulled over at the Speightstown fish market bar and said, "We can talk here. Let me buy you a drink."

"Fine," she said, getting out of the car. She followed him into the bar.

When their drinks were served, that sat in silence, sipping the drinks. Lyle finally collected himself and decided to come clean with her. "This is about the treasure," he said. "There is a man who wants to take it away from us and keep it for himself. He's a policeman, and he is a very dangerous man."

"Who is he?" asked Jenna. "What has this got to do with Eileen?"

"His name is Sergeant Smythe-Caulley," replied Lyle. "He's got Eileen and has threatened to kill her. Apparently, he has already killed Norman."

Stunned, Jenna just sat there. Lyle stared at her, not saying anything. Her mind was racing, unable to come to grips with what had just been said. Finally, she shook herself and said, "You better tell me everything from the beginning. I don't know how I can help, but I'm willing to listen."

For an hour and a half, Lyle reviewed the turn of events. He left nothing out, he was candid about his role in it, and Norman's theft of the coin and Trent's murder. Jenna was speechless as the tale unfolded. She realized that both she and Quincy had been totally unaware of what had been going on. She knew about Quincy's enmity with the policeman, and had an idea where it came from. She was also very aware that Smythe-Caulley was a trained killer. He finished with the scene with Eileen and the policeman and his demand that he kidnap Jenna.

"What about Ellis?" she asked. "Is he in on it?"

"No, he's in the same boat as you and Quincy," replied Lyle.

"My god, what are we going to do?" Jenna gasped.

"I don't know," said Lyle miserably. "If I go to the police, he'll kill her. He has nothing to lose. I'm terrified for her. Do you have any ideas?"

"I'd like to go and get Quincy; he'd know how to handle this."

"There's no time, I'm supposed to have you at Farley Hill right after dark, and that's only going to give us time to get there. He plans to threaten Quincy with harming you in exchange for the gold and frankly, I don't know that he won't kill everyone when he has it."

"I don't think he'll harm me before Quincy gives him the gold," she responded. "He's smart enough to know Quincy would kill him without reservation. He'll keep me alive, and if you play along with him, he might let you control me. That would give us a chance to do something to wreck his plan. I'll also tell him that I just placed one of the gold coins in my safety deposit box at the hotel. If something happens to me, he knows the police would find it when they go through my things."

"If we play along with the plan, I think I can protect you, at least until Quincy becomes involved," said Lyle uncertainly. "Quincy seems like a man who can handle tough situations. I don't know him really well, but I know enough to know he had been in many desperate situations and survived. Ellis I don't know at all, but he might pitch in and help Quincy."

"I'm willing to try to save Eileen", said Jenna. "Let's get on with it. I trust Quincy with my life, in fact, I just realized, I plan to spend the rest of it with him if he'll have me. He'll do something. Let's go before we lose our nerve."

"Great, I'm in," responded Lyle, getting up from the table. "Off we go. One thing, try not to talk back to the man, he has a terrible temper. No matter what, act terrified."

"It won't be an act," said Jenna, rising and following him out to the car.

They hopped in the car, and the short trip passed in silence. Everything had been said. When they parked next to Smythe-Caulley's Land Rover, Lyle reached over and squeezed her hand. Thinking that they might be watched, he jumped out and ran around the car, flung open the door, and dragged Jenna out. "Steady now," he said as he dragged her to the front door.

It was gloomy, but when Smythe-Caulley flung the door open, he was glad he had pretended to manhandle Jenna. The policeman grabbed her roughly and pulled her inside. He had the pistol in his right hand. He pushed Jenna up against the wall and pointed the gun at Lyle. Lyle looked around and saw Eileen motionless in the chair. He could see no obvious signs of trauma; she appeared to be unconscious, but breathing. Somewhat relieved that she was still alive, he turned to Smythe-Caulley, and said, "She's here, what now. Let Eileen go, and we'll be on our way."

"Not so fast," replied the policeman. "We have to have a little chat. Then, we're going to go to the gate house. There's a functioning phone there. We'll make a call and all come back here." He turned to Jenna and said, "I know about the gold. You and Quincy have not been too bright, letting the rest of the group in on your little find. Now you are going to turn it over to me and leave the island immediately. If you do not cooperate, I will dispose of you and pin a murder or two on Quincy. I can do it, just ask Lyle here."

Terrified but trying to think clearly, Jenna turned to Lyle and spat in his face. "You bastard, how could do this to me, to Quincy, we're your friends?"

Playing along, Lyle said, "Tough, Eileen left me no choice, and we want the gold. If you cooperate, I'll give you my word you won't be harmed. If you fight us on this, I can tell you it won't go well for you. Just look at Eileen over there."

Jenna glanced over at the unconscious girl and nearly fainted. It was obvious to her that Eileen was nearly dead. Numbly, she nodded to Lyle, turned to Smythe-Caulley and said, "All right, what do you want me to do?"

Smythe-Caulley explained what he wanted her to say to Quincy, and reiterated to Lyle that Eileen's health depended on his going along with the plan from start to finish.

"Do you both understand what's going to happen?" he asked. They simply nodded, and he said, "Right, let's walk down to the gate house. Lyle, you're in charge of her if she bolts, I'll shoot her then you then Eileen. Got it?"

"What about Eileen?" asked Lyle.

"She's not going anywhere for a while, I knocked her out. Play your cards right, and I won't touch her again."

"Ok," replied Lyle. He grabbed Jenna roughly and marched her out the door, followed by Smythe-Caulley with the gun held squarely at Lyle's back. They headed down the long drive to the guard shack at the entrance.

Unknown to the pair, he was the only one who would walk away from the coming meeting tonight. Jenna and Lyle were thinking furiously, both fully aware that their charade was passing muster with the policeman, but they would have to continue convincing him. They were absolutely sure he would not hesitate to kill them if he felt threatened.

Chapter 22 – Thursday Night
The Ultimatum

Totally unaware of the gathering storm, Quincy rowed slowly to shore; he watched the last of the sunset as he rowed the dinghy. Pity she had to go to town, he thought, we could have watched it together. It was turning out to be a great habit for the two of them. The green flash seemed to be a good omen for them. He reached the shore, beached the dinghy, and walked up the sand to the terrace. As he approached the beach bar, he spotted Ellis leaning against it having a rum punch.

He greeted him, and Ellis asked, "Join me for a drink?"

"Sure," answered Quincy. "Order me a gin and tonic. I'll just pop over to Jenna's room, and collect her. Order her a rum punch, too; maybe we can all have dinner together. I have to see if I can get Lyle and Eileen back as well. We have plans to make."

"Hurry back," said Ellis, turning to the bartender.

Quincy strode over to the guest wing, down the path to 104, and knocked on the door. There was no answer. Puzzled, he tried again; still no answer. Now, concerned, he turned toward the lobby and went to the front desk.

"Have you seen Miss White?" he asked.

"Yes," the pretty desk clerk replied. "She left with Mr. Lyle a few hours ago, and she has not got back yet."

"Thanks," he said. "When she comes back, please tell her I'm at the beach bar."

"Right Sir, I will," replied the clerk.

By now, thoroughly confused, he shook his head, and returned to the bar.

"I thought I'd lost you; let me order you a fresh one. Your ice has melted. Where's Jenna?" asked Ellis, as he turned to the bartender and signaled for another drink.

"I don't know," responded Quincy. "The front desk said she's gone off somewhere with Lyle. She apparently did not leave a message for me."

"Well, let's have a drink. She'll turn up soon. It's almost dinner time. Maybe they'll all show up together."

The two men stood looking out to sea, drinking quietly, chatting about the find, and exploring the possibilities for a salvage operation. Quincy realized that his growing misgivings about not contacting the authorities were dominating his thoughts. Cautiously he exposed his thinking to Ellis, and found to his delight that Ellis had come to the conclusion that a secret salvage operation would be all but impossible. It did occur to him, that what they had found so far, could most likely, be swept under the carpet, at least, partially. Gratified that he was not the only one with reservations, Quincy resolved to bring the subject up with Lyle when he returned this evening. As a group they could vent their ideas. He could make his final decision after the meeting, depending on what the group wanted to do. In truth, he had pretty well decided that he was going to speak to the Governor as soon as possible. He had no doubt whatever that Jenna would support him in his decision.

Before they could get into any detail on how to proceed, a waiter came up to Quincy and said, "Telephone for you, sir. You can take it in the lounge bar by the front desk."

"Thanks," replied Quincy to the waiter. Turning to Ellis he said, "Must be her, back in a minute."

"Right," said Ellis, I'll order us another drink."

When he picked up the phone, it was Smythe-Caulley.

"Evening, Major," he said snidely. "I trust I'm not disturbing you. Can you talk?"

"What the devil do you want?" Quincy demanded.

"Keep your knickers on, Major, and I'll explain. It seems that I've come into possession of something of yours; I thought that you might like to have it back."

"What the hell do you mean; something of mine?"demanded Quincy.

"Have you seen your girlfriend lately?" breathed Smythe-Caulley.

Rocked to his core, Quincy fumbled for words while he tried vainly to connect Jenna with Smythe-Caulley. All he could come up with was that brief incident at Bobbie's party. He was momentarily at a loss for words.

"What do you mean?" stammered Quincy, recovering his voice. "Is there some kind trouble I should know about? If you've harassed her again, you'll answer to me for it."

"It's rather more serious than that, I'm afraid. She has been connected to the theft of an illegal artifact."

Remembering that the coin was stolen from her room, Quincy responded. "She found an old coin on the beach when we were water skiing. Before she could do anything about it, it was stolen by a burglar. How did you find out about it? We have not yet had a chance to report it."

"Was it perhaps a gold coin?" asked the policeman.

Quincy's heart stopped for a minute. Nothing made sense to him. How could that miserable bastard possibly know anything about their find yesterday?

Smoothly, Smythe-Caulley continued. "It seems that a mutual friend of ours ratted you out Major. He not only told me about the gold, but he was kind enough to bring Miss White around for a little chat this evening. By the way, she managed to verify the story in astonishing detail. It seems that you have made a significant find. The old rumors have finally been born out. Pirate treasure at Sandy Lane is in fact a reality. Pity you'll not share in the bounty."

"Lyle," exploded Quincy. "That son of a bitch. Listen, you bastard, I'm coming down to the station to bring her back. We can talk about this in the morning. I will arrange for the gold to be delivered to you first thing in the morning. You can have my word on it. I'll deal with Lyle later."

"I'm afraid not, McKenna. She's not at the Garrison, and you'll not be taking her anywhere. In fact, unless you play ball, you may never see her again. The authorities are not involved in this. This is personal. Lyle is here with me, and he is minding your friend for me."

"What the hell do you mean, personal, Sergeant? If you hurt her, I'll kill you," yelled Quincy into the phone.

"Calm down, Major. We can come to some kind of satisfactory arrangement, I'm sure. After all, you have rather a lot of gold at your disposal. You just sit tight right there, and I'll ring you back by nine thirty this evening. My plan is to exchange Jenna White for the gold; then, you two will leave the island tomorrow and not come back. If you do, I'll see that you are both charged with the murder of Trent Carver. In the meanwhile, don't do anything stupid. Talk to no one, or Miss White will pay the price. I am not joking around."

He hung up. Quincy stared at the phone, shaking his head. He went around the corner to the front desk and said,

"I'm expecting a call back. I'm going out to my boat for a bit, but I'll be back at the beach bar presently, and you can find me there."

"Right, Sir, we'll call you when it comes in," replied the clerk.

Quincy turned and left.

Walking briskly to the beach bar, he stopped and said to Ellis,

"Come with me right now, we have to talk. They've got Jenna."

He turned abruptly and started down the beach toward the dinghy.

Alarmed, and confused by Quincy's abrupt statement, Ellis scrambled to catch up. He blurted out, "Who's got Jenna?"

Shoving off, Quincy replied tightly, "That bastard, Sergeant Smythe-Caulley, and Lyle Farmer, that's who."

"Who is Smythe-Caulley? When did this happen? Lyle? He's on our side, for Christ's sake, isn't he?" asked Ellis. Totally confused, he scrambled into the dingy, soaking his pants to the crotch.

"We've got to get her back before something happens. He knows about the gold. Apparently Lyle told him, and they obviously intend to take it for their own. They have threatened to hurt Jenna.

"What if we go to the government with this?" asked Ellis. "Then nobody gets it."

"He said that if I did anything, anything at all, to thwart him, he'd kill her. I have no idea yet where he's holding her. We have to play along if we want to get her back. When he calls again, we will have to act quickly and decisively."

Climbing aboard the Billfish, Ellis asked simply, "What can I do to help?"

"Just come with me, and watch my back. I'll do the rest. I've been trained for this type of thing. Unfortunately, so has that bastard."

"What do you mean trained for this type of thing?" asked Ellis, following him down to the galley.

"Both of us are ex-SAS. In fact, I'm active reserve. That bugger was cashiered not three years ago. We are both trained in the clandestine services. He's a right bastard, but he's no one to take lightly. He's good with a knife and a gun. I know, I've worked with him."

"Damn, I'm not much of a fighter, but I'll do what I can. I can at least watch your back. There are two of them, and I'm sure Lyle is nothing much. I'll square off with him when the time comes. You deal with the Sergeant."

"Right," said Quincy. "Let's see what we can round up for kit. I've no firearms, but I've got a thing or two that we can use. I assume you have some dark clothes you can wear."

Ellis nodded.

"I've got some old gear that will serve. Wait here, and pour yourself a drink; only one, mind you, we will need to be on our toes."

He disappeared into the master cabin. Ellis poured them both a drink and waited. In five minutes, Quincy was back. He was dressed in black trousers, a black T shirt, and worn, ankle-high, black boots. He carried a small canvas bag. He handed Ellis a sheath knife. Ellis slid it out of the sheath, and tested the edge on the ball of his thumb. It was so sharp he could shave with it.

"Don't cut yourself. Use it on the other guy." Quincy retrieved the knife slid it into the sheath, and replaced the knife in the bag and said, "Let's go, you can lace it onto your belt after you change. We should go ashore now. The crooked policeman is due to call back by nine thirty, and we need to lay out a plan of action."

The two men downed their drinks, turned to go, and Ellis said, "What are you carrying? I can't see anything."

Quincy reached up behind his back under the tail of his shirt, and pulled out a lethal looking dagger, about a foot long.

"Jesus Christ," exclaimed Ellis. "That's a real Fairbairn; they're a real piece of work. It looks well used. I assume you know how to use it."

"I've had a lot of practice," replied Quincy, as he slid it back into the sheath concealed under his shirt.

"Let's go. You go change and I'll wait for you at the bar. They're due to call back within the half hour."

They beached the dingy, Ellis departed for his room, and Quincy settled down to wait, mulling over what might be in store for Jenna and him this night. He was comforted somewhat by Ellis volunteering to watch his back. He also hoped that nothing bad would happen to anyone. His misgivings got the better of him, and he nursed a glass of water with lime and brooded.

Ellis returned, dressed much the same as Quincy, but wearing sneakers instead of boots. "Heard anything yet?" he asked.

"Nothing," he replied. "We wait."

Chapter 23 – Late Thursday Night
Farley Hill Plantation

Within fifteen minutes, another waiter walked over, and told Quincy that the call he was expecting was ready for him in the salon bar. Quincy stood up, grabbed the bag, and Ellis followed him into the room.

"I'm here," he announced. "Speak up you sod."

"Now," said Smythe-Caulley. "You are to come alone tonight, no later than eleven. Bring the rest of the gold."

"Right," said Quincy, ignoring the demand for the gold. "Where am I going?"

"Do you know Farley Hill Plantation?"

"Yes," he replied. "You must mean the old abandoned house next to the Mahogany Preserve?"

"That's correct," said the policeman. "Drive slowly up the entrance way; park where we can see you. The front door will be open. Get out and slowly come inside with your hands in the air."

"I can do that," agreed Quincy. "I'll be there. It will take me a little while to collect the gold, but I can make it, I think, by midnight."

"Don't be any later," said Smythe-Caulley, and hung up.

Quincy and Ellis walked briskly to his truck and climbed in. On the way, Quincy explained to Ellis that he had managed to delay the meeting until midnight. Carefully handled, that should give them the time needed to reconnoiter the layout of the old plantation house. He figured that with the drive time they might have as much as one and a half hours to check things out and make a plan.

"What a heap," said Ellis with a smile. "Are you sure we'll make it there?"

"Not to worry, she's a little tired, but she's game. Runs like a top. Here's your knife, best strap it on."

As Ellis laced the knife to his belt, Quincy started the truck, and pulled away in a cloud of smoke. Ellis had his doubts, but was willing to take Quincy's word for it. There was something about him that radiated menace. He was a man with a purpose. They discussed their strategy as they drove. Quincy and Ellis planned to park about a quarter of a mile away from the driveway, and reconnoiter the house. Then, once they knew the lay of the land, Quincy would return to the car, leaving Ellis in position. He would then drive up to the house at the appointed time. When the moment was right, on a signal from Quincy, Ellis was to provide a distraction of some kind. Hopefully, whatever it was that he was going to do, would distract the policeman long enough for Quincy to act.

They drove up Sailor's hill, turned toward Prospect, and stopped just short of the turn to Farley Hill. They parked in a wide spot on the road, half in the cane field and half on the narrow road. They left the truck's lights off, exited the car, and went forward on foot. It was ten fifteen on the dot; so far so good. In a few minutes they spied, in the moonlight, the long white driveway leading up to the old plantation house. On each side of the crushed limestone drive, lined with sixty foot tall, royal palms, the bushes provided some cover. The old limestone guard house stood just to the left of the entry adjacent to the drive. Overgrown bushes completely hid the once manicured lawns that swept from the entrance up to the house on either side of the drive. They bypassed the guard shack, and crawled through the bushes and around the structure until they reached the overgrown grass. Traveling slowly, bent over, using the bushes lining the drive as cover, they cautiously approached the abandoned house at the top of the hill. The old plantation house stood quietly in the moonlight. The moss covered limestone walls still looked good in the dim light. Except for the total absence of lights, the house looked perfectly normal and lived in. Only on closer inspection did the abandoned state become apparent. The shutters were gone, and the windows all broken. Quincy knew that the house had been all but gutted, but its grandeur had somehow managed to survive its abandonment. He had been through the house many times, and could, by closing his eyes still remember the layout of the ground floor.

When they spotted the front door, they stopped and crouched down. The door was closed, and there was no one in sight. Parked to the left of the house was Lyle's Vauxhall, and next to it, Smythe-Caulley's Land Rover sat with the passenger door hanging open, and the tailgate swinging down. There was no sign of life. The moon was not yet full, but they could see well enough to reconnoiter. Quincy quickly briefed Ellis on the layout and told him what to look for, but cautioned him not to venture inside the house until they were ready and positive that they knew the layout. They split up, crawling cautiously in different directions. Ellis went left, and Quincy went right. They moved as silently as they could, keeping out of sight of the windows. In fifty minutes they returned to the same spot. By the time he regrouped with Ellis, Quincy had made his decision; he was prepared to kill anyone who threatened Jenna. He wanted her back, permanently. The coldblooded decision calmed him, as he prepared for action. Running over his plan in his mind, he prepared to brief Ellis. Ellis too seemed determined, and that gave Quincy the boost he needed.

As they lay in the grass, screened from the house by some low shrubs, they went over the plan again.

"Here's what we do," said Quincy. "Ellis, there's a broken door at the rear of the house. The floors are all tile and marble, so they will be quiet if you don't trip over anything. Get into position just outside the doorway, and wait for me to get back. When you hear my truck coming, you can assume they will be concentrating on me. You slip inside, and start to work your way toward the front room. There is a hallway right off the kitchen, leading to your right. Take it as far as you can toward the front room. I'm sure the Sergeant will be waiting for me there. There are two rooms off the hall, make sure they are empty before you proceed. You don't want to be blindsided when we make our move. Try to get close enough to the front room to hear what's going on; wait for my signal. After I'm in, they'll soon find out that I do not have the gold with me. Then, the fun will start. I'll count on you for a distraction. Don't move until I do. Remember, he's most likely armed, and he's bloody dangerous. Do not be a hero. Just do what you can, I'll manage the nasty bits."

"Do not worry about me," whispered Ellis. "I'm no hero. I'll do what I can; you can count on it."

"Right. I'm off." Quincy simply vanished into the night.

Neither man had looked behind them. They had completely missed the man about twenty yards to their rear, crouched under a large grouping of overgrown Hibiscus. He had silently watched their every move. Crouched low, he remained deathly still; doing nothing, just watching.

Ellis was thoroughly spooked. What the hell have I gotten into? He thought, as he lay quietly in the grass. Adventure is one thing, but this is serious. I could get killed. Resolutely determined to hold up his commitment, he squared his shoulders and counted down the time. After ten minutes, he moved off carefully to his left, circling around the house to the rear. He cautiously crept up on the back landing and up to the door. He tried it and found that it opened easily with little sound. Satisfied for now, he left it ajar and settled down to wait for Quincy's truck.

The watcher moved silently up to Ellis's abandoned vantage point at the front of the house, and stared intently at the closed front door.

Within ten minutes, Quincy's truck could be plainly heard, gears clashing and exhaust ratline, it labored up the hill toward the house. Ellis could plainly hear it, and he was sure the people inside could as well. He realized that Quincy was deliberately making as much noise as he could, to cover for Ellis' entry into the house. He wanted all eyes on the front of the house when he made his move. The front door slowly opened, revealing a large black hole. There was not enough light to see into the front room. The observer on the lawn behind the shrub saw nothing except the moving door. He lay flattened himself behind the bush so that neither Quincy, nor anyone watching from the house would spot him in the truck's headlights. When the truck passed him, he rose to a crouch, and moved closer to the house.

Quincy drove up to the front door, and seeing that it was now open, strained to see into the dark room beyond. Even with the lights from the truck, he could see nothing. He shut the engine off, and turned off his lights, remaining in the truck until his eyes became adjusted to the dark. Realizing that the moon was bright enough to enable him to see clearly, he got out, set his bag on the hood of the truck, and walked slowly up the stairs, and into the house, with his hands in plain sight, hanging loosely at his sides. He could hear nothing; he could see nothing beyond the open door, so he slowly advanced into the entry.

"Stop right there, raise your hands, and stay still," said a voice from the darkness ahead. Quincy immediately recognized the voice of the Sergeant. He stopped, raised his arms, and stood quietly, saying nothing. For a moment or two, he could make out nothing. Gradually, the room came into focus; stark white, limestone walls climbed up into the dark, broken only on the left and right, by dark, wood-framed doorways. The wood was probably mahogany. When his eyes became accustomed to the gloom, he could make out on his left, that a naked woman was tied to a chair. In the dim light from the open door, he did not recognize Eileen. She was slumped forward. She appeared badly hurt and clearly unconscious. Further to his left, in a doorway framed by the dark wood, stood two people, and directly in front of him, in a niche in the back wall, stood the Sergeant.

By now he could see quite clearly at that distance; the policeman had a gun pointed, rock steady, at Quincy's chest. He recognized the Webley instantly; he had used an identical one for years during his career. He knew that, fully loaded, it contained six rounds. The naked woman and Smythe-Caulley stood out sharply against the white walls, but he had to strain to see the two dim figures in the doorway to his left. The gloomy hall behind the two concealed their identity. He surmised that one of them was Jenna.

"Quincy, be careful, he's got a gun," shouted Jenna from the doorway. That mystery solved, he could make out now that the other figure next to Jenna was Lyle. He was holding Jenna tightly by both arms.

"Shut up woman. Glad you could join us, Major. Did you bring the gold?" sneered the policeman.

"Not so fast, you bastard, let me make sure Jenna's all right, then I'll go back to the truck and bring in the gold. I left it sitting on the bonnet in my canvas duty bag."

"I don't think so," said the policeman, advancing on Quincy. "Stand aside and I'll look outside myself. When I'm satisfied, then we'll talk."

Quincy moved carefully to his right, about halfway between the entrance way and the doorway opening on his right hand side. Smythe-Caulley, keeping the gun pointed squarely at Quincy, advanced to the doorway, and turned sideways, keeping an eye on Quincy at all times. Apparently satisfied that Quincy posed no immediate threat, he quickly glanced out at the truck, spying the bag on the hood. He immediately turned back to face Quincy.

"That it on the hood?" he asked.

"Yes, it's all there as promised. If you want, I'll go get it. If you like you can get it and verify it's all there."

Smythe-Caulley turned back into the room, toward the rear wall, and turned slightly to his right facing Quincy; he raised the gun.

That's when all hell broke loose.

Chapter 24 – Wednesday to Friday AM
Norman

It seemed to take forever to sort what actually happened Thursday night. There was enough blame to go around, some credit, too, but it was to be grudgingly given, if at all. In the end, it was the Governor who put it all together and brought the sorry episode to an end.

Time wise, as near as Quincy could reconstruct the events of that evening, the entire confrontation at Farley Hill lasted less than ten minutes. At the time, it seemed to him that it lasted about thirty seconds. To the others, it seemed like hours had passed before quiet, once again, descended on the old house. To yet others, it made no lasting impression at all. They were dead, long past caring about what had happened, and why.

What had started off the final confrontation was that, out of nowhere, back from the dead, Norman rushed the open front door and tackled Smythe-Caulley to the ground. Where had he come from? Why did Norman get into the fight? Those who knew about Norman's involvement in the sorry affair were either dead, or in a coma. It took some time to sort it all out.

It seems that he had regained consciousness, Wednesday afternoon, floating face down, just off the cliffs, at the Animal Flower Cave. His side hurt; he knew that he had been shot. The bleeding had stopped. He turned, and looked back at the cliffs, and realized that he would die before he could save himself by having a go at the cliffs. There was no way to survive contact with the jagged coral; the waves would pound him to pieces. He noticed that he was drifting out to sea, and to the north. He realized that there must be a 'long-shore rip carrying him along. He remembered that North Point had a beach, and it was only a little ways away, perhaps half a mile, a mile at most. He could surely swim that far. If he could not, then he was done for. He set off, doing a side stroke. It spared the pain in his side, and he remembered his grandfather who claimed he could swim almost forever, using the sidestroke. As he moved further from the cliffs, the chop subsided and the deep swells took over; he put his heart into it. His rage at being shot by Smythe-Caulley drove him onward.

When he rounded the point, he could see the big rock standing off the shore. He turned his energy toward gaining the beach; as he struggled through the growing chop, he was heading into shallower and therefore rougher water. Battered by waves, he approached the rocks outlining the sandy beach. Taking in water, he struggled on. The next thing he remembered, he was laying face down on the sand, just above the wave line. He was dog tired, bleeding from a variety of wounds, apparently acquired when he crawled out of the ocean over the sharp coral. He had a dim memory of getting there. In fact, he was not sure at this point where he was, exactly. No matter, he was alive. He put his head on the sand, and slept.

Later that afternoon, he heard a shout, and, a few minutes later, gentle hands turned him over onto his back. He found himself looking up, staring into two faces. One belonged to a good looking, middle aged, blond, white woman, wearing a faded, old, blue, flowered, swim suit, with her hair tied carelessly in an untidy bun. The other face belonged to an old, salty looking black man. Norman fainted again.

When he came to, he was lying in an old canvas beach chair on the veranda of the North Point shooting shack. He was clad only in his khaki shorts, and they were in tatters. The white woman, Ruth Rider, who, it turned out, was the owner of North Point, and the infamous waterer of trees, was cleaning his wounds with a clean beach towel. He hurt all over. He blinked, rubbing the salt crust from his eyes, and looked up at her.

"Have you got a drink?" He croaked.

"Water, gin or rum?" she asked.

"Rum, I think. It seems more fitting; I've had my fill of water for the time being," he quipped.

She rose from his side, went over to the battered metal counter inside the shack, picked up a bottle of Mount Gay rum, and poured him a half glass full. She returned to his side, and handed him the glass.

"You probably need this. You're lucky to be alive. Just the one," she said, "You've had a bad time. You're the man that does the waterskiing at Colony Club, are you not? What the hell are you doing here, bleeding all over my beach?"

"Long story," he mumbled. "I'll tell you sometime. Many thanks for pulling me off the sand." He raised the glass, saluted her, and drained it in a gulp. Oddly enough, the rum did not revive him, it was lacking its usual kick.

"I'll be as right as rain in a day or so," he said.

"How about that hole in your side? What caused it? It's definitely not a shark bite, too small. It looks as if you have been shot." She said.

"It just looks bad. I fell on some coral at the Animal Flower Cave, fell out of the cave opening into the waves and got bashed around a bit. Look, it's not bleeding anymore. A couple of stitches and it'll heal up in no time. I managed to swim over to your beach, and that's all I can remember."

"Well, there's nothing more I can do for you here," Ruth said. "I'll drop you off where they can patch you up. It looks to me like you'll live. You'll be sore, but you'll live."

At that moment, the black man returned, and, between them, they loaded him into Ruth's white Opal station wagon. She said thanks and goodbye to the black man and drove off.

"I'm taking you to the St. Lucy clinic at the poorhouse. They can patch you up there," she said.

"Thanks. I am very grateful for your help. I think you saved my life."

"Nonsense; you're just beat up, not severely injured. Swimming ashore like you did, you saved your own life, and the swim will likely keep the soreness and infection down. Seawater is amazing on wounds. You were lucky to land on my beach. There's not another beach on the north part of the island until you get to River Bay, and that's a long swim."

"Well, anyway," said Norman, "I'm grateful, and I guess I'm lucky, as well; the sharks didn't get me."

She dropped him off, said goodbye, and drove away. He never saw her again. The sisters sewed him up, fed him, bandaged his cuts as best they could, and gave him a cot to sleep on. He fell asleep immediately, and awoke late next morning cold sober. In fact, he had never been as sober in his adult life. He was literally back from the dead. In the morning, he begged a shirt off the pastor of the poorhouse, and set out for Holetown. He got lucky and hitched a ride on an empty cane truck all the way to the Colony Club. He arrived at the entrance to the car park, just in time to witness Lyle handing Jenna into the Vauxhall. Why was she going with him? Something was going on, and it did not look good for Jenna. He crouched down behind a large hibiscus and strained to hear. "I have to first make a stop at Farley Hill," Lyle said as he closed the door. The car drove off. Norman's sixth sense was screaming; sobriety had raised his awareness. Norman knew instantly that somehow, Smythe-Caulley was in the middle of it. He had to find out what was going on. Fortunately, he reasoned, the Sergeant assumed that Norman was dead, and, therefore, would not be on the lookout for him.

The car pulled away, turned left on the beach road, and sped off. Norman glanced quickly around, spotting no one, he quickly ran over to the bicycle rack, and grabbed an unlocked Raleigh. Doggedly, he set off for Farley Hill. It was, probably, an hour and a half ride under normal conditions. In his present condition, who knew how long it would take him? Most likely he wouldn't be there until after nightfall. His rage at being shot and left for dead, perhaps for shark food, drove him on relentlessly. He had no idea that the two in the car had stopped for a drink. As it turned out, it did not matter. The events unfolded as the fates would have it anyway.

"Only about five or six miles," he muttered to himself. "No problem. I'm going to get those bastards. Wait until I get my hands on that Sergeant." His growing fury cancelled the pain in his side, and fueled his resolve to even the score.

He pedaled on into the evening. He arrived thirty minutes after Lyle and Jenna, and only ten minutes before Ellis and Quincy. He stopped short of his destination and ditched the bicycle in the cane field. He crept up to the entrance to the plantation house in time to witness Smythe-Caulley, Lyle, and Jenna walk down to the old guard house and go inside. He moved back to the cane field opposite the entrance and watched until the trio left the guard house and returned to the abandoned house on the hill.

An old truck passed him as he cautiously emerged from the canes. He started back across the road toward the Farley Hill entrance. While he was trying to come up with a plan, he spotted Quincy's battered Austin ahead, parked just off the road, partially concealed in the cane field.

Just past the car, he saw the two, black clad figures turn into the driveway, squat, and crawl through the bushes behind the guard shack away from the drive. Quietly, he followed, and when he too, reached the overgrown grass, he kept them in sight until they negotiated the steep lawn, and arrived at the abandoned plantation house. He hunkered down behind a large hibiscus bush and watched them reconnoiter the house. After almost an hour, the two men came back to the same spot and started to confer. They shook hands; then, Quincy simply vanished. Ellis remained, silently watching the house, occasionally consulting his watch. When Ellis finally moved away, Norman moved in, close enough to get a clear view of the front door. He saw the two vehicles, and knew that both Lyle and Smythe-Caulley were inside, probably with Jenna.

As he lay still, wondering what to do next, he heard and then saw Quincy's old Austin enter the drive and proceed noisily up to the house. He decided to follow Quincy to the house and access the situation from there.

When he saw Quincy enter the house with his hands in the air, he followed him onto the veranda, and flattened himself against the limestone wall behind the opened door. He heard everything. Smythe-Caulley was definitely there, and he was threatening everyone. Apparently, he still had that damned Webley. What could he do against the armed man who had shot him just two days ago? Suddenly, he heard the policeman tell Quincy to stand back. He was coming toward the open door. When the Sergeant looked out at the truck, he did not see Norman.

Norman saw him clearly. It was Norman who started the melee. Something snapped in Norman; he became enraged beyond all reason. Ignoring the fact that the policeman was armed, and without any conscious thought, disregarding his own potential danger, he moved. As Smythe-Caulley turned back into the room toward Quincy, Norman stepped around the door and charged the policeman, knocking him face first to the floor. The gun discharged, and the fight was on. Unfortunately for Norman, he had let rage overcome his common sense. He had tackled an armed trained professional. Early in the fight as he struggled with the policeman, he was clubbed insensible by the butt of the gun. Not really knowing who had attacked him, and where everyone else was, Smythe-Caulley got quickly to his feet. McKenna had vanished, and he could hear Lyle and Jenna running down the hall on the left side of the house. The man on the floor lay motionless; Eileen was still tied to her chair, apparently still unconscious. He was now concerned that Quincy had the drop on him. He glanced around anxiously, waving the gun at every shadow. Was Quincy armed? Was he alone?

Chapter 25 – Monday – Before Dawn
The Cliffs

When Smythe-Caulley went down, and as the pistol discharged, Quincy leaped for the right hand doorway, crashing to the floor and rolling out of sight. He thought that it must have been Ellis who had tackled the policeman. Lyle, unable to see clearly who was tangled up on the floor with Smythe-Caulley, and realizing that Quincy might be dead, grabbed Jenna by the hand, "We need to get out of here right now," he whispered to her, "He's just killed someone, and we're unarmed. Follow me."

He turned and ran down the hallway toward the back of the house, dragging her along like a dead weight.

From where he crouched in the hall, Ellis could not see what was going on when the fight started. He could only focus on the pair in front of him in the doorway. He started toward the couple, when suddenly they turned and came rapidly toward him. He leaped at the man, striking out at his head.

Suddenly, Lyle was hit on the jaw, and went down like a sack of grain. Dazed, he struggled to his feet. Ellis was on him, pounding him as hard as he could. Jenna was knocked aside. Her head hit the wall. She slid down onto her bottom, and sat there staring at the men fighting in front of her. She had no idea who the second man was. When the policeman went down and the gun went off, she had seen Quincy throw himself clear; she hoped that he had not been hit. From the entrance to the hallway, the gun fired again, someone screamed; there was a grunt, and a body hit the floor with a thud. Smythe-Caulley apparently had appeared in the doorway, saw the two struggling men in the hall, and fired blindly at them. He had hoped to hit someone in the gloom. He was not picky; whoever it was, had been slated for elimination anyway. The flash revealed to Jenna, the policeman, blood streaming down his face, still aiming the smoking pistol down the hall. After the flash, she was temporarily blinded; in the dark, only vague shapes were visible. She could barely see Smythe-Caulley silhouetted in the doorway to the main room, but she could make out a shape on the floor near her in the hallway. Someone else was crawling across the floor toward her. She was terrified, disoriented from the pistol shot, and shaking like a leaf.

From the direction of the main room, she heard Quincy shout,

"Where are you, you bloody coward? Come out and fight."

There was a crash, and Smythe-Caulley, still in the doorway, turned back into the room. He held his pistol in front of him, ready to fire. Relieved that Quincy was still all right, Jenna struggled to her feet. After a brief pause, another shot rang out. The flash revealed a motionless figure, prone in the middle of the entry room. Shattered wood flew everywhere, and Jenna could not see Quincy. Lyle struggled to his feet, wet with blood from the body at his feet. He had no idea who it might be, and he was now so terrified for his life, that he was willing to sacrifice anyone, including Jenna to save himself.

"Come with me, Jenna, he might come back. He just killed someone right here," snarled Lyle. "That man's gone completely round the bend. He'll kill us all for sure. To hell with the gold! I want to get out of here. He's probably killed Eileen, as well."

He grabbed Jenna by the hand and dragged her down the hall, through the door, and into the night. They headed straight for the woods behind the house. It was roughly fifty yards to cover. He could hear Smythe-Caulley running down the hall after them. They both ran like the wind. They knew they were running for their lives. Smythe-Caulley burst from the back door.

"Stop! or I'll shoot!" He fired into the night at the fleeing figures and missed. They ran harder, stumbling blindly through the bushes away from the house.

In the main room someone lay on the floor, stirring slightly, apparently semi-conscious. Quincy emerged from the side room, and conscious of the shattered doorway, stopped, momentarily, to make sure the Sergeant was not lurking waiting to finish him off. On full alert, and listening to the footfalls retreating down the hallway, he checked the prone man's pulse, and satisfied that the man, whoever he was, would live, he moved quietly to the naked woman in the chair. He could see that it was Eileen; her breathing was ragged but deep, and she had obviously been badly abused. He thought she was going to live. To disguise his whereabouts, he decided to leave her tied, and ran down the hall toward the back door. He tripped over another body and sprawled on the tile floor. As he fell, he instinctively tucked and rolled to the side. Sensing no movement, he recovered his feet and approached the prone figure. Realizing that he was standing in a pool of blood, he checked the man's pulse. This time there was none. He grabbed the corpse by the feet and dragged him through the back door into the moonlight. He could see that it was not the Sergeant. Ellis was dead, shot through the heart. Quincy placed his hand briefly on his friend's face, shut his eyes for a moment, and said softly, "Thanks, Mate, I'll get the bastard if it is the last thing I do."

He turned toward the woods just in time to get a fleeting glance at the figure of a man running into the tree line. He could see by the moonlight, it was Smythe-Caulley at a dead run, brandishing his gun. Quincy stood up and followed the noisy chase as the policeman disappeared into the woods.

Quincy knew he was heading into the mahogany forest. He was very familiar with it. In his spare time, he came here alone, to practice his clandestine skills. He needed to keep them sharp, because on the active reserve list, he could be recalled at anytime. If he were called up, his life would, once again, depend solely on his skills, his physical conditioning, and his instincts. He knew exactly where he was and where the policeman was headed. He quickly located the trail that ran through the woods to the escarpment at the edge of the forest. He started down it, at a brisk but silent trot.

He could hear two sets of noises ahead of him. Nearby, to his left, was the lesser noise. Ahead and slightly to the right, was a lot of noise. It must be Lyle and Jenna, he thought. Pretty soon they'll run out of woods to hide in. He ran harder, trying to be as silent as possible.

Fortunately, off the trail, the Sergeant could not move stealthily. His noisy progress was concealing whatever noise Quincy made, but he was gaining on the fleeing pair. It sounded to him like Smythe-Caulley had, over the intervening years, neglected his tracking skills. He blundered along in pursuit of the other two, gaining ground, but hardly concealing his pursuit. He was obviously unaware that Quincy was in the hunt. He had assumed that Quincy was either dead in the hallway or up ahead with Jenna.

Suddenly, Lyle and Jenna leading the chase, stopped abruptly. The only sound still within hearing, was the policeman blundering along on his left. Quincy knew the fugitives had run out of hill, and had fetched up against the steep drop at the edge of the forest. The escarpment, two miles long, was seventy five feet high near the old house. There was no safe way down.

For the moment, Quincy could not hear them at all. He could hear Smythe-Caulley slow down, and continue his pursuit much more quietly. He was obviously listening for the fleeing pair. Hearing no noise, he had grown cautious. He did not know who exactly he was pursuing, and he was worried that it might be Quincy who had spirited Jenna into the woods. Quincy went into his stealth mode and followed along, working parallel to the policeman; both men were heading for the escarpment. The woods were quiet until, up ahead, as he broke into the clearing, Quincy spotted Lyle and Jenna wrestling soundlessly near the edge. Immediately to his left the policeman also stepped into the clearing. The struggling pair was so engrossed in their struggle that they were unaware that they now had company.

Quincy knew that five shots had been fired. Smythe-Caulley had one shot left. From the time Quincy was a raw recruit, he had been taught to count the number of rounds fired. Lives depended on this knowledge, and he could do it in the middle of a raging gun battle. He always knew how many rounds he had, and how many his adversary had left. The Webley was impossible to reload on the run. This time, however, he didn't have a gun of his own. The Sergeant was a crack shot but he did not see or hear Quincy drop to his knees ten yards to his right.

There was still a chance to overcome Smythe-Caulley's one advantage. Quincy could not compete with the gun, but if he could get his hands on the man, he knew he could kill him. It was dim in the woods, and surprise was his best weapon. For all he knew, the policeman thought that it was Quincy lying on the floor of the main room. Smythe-Caulley stood tall, and slowly raised the pistol, aiming at the two struggling figures at the edge of the escarpment. He was taking careful aim. No doubt, he, too, knew that he had only one round left in the gun. His heart sinking, Quincy knew that he had no chance to close the distance between them. Quietly, he drew his killing knife, and slowly got to his feet, facing the policeman. It was unlikely that he could cover the ground between them before Smythe-Caulley could turn and fire. The man was a crack shot, and he did not want to throw his life away. He could see him clearly in the mottled moonlight. He was facing away from Quincy, with his entire right side exposed. I have to time this right, he thought, or Jenna will surely die.

The policeman advanced cautiously, step by step, planting his feet firmly so that he could keep the gun steady. As he closed the distance on the struggling pair, he kept his pistol aimed squarely at them.

"Stop," he shouted. "Or I'll shoot."

He was too far away for Quincy to try to rush him. The sound of a rush toward the gunman would give him away. He was Jenna's only hope. Holding his breath, he drew back his arm, and hurled his knife at Smythe-Caulley's chest. As the gun discharged, the policeman lurched to the side and fell silently to the ground. One of the two figures struggling at the edge of the cliff disappeared over the edge with a piercing scream; the other figure collapsed into the bushes at the cliff's edge. The need for silence past, Quincy ran to the fallen policeman. His Fairbairn had pierced the man's chest, just under his right armpit. It was buried to the hilt in his chest. Checking for a pulse, Quincy was satisfied that the bastard was finally dead; dead as a doormat, he thought with satisfaction.

Now concerned only for Jenna, he ran to the edge and looked down. In the gloom, he could see nothing save the tops of the trees in the forest below. A low moan came from behind him. Turning quickly, hoping against hope, he took two steps, reached down, located an arm, and pulled. The arm was small and bare. It was Jenna. She hadn't fallen to her death. He gathered her to his chest, frantically checking her over for wounds. Finding none, he picked her up, cradled her like a baby, and silently wept with relief. Breathing deeply, he set her down, lowered himself to the dirt next to her, and cradling her head in his lap, he waited for her to come to. He was spent with relief. He was anxious to get Jenna to safety, but he first had to know what had happened.

She stirred, looked up at him and said, "Quincy, what happened, where's Lyle? We were fighting, and I passed out." She quivered in his arms.

"Laughing and crying quietly, he explained, "Everything is under control at the moment Love. You're not hurt, Smythe-Caulley's dead; so is Ellis. Apparently Lyle fell off the cliff, so I assume he's dead as well. Eileen is unconscious, tied to a chair in the main room; I think she'll be ok. There's someone hurt on the floor in the entry; I don't know who it is. Whoever he is, he saved my life and gave us a chance. He's still alive, and he may be armed. We'd better steer clear of him."

"I'm still scared," said Jenna, "let's get out of here."

"Just a moment," said Quincy."

He pulled her erect, stood and walked over to the dead policeman. He leaned down, pulled his knife from the man's side and wiped it on the dead man's shirt.

"Good riddance, he muttered. "You have had it coming for a long time. I'm glad it was me that saw you off."

He slid the cleaned knife back into the sheath at his back, turned, and went back to Jenna. Quincy pulled her to her feet, and started to lead her off. She was still shaky, so he scooped her up and carried her back up the trail toward the house.

When they got back to the house, not wanting any more confrontation, he circled around to the front. He could see no movement, and there was nobody visible at the door of the house.

Quincy said, "Let's just leave, I'll call the police from the hotel, and they can sort this all out. We need to decide what actually happened."

He opened his truck door, and slid her on to the seat. Quietly, he closed the door, grabbed his small bag from the hood of the vehicle, and climbed into the driver's side. He stowed the bag under the seat, and started the Austin. He turned on the headlights, reversed the truck, and drove down the hill to the main road. Jenna sat quietly at his side, saying nothing, her hand gripping his thigh. She was hanging on for dear life with her head resting on his shoulder.

When he reached the car park at the Colony Club, Jenna was once again able to walk. They entered the hotel and realized that, at this hour, no one was up except the night watchman. Moving quickly to the empty front desk, he called the local police station and reported that there was gunfire at Farley Hill. Before anyone could ask him who he was, he hung up. They went silently through the hotel and down to the beach. He put Jenna gently into the bow of the dinghy, and shoved off. They never laid eyes on the night watchman.

A day later, when they had collected themselves, he placed a call to Government house and requested a meeting with the Governor.

The sun was high in the sky when they drove into the covered portico at Government House. At the gate, he said to the armed constable,

"Please inform Sir Robert that Major McKenna has to see him right away. I have an appointment"

"Right you are, sir," said the guard, saluting smartly. "Follow me, please."

He led them into the main hall and turned left into the library.

"You can wait in here. I'll call Lieutenant Charles his adjutant, and he'll be with you directly. I shall see if I can organize a spot of tea. The Governor should be available shortly.

"Coffee for me, please," said Jenna with a sigh. "Black, and as strong as you can make it!"

"Make that two please, with a whisky chaser," said Quincy, as he sat down.

After a brief discussion, Lieutenant Charles saluted smartly, turned and went in search of the Sir Robert. The Governor, attired in his typical tropical whites arrived, smoothing down his gray hair. Obviously windblown, he had apparently been out on the lawn in the wind. Smiling slightly, he advanced into the room. He appeared delighted to see Jenna, but, puzzled he turned to Quincy and said, "To what do I owe this honor? I apologize for keeping you waiting, but this day has been frantic. There has been a terrible tragedy at Farley Hill, and we're still trying to make heads and tails out of it. Are you aware of what happened, Major?"

Standing at attention, Quincy replied, "Yes Sir, I have heard some of it; I understand that people have been killed. Some of it may be my fault, I'm afraid."

"Well then, man, sit down and out with it. I'll get a cup of tea, and we'll try to sort through this mess."

It took Quincy a full two hours to relay the incidents leading up to the confrontation at Farley Hill. He left out the romantic bits, and failed to mention the gold at the bottom of Billfish reef. He did, however lay the doubloons on the table as evidence of their find. He had held back the gold coin and the bag on the bottom of Billfish reef. He was not sure why. He could always retrieve it later if it seemed the right thing to do.

By the time he finished recounting the story Sir Robert was trembling with suppressed rage. He was livid that one of his serving officers had run amuck. It had happened on his watch. He was chagrined that he had not seen it coming, and embarrassed that, for the first time in the colony's history, a government scandal would tarnish the rule of the British Crown. He was upset that Quincy had not come directly to him, but appreciated that he wanted Jenna to be recovered before she had to face the issue. He needed to make sure that Her Majesty's Government was going to maintain the high standards expected of it. He must let the chips fall where they may. It took a week or more to confirm what had actually transpired that evening. In the end, the furor died down.

The exact details were kept within the confines of the constabulary, and the dead were buried quietly.

One positive note emerged from the sorry affair; the Crown and the island treasuries would be enriched by the find. Just how much would evolve during the salvage operation. Long overdue, Her Majesty's Constabulary was now spared the embarrassment of a very bad officer's conduct. They were rid of Smythe-Caulley for good. Quincy was once again restored to the Governor's favor, and Jenna had emerged as a reluctant heroine.

Everyone maintained a proper, British, stiff upper lip; even Jenna!

Epilogue – Three Months Later
Sandy lane

The constable looked out from the beach, and saw a beautiful sight. A fully rigged ketch was coming south around the point under full sail with a following wind.

"Ten knots at least," he muttered.

He smiled, and tapped his companion on the shoulder, pointing to the Billfish. Together they walked along the sand as the yacht started to shed sails, and prepare to drop anchor. It threaded its way delicately through the cluster of boats already at anchor about one hundred yards off the beach. The constable spied Jenna at the helm, waived, and broke out in a large grin.

"She's coming along quickly," he commented. "She'll be as salty as Quincy before you know it."

Quincy walked forward to the bow, and let the anchor go with a splash. He returned amidships to finish tying up the main sail and prepare his boat for anchorage. Jenna left the cockpit, and started tying the other sail to the stern boom. They met amidships, stopped to share a kiss, and a pat on the rump, and went aft to get into the dinghy.

"Looks like the dredge is still going full blast," Quincy observed. "Let's go to the beach and see if we have permission to start salvaging the wreck."

He rowed briskly ashore to where the two men were waiting with smiles on their faces.

"How is our newest salvage crew doing today?" the constable asked cheerfully." Are you ready to go to work?"

"You bet," smiled Jenna. "I get to try out my new scuba skills. He's going to do all the heavy lifting, though. I'll supervise."

The four shook hands, and stood chatting for a while. Finally, the noise ceased; the dredge had finally, shut down. In thirty minutes the water would clear, and they could go to work. Quincy smiled at Jenna's previous remark. As the head of the new treasure salvage operation, he would do little more than supervise, and keep an eye on the items they retrieved from the sea. His new diver, looking suspiciously like the Norman of old, was turning out to be a rare character. He suspected he might have sticky fingers.

After the shootout at Farley Hill, Norman had vanished. Despite Quincy and Jenna's attempts to help him by telling the authorities of his heroic intervention nothing was ever mentioned, officially, about Norman. Smythe-Caulley was banished to a pauper's grave, without ceremony. Lyle Farmer and Ellis Caulfield were buried side by side in St. James Parrish church yard. Eileen, somewhat recovered from her ordeal with Smythe-Caulley, had moved to England. She had apparently discovered some distant relatives there.

Two months later, a man named Frank Downes showed up at the Colony Club, and moved into the old shack on the beach. He carried a newly minted, Barbados passport. He was thinner and paler than Norman, and he was completely sober. Nothing was ever said. He asked for, and got a job, as assistant to the new salvage chief. He spent his first month on the job teaching Jenna to dive. He was a superb instructor, and a good worker; always on time, and always sober. He worked as long as needed each day, and then disappeared up the road at night to see his girlfriend, Cora. He was back on the job every day at seven AM, sharp, six days a week. After a month, he moved out of the shack, and into Cora's house. A week later, the Colony Club had the shack demolished, and planted a stand of sea grape in its place.

The old Norman had vanished for good. Jenna never returned to New York. She never missed her old job. She seemed to be quite content to serve as the first mate of the Billfish. Quincy never told anyone how, or why, he had been awarded a substantial sum for finding a rare sunken treasure. Simultaneously, her majesty's governor, Sir Robert Arundell, had awarded Quincy a handsome salvage contract. He continued to wear his dress whites for special occasions, and, rumor had it that he would, someday soon, be married in full dress.

After a busy first day of salvage, Quincy and Jenna were relaxing in the cockpit of the Billfish. Jenna turned to Quincy and said, "One of these days, we should pop back over to Billfish Reef, and retrieve that old service bag of yours. It might come in handy some day."

"Let's let sleeping dogs lie. Who knows? Perhaps someday when we're married? You might like a proper house. We'll see."

He smiled at her, and they clinked glasses, and turned, once again, to the sunset, waiting patiently for the green flash.

Back Cover

Barbados 1956

Jenna White, thirty five, is a successful New York attorney. Overworked, frustrated, unfulfilled, and tired to the bone, she flies off to Barbados for a much needed break. Totally unaware that she will be caught up in a series of disastrous events resulting in greed, death, and the discovery of the love of her life, she starts to unwind. Enjoying herself for the first time in a decade, Jenna meets and spends time with a variety of attractive men; Ellis, a rich American playboy, Norman, a handsome Aussie derelict, and Quincy, a British charter boat captain. On a water skiing trip, Jenna unearths an old coin on Sandy Lane Beach. It turns out to be an old Spanish Doubloon, one of the infamous Pieces of Eight so often mentioned in connection with pirates of old who frequented the island hundreds of years ago.

Innocently showing the coin to her new found water skiing friends at the beach bar, Jenna sets off an explosive chain of events that finds her group of water skiers setting out to locate a long lost treasure. Norman conspires with a crooked cop, ex SAS Sergeant Smythe-Caulley, to steal the treasure when it is found. Into the mix charges Quincy, also ex SAS, and the nemesis of Smythe-

Caulley. He sweeps Jenna off her feet and champions her search. Greed quickly leads to murder when the small group finds a rotting chest of gold coins on the reef off Sandy Lane Beach. The confrontation between Jenna and Quincy, the hapless bystanders, and the murderous and vengeful Smythe-Caulley, culminates in a deadly showdown at the abandoned, but still elegant, Farley Hill Plantation House.

Stuart Leland Rider lived in the tropics from 1946 to 1960. He spent most of those years, on and off, living on the island of Barbados.

While the characters are fictitious, they are based on people who populated the island at the period covered in the book. Actual historical figures are interspersed throughout the story. All the places are real, and still exist today. You should visit them. The best part about Barbados is her people, they are happy and welcoming.

A successful commercial developer, Mr. Rider is the author of six successful business books. This is his first book of fiction. There will be more to come.

Made in the USA
Charleston, SC
26 July 2013